the Eighth Wonder

the Eighth Wonder

Kimberly S. Young

authorHOUSE®

AuthorHouse™
1663 Liberty Drive
Bloomington, IN 47403
www.authorhouse.com
Phone: 1-800-839-8640

First published by AuthorHouse   01/30/2012

ISBN: 978-1-4670-7129-1 (sc)
ISBN: 978-1-4670-7130-7 (hc)
ISBN: 978-1-4670-7131-4 (ebk)

Library of Congress Control Number: 2011962956

Printed in the United States of America

Praise for *the* Eighth Wonder . . .

"A deeply moving story with a Bridges of Madison County quality."

~ *Rehka Gajanan*
Humanities Professor, University of Pittsburgh at Bradford.

"Kimberly Young's richly drawn characters pull the reader
in for a poignant and compelling read."

~ *Beth Andrews*
Romance Writers of America Award Winning Author of
A Not- So- Perfect Past

"Kimberly Young has constructed an amazing first novel about unexpected love
and the strange chemistry of May-November romances. This is no bodice-ripper
or sappy saga of moonstruck entrancement. Her characters are deep,
and the reader roots for them."

~ *John M. Hanchette*
Pulitzer Prize-winner and St. Bonaventure University journalism professor.

"The Eighth Wonder is a warm and poignant tale that stirs us to do some fresh
thinking about the answers to the timeless questions about love."

~ *Kevin Quirk*
Author of Your Life is a Book—And it is Time to Write It
and co-author of Brace for Impact

"A well-crafted love story."

~ *William P. Robertson*
Author of the Bucktail novels

"The Eight Wonder is a poignant story of discovery. Discovery of unexpected
places, people and what really matters in a life where one learns
to look beyond first impressions."

~ *Linda Devlin*
Director, Forest Press and Allegheny National Forest Visitors Bureau

In loving memory of Bill Meyer (1926 to 2001)—
the greatest dad a kid could ever have.

Hence rose the saying, "If I love you what is that to you?" We say so because we feel that what we love is not in your will, but above it. It is not you, but your radiance. It is that which you know not in yourself and can never know.

Ralph Waldo Emerson

CHAPTER 1

Nicole

The Kinzua Bridge had changed everything in her life. As the familiar smell of wood smoke filled the cabin, Nicole Benson gazed out the window at the rusted steel girders of the fallen bridge in the distance, the bridge called the Eighth Wonder of the World but which had much more meaning for her than a mere wonder. The large potbelly stove smoldered as she glanced at the empty wall where his lithograph once hung, and she sensed the quiet, much as she did on that summer day when she first came to Bradford.

A warm breeze through the open window caressed her cheek as she stretched back in the chair and took a deep breath. The scent of pine and the fresh air from the Pennsylvania woods brought back memories of hiking with him through the area.

Spring had thawed into an early summer, and the valley was lush with green but peppered with tints of brown from the trees ready to bud. Half giggling, half choking back a tear, Nicole realized that she actually could tell them all apart now and began rattling off their names: hickory, maple, oak, cherry, and hemlock—miles upon miles of hemlock.

Getting up from the desk, she longed to feel his touch again as she stood at the window to soak in the view, the view they had looked at together so many years ago.

"As I write this, I struggle with the same temptation to call I have felt every day since you left. It was so long ago, but I remember every moment as if it were yesterday."

It had been more than a decade since she had seen him, and yet she could hear his voice as the words from his letter sprinkled across her mind like the morning mist over the hills.

"I am sitting at our kitchen table on a cool day in autumn, the season of the year that I most associate with you, especially after the leaves have turned."

She had already memorized every line, every word, every nuance, though it had been only days since his letter had arrived at her office. Eleven years after she saw him last, she could still remember his deep green eyes, his smile, and how his face seemed so kind. She could still picture him sitting on the porch of the cabin watching the sunset over the valley in the late afternoon as she brought out their coffee with a splash of Bailey's. They spent their evenings here talking through the night. He understood her heart more than any man had or could.

She could only speak of it now with a sense of clarity that comes from age and wisdom that she certainly didn't have before that year. Caught up in materialistic pursuits, driven by all that Wall Street had to offer, Nicole had completely forgotten the humble beginnings of her working-class roots. When she felt the calling to teach, she thought that she had changed, that she was doing something noble, when all she did was exchange her materialistic needs for the prestigious rewards of her new academic pursuits.

For any woman, the questions of love, marriage, and children run deep and Nicole was no exception. She examined each with the thoroughness of a skilled surgeon.

Sitting over coffee with her female colleagues at the university, listening to them chatter on about their sons' baseball games or their daughters' school dances, Nicole once felt like a leper because she didn't fit the role of a good wife and mother, but now, she felt a gentle peace. To be honest, she didn't know she had the power to love, to give of herself so unselfishly in every way a person can until he gave her the faith and courage to try.

"As I gaze out from our front window at the Kinzua Bridge, I am constantly reminded of how it pales in comparison to your beauty."

"Would he still think so?" Nicole thought, looking at her reflection in the glass as she ran her fingers through her hair, trying not to think about the small patches of gray or the wrinkles that had started to set in.

Nicole reached for her bifocals on the end of his antler-legged table, and then she sat back at the desk and turned to the keyboard of her laptop when a hard gust of wind rattled the front window. A bronze haze filled the hillsides from the late morning sun. Staring out the window, she felt herself choke up as fragments of the once tall steel girders lay crumpled on the ground at the bottom of the gorge. Nicole remembered reading about the tornado while sitting at a faculty department meeting. Just before the meeting was about to start, Nicole scanned the Internet, reading about the local news of Bradford when she read the headline 'Viaduct Tumbles'. The tornado had pummeled through the center of the bridge slicing down ten of the twenty towers, eventually taking down four more towers. It took less than 30 seconds to destroy a bridge that had stood for over a century.

Staring at the shards of twisted brown rusted metal that looked like broken bones of a once grand structure. Train tracks dangled like twigs over the valley. Nicole remembered the majesty of the historic railroad bridge that once had pierced the wilderness soaring like an eagle over the valley. Reminded of its splendor and of its beauty, she smiled.

"Yes," she softly murmured. "It truly was the Eighth Wonder of the World."

They had met in the summer of 1997. Nicole had just graduated from NYU with her Ph.D. in political science. As she drove through the woods, she imagined being a professor at a prestigious Ivy League university. She pictured telling her classmates where she was headed after graduation, letting names like Harvard, Yale, or Princeton roll off her tongue. In fact, she'd had other job offers, at Tufts in Boston and at Temple in Philadelphia—better schools in better places. Instead, she had taken a one-year teaching job at McKean College in Bradford, Pennsylvania—a small liberal arts school none of her friends had ever heard of located in a town that was only a tiny dot on a map.

As she ventured deeper into the wilderness, she still wasn't sure if she was making a valiant attempt to spend more time with her father before he died or running away from yet another failed relationship.

"Oh hell," Nicole said aloud. At that point, she had moved over ten times in the past fifteen years. So much so, her friends and family started to write her address in pencil. Not only were her apartments temporary but so were her jobs and her relationships. She didn't even own a pet for fear of too much commitment. The closest thing to something permanent in her life was a houseplant that she bought during her freshman year of college.

As she turned off the highway, slivers of the late afternoon sun squinted through the trees. Her old Nova rattled and coughed as she turned into the driveway of the house where she had rented an apartment.

As Nicole looked up at the gingerbread porch and framed steeples, the movers unloaded the last of her belongings. Bradford had one advantage, she thought. It was cheap. For less than a third of what she paid for a studio in New York, she had rented a large two-bedroom apartment that took up the entire second floor of a restored Victorian mansion, complete with a fireplace and a balcony. She never could have afforded such luxuries in the city.

She grabbed her camera bag from the back seat, swung it over her shoulder, then picked up her laptop case and headed up the stairs. The smell of thick musty carpet permeated the mahogany stairwell in the foyer. The flowered wallpaper was made of silk, but it was thin and peeling in places. She climbed the steps, each creaking like she was in an old horror movie, as she made her way to the top. Walking down a short hallway, she reached her front door, which was already open.

Two movers dressed in flannel shirts, camouflage ball caps, and jeans were inside. One mover was stacking a large pile of cardboard boxes marked "books" against the wall of the living room.

"You a student or something?" he asked as he hoisted up another box.

"Nope, a professor," Nicole replied as she looked at the dozens of book cartons that represented her life. She had spent most of her adult life in school, supporting herself while accumulating debt. In between taking classes, she had slaved away, writing and rewriting her dissertation. She had often questioned

4

giving up a promising corporate career on Wall Street to live as a poor graduate student, eating five-for-a-dollar Ramen noodles and Chinese takeout, worrying about how she would pay for books, rent, and the occasional luxury of Jimmy Choo shoes. Fashion was still a priority, a leftover extravagance of working in the corporate world where looking good was part of the culture.

On especially depressing nights, when she couldn't stand to write another word of her dissertation, she used to take long walks through the city with her camera, snapping random photos of a policeman, a hot dog vendor, a building, whatever caught her eye. She liked to fantasize about driving a Lexus, owning a Rolex, or shopping at Saks or Neiman Marcus, something to show that she had finally made it. Instead, she drove a used Chevy Nova, wore a Timex, and still shopped at Filenes and Stein Mart.

Studying in the library alone at night, she had often wondered how it was that, at thirty-five years old, she was still wandering through life on her own while attending her friends' weddings, housewarmings, and baby showers. Even her younger sister was married and had two children. All Nicole could focus on was graduating and starting her career.

"A professor?" The mover turned to look at her. "I think of some gray-haired guy with a beard."

"Yeah, I get that a lot." Nicole smiled politely. "I don't exactly fit the stereotype."

Most people on campus mistook her for an undergrad, and people usually guessed that she was in her twenties. Occasionally, she still got carded walking into a bar. Her long dark hair hadn't even started to turn gray, while most of her friends already paid for a monthly cut and color. Dressed as she was in her faded NYU baseball cap, a white sleeveless T-shirt, a grubby pair of denim shorts, and a worn pair of Nikes only accentuated her youthful looks.

"So how'd you end up out here?" he asked, wielding his pudgy body around to gather up another box.

"It's near my dad. He's in Buffalo."

"You'll be used to the snow then." He laughed. She noted that he had thick, stubby hands for a large man as he lifted the last box.

"So I've heard," Nicole said, dumping her camera bag and laptop case on the sofa. "When I told people I was coming to Bradford, if they'd heard of it at all, they said, 'Oh, you mean Brrrrradford.'"

"Ah, you'll love it here," the mover said with a hint of sarcasm. "My uncle's got a hunting camp in the forest. He says it's the best deer hunting around."

"Well, since I left my gun cabinet back in New York, I doubt I'll be doing much hunting."

"Not much else to do around here then," he chuckled.

Nicole knew she could survive the brutal winters after living through blizzards growing up in Buffalo, but she didn't know if she could survive losing her father. Constantly relocating for another job, another school, never having that sense of permanence or home, was hard for her. Nicole was always packing and unpacking, only taking what she really needed and leaving what didn't fit in storage, and she seemed to live her life out of boxes. Her father marveled at her ability to pursue her dreams, but he was the one constant she had. He was so proud that she was the only one in the family to graduate from college and bragged to his friends that his little girl was going to be a doctor.

A well-read but uneducated man, he was ten-times proud when she was accepted at Fordham. Nicole could still remember how her father held back the tears as he said goodbye in front of the Greyhound Bus Station. There was also a lump in the pit of her stomach as the bus pulled away. On a partial scholarship, and with little more than she could carry on her back, she had headed for New York City. It was a hard transition for Nicole, being so far away from home and her father, but soon enough the noise, confusion, and congestion of the city became a way of life.

Bustling through the streets of Manhattan, keeping up the pace to which her entire life had been set, Nicole never realized how distant from him she had become, how guarded she was when they spoke on the phone, until he got sick. He had pancreatic cancer. It was inoperable and quick.

"Well, that about does it," the mover said, handing her a clipboard and a pen from the back pocket of his jeans. "I just need your signature by the X."

He tore off a copy for Nicole, tucked the clipboard under his arm, and started down the stairs. "Good luck to ya."

"Thanks." Nicole waved goodbye as she closed the door behind him.

From the bedroom window, she watched the moving van pull away from the curb and slowly disappear down the road. Her stomach started to turn.

She felt as if her life had suddenly come to a screeching halt. Bradford was a cold, economically depressed, and dreary little town. For the first time since living in New York, or anywhere, she was going to be completely isolated from her urban escapes. There were no museums, no bookstores, no coffee shops. There wasn't even a Wal-Mart, and Nicole nearly shed a tear when she found out only because she thought, if even that corporation could not find the place to set up shop, what else could possibly be here. Buried in the rural foothills of the Appalachian Plateau and surrounded by the Allegheny National Forest, the only things Bradford offered were hunting, fishing, and camping—none of which remotely appealed to her.

She wandered from room to room to take a quick mental inventory. There was a green plush sofa she inherited from a former roommate, a couple of white plastic end tables from Big Lots, some bookshelves and lamps from Ikea, a kitchen table with mismatched chairs and a worn wooden desk she bought at a flea market, a lumpy futon she used as her bed and several milk crates stuffed with textbooks that also doubled as nightstands. She did not own one new piece of furniture and hardly enough of these hand-me-downs and pieces of plastic faux furniture to fill the extra space of her new apartment. Nicole felt more like a vagabond than a newly minted Ph.D.

She climbed over several boxes as she made her way to the bathroom, and she felt slightly better as she splashed cold water on her face. Her towels were still packed away and so she wiped her face on the bottom of her T-shirt. Then she searched for her portable stereo. She found it hidden underneath her ironing board, which was folded flat and lying on the floor. Her CDs were buried somewhere in the sea of brown cardboard, and so she tried to tune in the radio. All she got was static, except for Alabama and a Willie Nelson song that she couldn't stand. She hated country music. She clicked on the AM dial to see if there was something more palatable and discovered WESB 1490—Bradford's rock station.

"I didn't think a town of ten thousand was big enough to have its own station," she said to her wilted houseplant, which was sitting on the kitchen table amongst boxes filled with dishes and pans.

Nicole plopped down on the sofa, exhausted from the drive and hummed a poor rendition of Stevie Nicks while the radio played "Landslide" by Fleetwood Mac in the background. *"I took my love and I took it down. I climbed a mountain and turned around. And I saw my reflection in the snow-covered hills 'til the Landslide brought me down. Oh, mirror in the sky—What is love? Can the child in my heart rise above? Can I sail through the changing ocean tides? Can I handle the seasons of my life? Mmmm . . . mmmm . . . I don't know."*

Could she handle the seasons of her life? Suddenly Nicole wasn't sure.

Nicole reached inside her purse for her cell phone. There was no signal. She went into the kitchen, then to the bedroom. Still nothing. She went from room to room, hoping to hear a signal or any type of sound that meant she wasn't completely isolated from civilization.

Finally getting reception when she stepped onto the balcony, she hit speed dial. "Hi, Dad. It's me," she said. "I'm finally here but this place feels a little like being in an episode of Northern Exposure."

"Is it that bad?"

"It's like redneck city here—I don't exactly blend in." She laughed.

"How's the apartment?"

"It's good, much roomier than my studio. I still can't believe how cheap rent is here."

"Well, that's a good thing."

"I guess." Nicole paused, remembering the reason she had come to Bradford in the first place.

"Honey, I'm sorry. You know you didn't have to move to be near me," her father said with a sigh.

"Please, Dad. We've been over this before. I only wish I could be closer. I'm only a little more than an hour's drive away. Before long, I will be off again to some new place. Remember the appointment is only for a year."

"I didn't mean about that. I meant you didn't have to refuse those other job offers."

"Yes, I did." Her voice became stern as the guilt resonated inside her. She had always been too busy to visit or even call. She had visited him for a weekend here and there in between semesters, and sometimes on summer vacations, but she hadn't really been home in seventeen years.

Part of the reason she did not return often was that she didn't want to be home. She had her friends, her life, and her studies in the city. She couldn't give that up, even for him. She wanted to lead the exciting life. Even if the exciting life merely meant, in reality, that she was going to NYU, she was in Manhattan and on the cusp of the glamour and culture. Her schedule was entrenched in all that *is* New York: the theater, the lectures, the arts, the shops, and the restaurants. It was all so hard to resist. But the bigger reason remained: she did not want to go home, but rather, to keep her distance from the pain she felt growing up.

Nicole had watched her parents suffocate in a lifeless marriage. Her father worked as an electrician, not so much because he liked the work but, as he said often, it was a good job with good benefits and an honest living. Her mother worked as a waitress and felt cheated by life, felt stuck in a blue-collar neighborhood of Buffalo raising two kids. Being the oldest, Nicole had sensed her mother's longing and disappointment, sensed that she was going through the motions of motherhood, which seemed to be more of a burden than a joy.

Her father took it the hardest when her mother decided to leave. He wore his wedding ring for years after the divorce. But Nicole wasn't all that surprised. Part of her almost felt relieved.

Nicole was fifteen when her mom walked out, and her sister, Allison, had just turned seven. Their father became their only anchor. After she left, he did his best to raise two girls alone. He taxied them to swimming lessons, choir practices, and high school dances. He gave them dating advice, took them shopping for prom dresses. Nicole had to admit, in spite of their mother being gone, he made their lives normal.

Her mother had missed birthdays, holidays, and all their graduations. Eventually, Nicole got used to her mother not being there. It was hard at first, but she had somehow worked through the anger and disbelief to feeling numb about the whole experience. The hardest part was telling people where her mother was. Distant relatives would ask, "How's your mother?" Or strangers would say, "Your mother must be so proud of you." Nicole never knew what to say and so she said nothing at all.

"A visiting professorship at McKean College works for me," Nicole said. "I'll still get teaching experience to put on my resume, and this position gives me time to put my life in order." Nicole was trying not to think about it all again, that feeling that her life was on hold. She did not want to be so self-absorbed right now, when her father needed her. Yet the move had brought those feelings back and she knew that all she could do for now was hold them off a while. "It hasn't been any kind of sacrifice, and I haven't been there for you as much these last few years as I should have been. I want to do this. I can help you. I can see the chemo is already starting to get to you. Allison has the boys to take care of, and Jean is no kid and can't do it all herself." Jean was her father's girlfriend.

"Don't you worry about us," her father said. "We have been managing very well and I am feeling better. Speaking of Allison, have you called her yet?" he asked, almost as if he wanted to change the subject away from his health.

"Nooooo." Nicole sighed, knowing how much her father wanted them to have a closer relationship. "I'm not sure we'll ever be something out of a Norman Rockwell painting."

"She did come up with John and the boys for your graduation."

"I know. I loved introducing her to my friends. It was the first time she had visited me in New York. I know it's hard now with the kids, but it's more than the fact that she never came to see me. I don't think she'll ever fully understand why I decided to get a Ph.D. instead of a husband."

"You're probably right," her father said with a slight laugh, knowing that Allison had long believed that somehow marriage and motherhood completed a woman.

"But she is still your sister," her dad said.

Her sister had led such a completely different life than Nicole. The only things they had in common were their love for Shawn Cassidy growing up as teenagers and their mutual addiction to Ben and Jerry's Chunky Monkey ice cream. Allison got married to her childhood sweetheart after high school. They moved to Greensboro, North Carolina eight years ago. John was a carpenter, and he found better jobs in the South. They quickly started a family and Allison was busy raising Craig and Josh, both handfuls at ages two and four. Nicole was close to Allison growing up, but phone calls and letters slowly dwindled as their lives went in vastly different directions.

"All she does is question why I broke up with Michael. She thought he was the perfect guy for me. She never got that he was shallow."

"It's her reality."

"But it's not mine. Why is it that I always have to be the one to understand?"

"Because you are smarter."

"If I am so smart, how did I waste two years dating Michael?"

Glancing over at her camera bag on the sofa, Nicole thought of last Christmas Eve at Michael's apartment, how surprised she was when she opened his gift. It was a new Nikon FM2 with a telephoto lens, the same one she had wanted since taking up photography in college. Michael had pulled her close and they had kissed. Nicole was still amazed by the gift even as she stared at it now because Michael was always more interested in making love than looking at her photography.

She had met Michael at a Monet exhibit at the Museum of Art. He shared her dream of someday going to Paris to see the Louvre. Over coffee at a nearby café, she learned that Michael was a neurologist at NYU's Medical School. It was true, Michael was good looking, wealthy, and ambitious—exactly the type of man Allison thought she should marry.

He showered Nicole with flowers, dinners at elegant restaurants, and evenings at the theater. He helped her move into her latest apartment and loved to take her on lavish vacations. For their last anniversary, he took her to Tavern on the Green in a horse-drawn carriage, the one place she had wanted to go because it was in all the movies. Last Christmas he had taken her to Palm Beach to meet his parents.

Thirty-eight and single, Michael had talked about getting married and he clearly expected to settle down. He assumed Nicole, thirty-five and also single, would want the same thing. As a first step, he talked about moving in together, but Nicole always wanted to wait, at least until she finished school. Deep down, she wasn't sure if she really loved Michael, or if she was settling because she was merely tired of being on her own, tired of the loneliness and responsibility.

"We're just different, Dad," Nicole said. She had to admit that, sometimes, she was envious of Allison for the choices she made. She found herself wondering how much easier life might have been had she also gotten married, if she had someone to take care of her, had a family of her own. But then there was always the kicker to these thoughts, the fact Nicole had not just put these things off but seemed to be actively avoiding them. She could have gotten engaged to Peter, her college sweetheart. He had asked, but again, Nicole wasn't ready to commit. At that age, she thought that she was just too young or too immature to settle down, but only years later did she realize her refusal to become involved with men, beyond a certain level of involvement anyway, had become a pattern.

"Well, I should unpack," Nicole said, changing the subject. "I'll call you in the morning."

"Okay, honey," he said. "I love you."

"I love you too, Dad," Nicole said, wondering why she always deflected every feeling, as indicated by the fact that her father always said it first. She came back inside, climbing over a few boxes stuck in the middle of the kitchen floor. As she looked over all the boxes in her living room, unpacking seemed the only thing to do.

She emptied a box of T-shirts into her dresser drawer, tossed some bed sheets in the linen closet, and laid out her hair dryer, make-up case, and curling iron on the bathroom counter. She consoled herself with the thought that slowly her mess was transforming into more neatly organized clutter.

Nicole dragged several milk crates into the spare bedroom, arranged her bookshelves against the wall and placed her laptop on her desk. The room was starting to look more like a home office. She made a little space for herself on the floor and dug through an assortment of textbooks on subjects from the presidency to the constitution, to biographies of Lincoln, JFK, Roosevelt, and Truman, and to a few romance novels—her "mind candy" as she called them.

Rummaging through her books, she laughed because all she really had to show for all those years in school were boxes full of paper. As she stacked the books she was leaving at home, she stumbled upon her dissertation. Admiring the black binding and her name, *Nicole Benson, Ph.D.* engraved in gold letters on the front, she caressed the thick volume of three hundred pages and questioned if it had been worth the sacrifice.

Suddenly starved, she looked at her watch. It was almost seven o'clock. She hadn't eaten anything since an Egg McMuffin that morning. She got up from the desk, pulled a clean T-shirt and a fresh pair of shorts out of her suitcase, and took off her baseball cap to comb her hair. Dabbing on a thin coat of lipstick, she grabbed her purse and keys and walked downstairs to her car, mildly curious to see downtown again. She hardly remembered the town from the day of her interview. At the time, she had tried not to look too closely or she might have talked herself out of coming.

She turned down Main Street, a depressing little strip of decrepit old buildings, many with chipped paint and worn siding, and empty storefronts. The hallowed remains of what might have once been a vibrant town, she thought.

She parked her car at one of the many empty meters. Nicole laughed—a quarter bought an entire hour. That wouldn't even buy ten minutes in New York City.

As her feet moved along the pavement, her heart felt the decay of the vacant buildings. The town seemed so lifeless, until she looked up and saw a big neon sign on top of a large glass and chrome building. In bright pink neon letters the sign read: "Home of the ZIPPO Windproof Lighter." And the words "They Work" flashed as a large, pale blue, neon lighter flickered on and off in the middle. It was the only sign of life in the town. She thought of being at Tufts or Temple. The feeling of dread returned at the thought of starting her job at McKean College.

As she looked for a place to eat, she desperately craved a burrito from the Fresco Tortilla Grill, one of her regular stops near NYU. The only takeout places she found were a dumpy looking Chinese restaurant and a Subway, where she ordered a turkey sub as she reminded herself that Bradford was only temporary. On the way home, she decided to pick up a little something to help ease the unpacking process. She stopped at a nearby convenience store where a teenager who barely looked up from his comic book stood behind the counter.

"What do you mean, it's illegal?" Nicole exclaimed when she asked where to find a bottle of wine. She was told that wine and liquor were only sold at something called a State Store in Pennsylvania.

What kind of backwoods state is this? Nicole thought as she asked, "Where can I find one?"

"There's one just around the corner," the clerk said as Nicole hurried out the door.

Minutes later, Nicole was back at her apartment and sipping a glass of merlot, enjoying the first sense of relaxation that she had felt all day. She ate her sub at the kitchen table, and after supper, she gave up on the idea of unpacking and sat on the balcony with her wine.

It was quiet, except for the peepers chirping in the neighboring fields, and Nicole marveled that she had not seen so many stars in the sky for years and that the night sky had never looked clearer. She found Orion and remembered summers at home with her dad.

In the evenings, they would sit on the porch as he pointed out constellations. Orion was her favorite. She had talked to her father about every boyfriend and every breakup. She confided in him about every job offer and every career decision. He wondered aloud a few times why Nicole had confided in him. After all, he said, "He was just an electrician with a high school diploma." Sometimes he didn't understand all the dynamics involved with a new job offer in the business world or the nuances of being a single woman living in Manhattan, but he supported her. He always did, no matter what she chose, even when her friends and her sister didn't understand her choices at all.

Looking out over the fields as she leaned against the wooden rail of the balcony, Nicole watched fireflies flicker like Christmas lights in the dark. She felt a lump in her stomach start to swell. The more she thought about all the little things that her father had done for her, the more she realized that the move was a pilgrimage home—one that she needed as much as he did.

Nicole awoke to the cooing of two mourning doves roosting on the ledge outside her bedroom window. She ignored the pigeons that usually littered the streets in New York, but something about the familiar sound of the birds cooing made her happy to have their company as she dressed for the day. She didn't even turn on the radio. Digging through her garment bag, she found the same navy blue Liz Claiborne pantsuit that she had worn for her interview; it was the only article of clothing that wasn't wrinkled from the move.

She skipped her usual morning coffee to leave early, giving herself plenty of time, but then got stuck behind a school bus. For nearly three miles, the bus seemed to stop in front of every house on the way to the campus, and so she arrived a few minutes late for her faculty orientation at McKean College. Inside the conference room, the president of the college, a tall, thin man with grey hair and horn-rimmed glasses, greeted her. She exchanged a few pleasantries with the others gathered there and then immediately looked for the coffee. It tasted like warm sludge but it soothed her nerves.

Nicole was standing alone in the corner with her coffee, missing her small luxury of a vanilla latte at Starbucks, when President Sampson hastened everyone to be seated. He then formally introduced the group of eleven faculty members while breakfast was served. Nicole noted that, in spite of normally feeling old, she was the youngest faculty member in the room. She picked at the stale pastry and cold eggs and craved a good Manhattan bagel as she tried to make small talk with those at the table. After the caterers had cleared away the plates, President Sampson stood again to address the group.

"The college has just instituted a mentor program for new faculty," he began. "Each one of you will be assigned a mentor from among our senior faculty."

An assigned mentor? It felt a little like being back in third grade as he read off the list of names. It was in moments like this that Nicole wondered how differently her life might have been had she stayed at Citibank. After graduation, she spent years trying to get ahead, slowly trying to climb the corporate ladder. College graduates with no experience were a dime a dozen. After several years of working entry-level jobs that never went anywhere she felt like she finally had made it. In a few months, Nicole went from an assistant in their Mergers and Acquisitions Division to an account manager. They gave her a plush office with a skyline view and bonuses for every new client. No one but Nicole's father understood when she decided to quit. At twenty-nine, and with no one else to pay the bills, her friends thought she was crazy to give up a promising corporate career. Her sister thought she should go back to school to get an MBA, and her boyfriend at the time, a young attorney from Brooklyn, thought she should try law school. Nicole wanted to teach.

"And Dr. Benson, your mentor will be Dr. Carol Greysen," President Sampson said, jolting Nicole from her drifting thoughts.

Nicole looked up to see a woman with short gray hair and thick glasses waving at her. Nicole immediately guessed that Carol was in her late fifties and noted that her outfit looked like something off the Goodwill rack. As she glanced around, Nicole quickly realized that fashion was not a high priority among most of the faculty. She doubted any of them had ever heard of Calvin Klein.

After a day full of dry presentations, Carol walked over to Nicole. "It's so nice to meet you dear." Her voice sounded faintly British as she extended her hand. "I'm from Manchester. Dad was a professor at King's College. Mum was a poet laureate. You could say academia is in our blood." Carol laughed. "Don't think I've always been in this dreadful place, oh my, no. We moved to Chicago after Dad retired. I did my graduate work at Loyola. English *Literature*," she said, emphasizing the last word. "And you?"

"I just graduated from NYU," Nicole said as she shook Carol's hand and felt comforted that she too had urban roots. But Carol's demeanor wasn't much like the people she knew in New York: cold, distant, and avidly avoiding any eye contact. She had met her type before, however, the eccentric academic type whose habit of blubbering on about themselves constituted small talk.

"What's your discipline?" Carol asked as she pulled up a chair close to Nicole as if the answer could reveal everything about one's character and convictions.

"Political Science."

"Oh, I just love American politics," exclaimed Carol.

"To most people the study of government sounds boring," Nicole replied.

"Nonsense. Your American government system is quite intriguing, so much different than the Royals. And after the whole Princess Diana thing, I think that Charles and the Queen Mum didn't quite know how to handle it, a bunch of isolated snobs if you ask me. They were all fodder for the tabloids. I find Americans are so much more forthright and open," Carol laughed. She was bubbly like a bottle of champagne ready to explode. "So, what line of work is your father in?"

"He's retired now. He was an electrician. You could say academia isn't in our blood."

"And your mother?" Carol asked.

Nicole bristled. That topic was definitely off limits.

"She's gone," Nicole said, giving her stock answer. It was easier to have others believe that her mother had passed away than to admit that she had been abandoned.

"That's dreadful. I'm so sorry, my dear."

"It's okay. It was a long time ago." Nicole leaned back in her chair. She could hardly remember her mother's face. All that came to her was a vague recollection of a woman with dark curly hair and brown eyes. She wondered if she would even recognize her if she bumped into her today.

In the span of ten minutes, Nicole learned that Carol was twice divorced, once because her first husband was an abusive bastard and once because husband number two ran off with a younger woman. She learned that Carol never had children but had a niece she was close to in Florida, and that last year, while on sabbatical in London, she had an affair with a young Oxford scholar who shared her love for Chaucer and they made love all night near the Thames River.

Nicole had always felt uncomfortable around confessors, as she tended to label anyone so inclined to tell another person such things. She found herself cringing, wondering if Carol told everyone these intimate details.

"So, you're here by yourself?" Carol abruptly asked.

"Just me."

"You must come for dinner tonight," Carol said.

"Tonight?"

"I make a great beef stroganoff," Carol insisted.

Initially Nicole was going to decline her offer, but then she decided that she liked the idea of a meal that she didn't have to cook and agreed to be at Carol's by six. Nicole spent the rest of the day taking the new faculty tour of the campus and completing the orientation. She just made it home in time to change into a pair of jeans before she had to be at Carol's.

Carol lived in one of the nicer neighborhoods in town, in a large three-bedroom home behind the local hospital. She gave Nicole a quick tour.

Nicole worried that they'd have nothing in common, as Carol was more Early American and she was more Modern Contemporary in their respective tastes, but dinner was relaxed. Carol described her own difficulty adjusting to Bradford and entertained Nicole with gossip about which faculty members were having sex with which students. She discussed feminism at such great length and in such a way, invoking the most radical of feminist theorists that Nicole started to wonder if Carol hadn't converted to lesbianism, but she decided it was rude to ask.

"You don't seem the academic type." Carol turned to Nicole, dishing out the last of the stroganoff. "It takes a special breed."

"I loved the study of government and thought about teaching even as an undergrad but I never told a soul, not even my father. I loved everything about legislation and the Constitution but I didn't know what to do with that knowledge after graduation. I thought about law school for a while but I didn't have the killer instinct. Wall Street at first seemed the safest choice."

"What happened?" Carol asked.

"I hated office politics and power lunches. I hated always trying to land the next big account at the office. I quickly learned that ideas only mattered if they made money in the business world. I knew I'd never be happy with that kind of life, not in the long run."

"Well, my dear, you'll be most unpleasantly surprised," Carol said in her droll accent. "The politics in academia are more vicious than business because the stakes are so small." Carol laughed at her own joke.

"So I am learning." Nicole smiled.

As Nicole helped clear the dishes, she realized that it had been a long time since she had a home-cooked meal. Usually, dinner with friends meant that food was catered, ordered out, or eaten in crowded restaurants.

After dinner, Carol poured herself another glass of wine and took out a pack of Camels. "Hope you don't mind?"

"Not at all. I'm a closet smoker, so do you mind?"

Nicole never shared her smoking habit unless she absolutely trusted a person or was among a group of strangers. But in this case, she felt like she already knew Carol's most intimate secrets.

"Funny, you don't look like a smoker," Carol said, handing her the pack.

"I get that a lot." Nicole smiled. She always assumed it was her bookish ways that made her look too smart to smoke.

"I suppose I'll have to buy one of these now." Nicole reached for Carol's Zippo lighter and lit her first cigarette of the evening. The lighter was far different than the cheap Bics Nicole used, and when she couldn't figure out how to turn off the lighter, she exhaled a deep breath to blow out the flame.

"That's why they call them windproof." Carol laughed, grabbing the lighter to close the lid. "Even people who don't smoke own Zippos around here," she said as a cloud of white smoke blew into the air. "So what are you doing this weekend?"

"Unpacking, most likely." Nicole turned, looking directly at Carol. "Why?"

"The Crook Farm Fair is this weekend. I thought you might like to go."

"The what?"

"It's a fair held at a darling little historic farm from the 1870s that's been restored. The Bradford Landmark Society preserved the farmhouse. Every year they host a fair that is simply wonderful. They have the best fruit jams, marmalades, and rhubarb pie. I always pick up a couple of jars of bread and butter pickles."

"Bread and butter pickles?" Nicole was almost afraid to ask.

"Oh, you'll just have to try them." Carol laughed.

A country fair didn't sound like Nicole's idea of fun. Besides, she was not much for trying new things. Like Carol's invitation for dinner, however, she was about to decline the offer and explain why she needed to stay home to unpack, but the thought of spending the weekend alone gave her a chill. This odd woman with so much energy and no secrets might just lead the way to . . . Nicole gave up the thought since she had no idea what might transpire. But she decided that she might learn something intriguing about this place, something that she could use to aid in her survival for the next year, and she accepted the invitation.

The Crook Farm was a journey back through time. Arriving promptly at noon, Nicole drove past the split-rail fence into the entrance, parking her car in a large grassy field. She could hear a bluegrass band as she walked down the gravel path toward the farm. The whole scene would fit inside a Manhattan square block. There was a small rustic bank building to her right and a one-room schoolhouse to her left, next to an old-fashioned general store with children running around on the wooden porch in front. In the distance a ways, she saw the renovated farmhouse Carol mentioned, and she pictured the early pioneers standing on the small wooden slab porch of the vintage home. Nicole almost expected to see Laura Ingalls running across the prairie any minute.

Dozens of white tents covered the farm area where vendors were selling homemade bird feeders, homemade wicker baskets, wooden ducks, and, of course, dozens of jars of bread and butter pickles. The scene was a far cry from the street vendors in New York selling tacky oil paintings of Elvis and fake Rolex watches.

Clumps of people leisurely browsed each table, and Nicole imagined the women in corsets and petticoats and the men in derby hats and frocks. She watched people clapping their hands to the Wily Milo Old Time String Band, which made her want to run, but she had promised to meet Carol at the old schoolhouse and so headed in that direction.

At 12:30, there was still no sign of Carol. She peeked inside the dim schoolhouse and saw a black potbelly stove in the center of the room and several rows of ancient wooden desks all facing a slate blackboard. The room even smelled aged. Nicole sat on the wooden step outside to wait for Carol. From here she could see several picnic tables under a large tent just in front of a turn- of- the- century barn.

A man hugging a group of elderly people caught her eye. She watched how his broad shoulders moved with ease as he bent down to kiss the ones in wheelchairs and how his touch was like that of a son. She wondered how he knew all those old people as he helped another woman with her plate of food and another with her napkin. He wore khaki pants and a cream-colored button-down that nicely fit his tall build. He had youthful features and thick auburn hair accented with gray at the temples. Something about his face made him seem kind.

"Sorry I'm late." Carol's voice startled Nicole from her reverie. Carol was dressed in a large green hat, a pink top, and bright orange shorts. She looked more like a large floral pansy.

"I couldn't find my keys. Then I had to stop for gas. Oh, and then I had to go back home because I forgot my purse."

"It's fine." Nicole's perfectionism would never allow her to be that disorganized, but she knew only a few people on the planet were even remotely organized and so usually forgave that negative quality in others.

Carol grabbed Nicole's arm. "I can't wait to show you around."

Nicole decided to make the best of the afternoon. It seemed that every booth had its own homemade jams and jellies for sale. Carol bought three jars of pickles, which Nicole promised to try. Carol dragged her inside the restored farmhouse where a woman wearing an apron and colonial mop hat with white lace trim greeted them. The woman explained that Erastus Crook had built the farm, which included a barn, corn crib, carpentry shop, oil tank, boiler house, and pumping rig. Nicole tried to look interested but found her mind wandering to all the unpacking that she still had to do.

It was almost two-thirty, and Nicole hadn't eaten all day. Even though she wore shorts, she was not only hungry but dying from the humidity. Carol treated her to a hot dog, corn on the cob, and lemonade at one of the food stands. They bumped into President Sampson and his wife waiting in line and exchanged pleasantries. After they ate, Carol made a dart for the Amish quilts. Craving a funnel cake, Nicole walked across the farm. She made her way past the bluegrass band to the funnel cake stand, ordered two cakes with extra powdered-sugar, and grabbed a handful of napkins.

She carefully balanced a funnel cake in each hand as she made her way back toward Carol, who was now trying on an Amish shawl. Nicole leaned over to take a bite of one. The taste reminded her of her father. Nicole was seven when her father took her to the Erie County Fair for the first time. She was scared by a circus clown. Her father made her tears go away with a funnel cake. Nicole wished it were still that easy to make her happy.

Suddenly, a baby stroller crashed into Nicole's arm, sending her funnel cakes and napkins flying to the ground. The mother, oblivious to the accident, continued walking.

"Here, let me pick those up for you," a voice said from behind her, and a man bent down to grab her fallen napkins.

"Thank you." Nicole turned to the man as she picked up the broken pieces of cake from the grass, surprised to see his face. It was the same man she had seen hugging all the old people, except now he had on a pair of bifocals.

"I saw the whole thing. You could probably sue." She studied his features more closely. He had a warm smile and more gray at his temples than she had noticed from afar. He was tall with broad shoulders, making him seem rugged, and yet he had a boyish face. His bifocals made him seem distinguished without seeming old. Something in his deep green eyes instantly charmed her.

"I suppose rudeness isn't limited to us New Yorkers." She finally stood and then, as if by instinct, noticed his wedding band as he handed the napkins back to her.

"Thanks again." She smiled and juggled the funnel cakes to free one hand. "I'm Nicole Benson."

"Nice to meet you," he replied as he shook her hand. "Tom Ryan." He pointed to her shirt. "You spilled a little sugar."

"A little?" She laughed, looking down to see her navy blue polo shirt covered in white. She started to brush off the sugar, which normally would have made her feel embarrassed, but she noticed that Tom had politely looked away as she started to wipe off her shirt.

Tom offered to hold her funnel cakes, and when both her hands were free, he asked, "Is this your first time at the fair?"

"Yes, I'm still getting used to all the trees," Nicole replied, continuing to wipe at the sugar.

"Oh, the trees." He smiled. "Did you know that Bradford was once a timber mecca?" he asked as he looked past the fairgrounds and into the woods. "In the 1820s, the town was occupied by lumbermen and was a main supplier of wooden rims for bicycles and carriages. And at one time, half of all the toothpicks in the world came from here."

"That's a lot of toothpicks." Nicole laughed, making a bigger stain as the white powder smeared.

"See that?" Tom asked, ignoring the mess she was making. He pointed to a rusted metal pump jack. "That's an oil pump. It was oil that put Bradford on the map. By the late 1800s, the area became known as the High Grade Oil Metropolis of the World."

Tom's eyes then turned to Nicole and his gaze lingered on her face, lingered in a way that had not happened in years, if ever. Michael certainly had never looked at her that way.

"Wow, I've only been here a few days and I've got an entire history lesson about my new digs," Nicole said, impressed by Tom's passion for the area. Then she noticed a button on his shirt that read Co-Chairperson.

"Are you some type of official for the fair?" Nicole asked, but before Tom had a chance to answer, Carol suddenly appeared.

"Meeting our new faculty, Tom?" Carol asked. Nicole was surprised that Carol knew Tom. She then learned that they served together on the board for the Bradford Landmark Society, the group that ran the Crook Farm Fair, for several years.

"Tom's an administrator for one of the largest nursing homes in McKean County," Carol explained. Now Nicole understood his connection to the elderly. Nicole recounted the stroller accident to Carol, pointing out her shirt coated in white. Carol laughed and couldn't resist showing off her new Amish shawl.

Nicole thought the shawl unattractive, even downright ugly, but she kept that opinion to herself.

"It was only sixty dollars," Carol gushed. Of course, Nicole thought she overpaid.

Tom looked at his watch. "I didn't realize the time. It's my turn to clear off the picnic tables." He tossed away the remains of the funnel cakes in his hand. "You should get another funnel cake. Tell them it's on me," he said before he turned to leave.

"Thanks again." Nicole smiled and waved goodbye.

Nicole looked over her shoulder and noticed that Tom had turned to look in her direction as well. Was he looking at her? She could not tell if he had merely glanced over his shoulder or was actually looking directly at her.

Nicole had no way of knowing, but as she disappeared into the crowd and Tom went about the mundane tasks required to close the fair for the night, her image kept returning to him. This was the first time that he could remember that any woman kept appearing in his thoughts as if against his will.

CHAPTER 2

Tom

It took Tom longer than usual to get the fairgrounds cleaned up. They were short a couple of volunteers, but he didn't seem to have his mind on the task at hand. The woman he had just met kept appearing in his thoughts, but he assumed it was merely the fact that she was pleasant and beautiful, something of an exotic creature among the locals. By the time he finished the short drive home, Rose had gone to bed so the house was very quiet. He took a beer from the refrigerator and dropped into a chair in the living room to unwind. The events of the day kept flashing through his mind. Why was he continuing to dwell on the young woman he had met at the fair? That kind of obsessive thinking, let alone about a woman, let alone one younger than he, was so out of character. Tom now thought about his marriage instead.

For the first fifteen years of their marriage, he and Rose were very close and had what seemed to be common interests. When they first met, they went biking in the summers and ice skating in the winters until Rose sprained her left ankle. Tom was even one of those guys who didn't mind going shopping, and Rose loved that about him. They would go to the mall and spend the afternoon together, sharing a nice dinner out in the evening. The arrival of their son Robert seemed to strengthen their relationship. They would have a picnic lunch at the park and visit the zoo, and one summer, Robert and Tom being history buffs, had taken a trip to Washington, D.C. But everything changed when they lost their daughter, Lisa, to leukemia.

He reached for the television remote on the coffee table and clicked through the channels. There wasn't much on that late in the evening except for infomercials, reruns of *Law & Order*, and the news. He watched CNN as the anchor ran through the top news stories of the day. His mind wandered and he thought again about meeting Nicole. What brought a woman like her to such a remote town and from New York City no less? She surely had other choices. A well-educated woman like her would expect more than this town in the woods had to offer after all those years of education, he thought. And what if she didn't move here alone? What if he ran into her again? How would he react? The questions began to wear on him, so senseless given that he had no answers, but especially given the topic. As the television flickered in the background, he wondered why he was thinking of her at all and began to feel ridiculous. He looked at his watch, finished his beer, and went to bed. He assured himself that his head would be clearer in the morning.

He awoke to the smell of bacon. Rose was in their kitchen, a kitchen that they had remodeled the year before. Instead of old metal cupboards, Formica counters, and linoleum floors, they had put in cherry cabinets, granite countertops, and ceramic tile flooring. They thought it would help them move on in some small way, to forget about Lisa for just a bit if they renovated the house. But her bedroom remained the same because even entering it was too difficult for Rose to face, let alone changing it. She had screamed at him in a moment of despair that her daughter's death wasn't something that she could simply forget with a few coats of new paint and new furniture for the room where Lisa had slept and played.

Cooking bacon was a task that Rose had done a million times before. She loved getting up early, still in her nightgown and bathrobe, cooking breakfast for the children and then getting them ready for school. Her role was to be a mother. It was what she had loved about life.

Rose had tied her thick red hair into a ponytail keeping it off her face just like she wore it when she worked at the hospital. Her maiden name was O'Malley. Her grandparents came from Ireland and settled in Pittsburgh working at the steel mills. Her father had insisted Rose and her brother, Richard, both get some type of college education. Rose immediately chose nursing.

She had enjoyed being a nurse, taking care of others was her nature, her calling, but she loved being a mother more. As Rose stood at the stove, it still seemed empty being there without Lisa sitting at the kitchen table. Lisa had loved learning how to cook. Rose was a willing teacher. Rose would bake cookies before Lisa's Brownie meetings. She would make fresh bread each week for Tom and the kids. She would make homemade pizza for Robert and his hockey teammates after school games. Lisa would be her sous chef mixing batter or chopping vegetables.

As the bacon sizzled in the pan, Rose sighed. Those days were long gone.

"Remember when we redid all this," Tom said entering the room. There was no kiss. They hadn't kissed in years.

"I sure do," Rose said. "It took months before I felt comfortable cooking again in here."

Rose turned her body, scraping the last of the scrambled eggs onto a plate with a few slices of bacon on the side.

"I hope you wanted bacon," Rose said, putting some on the plate next to the scrambled eggs and wheat toast.

"That's fine," Tom said, pouring coffee from the Mr. Coffee maker and pulling up a chair at the walnut table, another new item they had added.

"Have you heard from Robert?" she asked, putting the plate in front of Tom.

"Not since last week. He was studying for midterms."

"He works too hard."

"Yes, you are always the worried mother. He can handle going to school. It's only part-time." Robert was twenty-three and had graduated from the University of Pittsburgh with a degree in finance, and he was now working on his MBA at night.

"He has such a big job at the bank," Rose said.

"He's single and he'll figure it out."

Their conversations were always the same, usually about Robert and sometimes about the bills and household finances.

Tom wolfed down the eggs and bacon. There was silence as they ate. He looked at the sun shining through the kitchen window, skimmed the headlines of *The Bradford Era*, and almost twenty minutes later finally broke the silence between them.

"I think we should have a few nice days," he said, picking up his plate and heading toward the sink. "Weatherman says it shouldn't rain until next week."

"Oh, that's good," Rose said, almost absent-mindedly. "I'm going to pick some blackberries to make some pies. I thought I'd bring one to Robert when I visit him this weekend."

"He'd like that," Tom said, finishing his coffee. He was ready to go to work. In spite of the few words between them, Tom felt tired out by the small talk.

He got up from the table and climbed the stairs. He turned down the hallway and walked by Lisa's room as he made his way to the bathroom. He peeked inside. It had been months since he had done that. He missed her. Each day, each night, he wanted her back.

It had been six years since Lisa's funeral, and Tom still couldn't bring himself to talk about her death. Staring at her bed, he was reminded of how he and Rose had tucked Lisa into bed as part of their evening ritual after dinner. Now, they seemed to have separate times for going to bed, like they both were trying to avoid being reminded of Lisa. Through the years, Rose had focused her energy on Robert, putting her heart into their son. Tom had focused his energy on his hunting camp, putting his heart into the woods. But there was no escape. He remembered Lisa's smile as she tagged along beside him with her Barbie knapsack and pigtails. She loved the woods too, the way the snow covered the valley and how the icicles glistened in the trees.

Lisa's bedroom was blue, her favorite color. She had hand painted a mural of various fish species, and there were fish peel-and-stick wall decals scattered around too. She loved fish after visiting Sea World. She had a painting of Shamu the whale she made in first grade and photographs of their dog, Pepper, a cocker spaniel that died years before she did. Next to the bed, she kept a large cork bulletin board where she hung artwork from school, pictures, ribbons, and awards. Her favorite award, first place in the reading contest, hung in the middle of the board. Tom looked around the room one last time. He felt the tears well, as they did every time he peeked in here. Her knapsack was in the same corner she'd left it the night they had to rush her to the hospital. The leukemia had progressed too quickly. There was nothing more the doctors could do.

Lisa had come along several years after Robert. It only took a few months before she became Daddy's little girl, and as she grew up, she was a bit of a tomboy and little girl all at the same time. When she got old enough, she went for treks with him in the woods when they would go to camp, where Tom spent weekends updating the kitchen and building the loft into a real bedroom.

Lisa knew that trips to camp would always include a walk in the woods in search of deer, turkey, or grouse. By the time she was in kindergarten, she was able to identify the tracks of all the various local wildlife. He would take Lisa whenever possible. The routine was to work on cabin upgrades while Lisa took a nap. When she woke up, they would take a walk, which were much shorter after she became ill because she would get tired very quickly. As the sickness wore on, she would sit on the porch with a blanket over her shoulders and watch the changing leaves. In the winter, she would sit in front of the fire. By spring of that year, she had gotten too weak to make the trip to camp, and by the summer following her diagnosis, the day Rose and Tom dreaded finally came.

Tom closed the door to Lisa's room behind him and made his way to the bathroom. He combed his hair and shaved, and on his way out of the bathroom, he grabbed his tie and jacket from the bedroom. Looking over the room, he remembered when they first moved back to Bradford, how he and Rose had been much closer. They went to the movies, went on picnics, and took walks together. The world for them could not have been better. Rose loved her job as a nurse at the hospital, and Tom was settling in as the director of the nursing home. Robert was in high school and Lisa was in second grade. Both of the kids were doing well in school but Lisa seemed to be as absorbed in learning as she was entranced with the forest. She loved school, especially English. She had won second place in the elementary school's spelling bee. She always had a new word that she would share with them over dinner. That fall, when Tom had taken Lisa to camp, she began to complain of being tired and to show signs of an infection and a fever. Rose took her to see a pediatrician when they returned but he was unable to immediately determine a cause for Lisa's fatigue.

When Lisa was in the third grade, she began to lose weight. She was never a big eater, but they took her to the doctor just in case. The doctor ran a battery of tests and they were shocked when he told them that Lisa was suffering from leukemia and the disease had been progressing rapidly. The cancer was aggressive, and even with treatment, the doctor told them that Lisa did not have long to live.

Rose broke down crying at the news. Tom tried to be strong and didn't say a word. They drove home in silence. They didn't know how to tell Lisa. What could they say? How to explain? They waited a few months before they told her. At such a young age, they feared that Lisa would not understand what was wrong with her. They worried she would be scared, and she was.

At first, Lisa understood she was sick and wasn't feeling well. Once the chemotherapy treatments started, she had more problems coping. Going back to school after her diagnosis was a good thing because she was with her friends and that kept her mind occupied, but then she became more sick and fatigued with each treatment. She was unable to concentrate on her schoolwork. She was not doing well, especially in English, and that almost crushed her more than having cancer. Her friends noticed that her hair was thinning and she had lost weight, and at such a young age, it was hard for them to understand what was happening to her.

It was hard to come to grips with the prospect of losing Lisa. They tried to keep Lisa's life as stable as possible. Although she was aware of her condition and understood the outcome was not likely going to be good, Lisa was incredibly brave.

The priest came up to Tom at the church as he passed the casket and whispered, "God takes the most beautiful flowers for his garden." He wanted to believe that Lisa was in a better place, but she had left a void at his side and he was not so sure he didn't begrudge God his flowers.

Fully dressed now, Tom walked down the hallway, these thoughts heavy on his mind. He took one more look into Lisa's room, why, he wasn't sure. Then he remembered the date, the first of September, the anniversary of her death. Now he understood why he was thinking so much about Lisa.

Rose was still in the kitchen cleaning up breakfast when he came downstairs, as he put on his boots in the foyer and grabbed his overcoat.

"See you later," he said to Rose, and he kissed her on the cheek as he always had since they'd been married, now out of habit. "It might be cold up in the woods, even this early in September."

"Have a good day at work," she said as she always did when Tom left in the morning, and she stopped wiping down the counter for a moment to let him kiss her, also out of habit.

As Tom drove to work, he noted that the crisp air carried a hint of a coming change of season. Fall was his favorite, the changing colors of the leaves and hunting season. He hoped that he would have an opportunity to get out some this season. The short drive to the office didn't give him much time to get his head into the work that lay ahead of him that morning. There had been too much on his mind before he left the house. As usual, he stopped for a cup of coffee at the convenience store to get his thoughts together before pulling into the parking lot of the nursing home.

Tom had been the assistant manager at one of the largest nursing agencies in Pittsburgh. His mother was alone after his father died. When her health began to fail, he felt it was time for him to come home to Bradford. He took a job as manager of the local nursing home while Rose was able to get a nursing position at the Bradford Hospital.

The nursing home was one of the largest in McKean County, which kept him busy in meetings with the administration and his staff most of the week.

Tom now looked over the paperwork spread across his desk. There was a pile of Medicare forms to finish. Mildred's medications needed to be checked. He had a meeting with his board of directors to review the budget. He needed to keep his mind occupied.

He enjoyed working with the elderly. They reminded him of the simple aspects of life. He loved just walking through the hallways talking with the residents. One resident, a strikingly beautiful woman in her eighties named Carmen, always waited for him to arrive. She had a smile as bright as the sun and gorgeous shimmering silver hair. Her attire was always impeccable and she had the grace of a swan as Tom wheeled her to the beauty parlor down the hallway, as he did now. He also cried and prayed with another resident who reminded him of his mother. She was very broken, sad because she had just lost her forty-three year-old son to a massive heart attack and five days later lost her husband of forty-five years. She was a very large woman with a broken leg, and she was bedridden, unable to do much of anything for herself. He helped a couple of residents suffering from Alzheimer's who were wandering around the hallways back to their rooms, and he visited a couple of patients who suffered from terminal illnesses to help them cope with the pain. It was residents like these that put his life in perspective and made his work meaningful. While he loved working at a nursing home, when he became an administrator, the job became more about the paperwork than the residents and he spent less time on the floor and more time in his office, at board meetings, and at conferences. But there were days when he set the administrative tasks aside and spent time with the residents, like today.

No matter what else he was doing this day, however, he could not shake the image of his daughter on the porch of the cabin watching for the deer. Even when she became sick from the chemotherapy, she loved going to the cabin. She curled up by the woodstove and read or colored, and she could forget about her illness, even for a few moments, in the solitude that the cabin offered.

He grabbed his overcoat, told his secretary he was leaving, and headed for the Kinzua Bridge. Seeing Lisa's room again had made him remember the first time he talked to Rose about Lisa, and now he could not shake the memory. A couple of months after the funeral, they were sitting at the kitchen table on a Saturday morning. Robert had just left for college in Pittsburgh. They were alone for the first time in weeks, empty nesters for the first time without Lisa.

"How are you doing?" he asked.

"What do you mean?"

"You haven't said a word about the funeral," he said, in a quiet tone.

There was a long pause.

"I answered all the sympathy cards. We had so many memorials. My mother was a help. She kept a list. I think I have written to everyone."

"I meant about Lisa," Tom said tentatively.

Rose got up from the table and started clearing the breakfast dishes. Still, she said nothing.

The water poured from the kitchen faucet as Rose washed the dishes, carefully placing each on the draining board. All Tom heard was the clinking of the glassware.

"I'm not sure I can," Rose finally whispered, and then she was quiet again.

She washed both of their plates, their silverware, and her coffee cup as Tom sat at the kitchen table in silence. He finished his coffee and put the cup in the sink as she continued washing dishes and wiping down the counter. He went upstairs to take a shower and they never said another word that morning.

Tom made a few more attempts to help Rose deal with her grief, but all he seemed to accomplish was to cause her to become more withdrawn. Bradford was a very small town. Some of Rose's co-workers would tell Tom when he ran into them at the grocery or the gas station that she seemed to be in a fog. They said she did a professional job but didn't seem to have the same concern for the patients as she did before Lisa's death. It seemed impossible to rebuild what Tom and Rose had together before the kids came along, and they started to retreat into their own social circles. Rose had her book club friends and her knitting group. Tom had his hunting friends, his work and volunteering in the community. They tried to cope in their own ways, but it seemed hopeless that they would ever be able to deal with their grief together as parents.

Tom drove to the bridge now, feeling that usual pang of anxiety. It was very difficult to go back to camp after Lisa's death. Sometimes he would make the trip to the cabin with every intention of making some improvement that was badly needed, but he would spend the day sitting or roaming around in the woods with no real plan or purpose. He would dwell on how much Lisa enjoyed the cabin and how much he missed her. She had left a hole in his heart that he knew was going to take a very long time to heal, but sometimes he wondered if the wound ever would heal. She always would be the little girl who tagged along on walks in the woods with her pink backpack and her wondrous curiosity.

He pulled the car off the hard road, and as he pulled into the driveway, he felt sad. He hadn't been at the camp in weeks. He turned off the engine and sat there for a long time staring at the front of the cabin, remembering so many good times that he shared with his father and his daughter at this place. Then, unexpectedly, he thought of Nicole, how a city woman like her had probably never been to a cabin this far out in the woods. If she had, it was probably with a group of friends on ski trips or camping trips to get away from the hustle and bustle of the city. He felt resentful that he was thinking about her, as if she had intruded where she did not belong. He had no reason to be thinking of her.

The air was dry and the skies were clear, not one cloud in sight, a good day to be on the trail. Tom got out of the car, tied a loose lace on his shoe, and started through the trees, through brush and gravel until he got to one of the trails. He remembered a backpacking trip through the woods with his father as he hiked.

It was far different than the weather today. Tom couldn't have been more than eight or nine. They were trudging through the woods near this very path, and Tom's head hurt and his stomach was weak. He was getting over the flu but had insisted on going hiking with his dad. Backpacking might have seemed like a cruel punishment to most kids his age, but Tom insisted.

It was an easy hike. They had started early in the morning after breakfast, heading toward the bridge. It was several miles, but Tom wanted to see it. They had only gone a mile when Tom wandered ahead of his father a couple of hundred yards.

The forecast had been for clear skies and temps in the mid 40s, but as they hiked, the temperature dropped, clouds moved in, and it started to snow. Zero visibility snow. The trail was poorly marked and staying on it became difficult as Tom and his father had turned to walk back to the camp.

Tom had looked back and couldn't see his father at all, just snow. Tom continued to walk down the dirt path, careful to watch the trail markers as the snow swirled around his face, the evergreens coated with thick powder. The trail eventually disappeared in the building snow.

Tom became scared and the snow felt like sand on his face. He wasn't sure if he was heading in the right direction. His backpack seemed heavier. He felt like he couldn't breathe. Suddenly, appearing from the snow, his father's face was in front of him.

"Grab my hand. Did you think I would lose you in all this snow?" his father said reaching for Tom and tossing his backpack on his shoulder.

"No," Tom said. "I knew you'd find me."

On the way back to the camp, Tom's father talked about safe hiking practices in the colder months, how they needed to dress in layers, which they had done, bringing along plenty of water, which they had, and keeping a flashlight, which they had brought too.

"You have to avoid eating snow as a source of water," his father said, calming Tom's fears about being lost. "The body has to expend a great deal of energy to warm even a small amount of snow or water."

They made their way back to the camp safely, and Tom always remembered that morning. Tom's father had taught him everything about the woods, hiking, and the trails that surrounded the Kinzua Bridge. In that one moment, on that single trip, his father had made the woods seem safe, no matter what. It was ironic that his father died in a hunting accident when Tom was only eighteen. Tom had taught the same things to Lisa that his father taught him all those years ago.

That was perhaps part of what made Lisa's death so unimaginable. Like most parents, Tom expected to see Lisa grow and mature. Naturally, he expected to die first and leave his children behind. That was the natural course of life's events, the lifecycle continuing as it should. But worse than the fact that a child had preceded a parent, she had been his apprentice in the woods, as he had been his father's. Now, they were both gone. His grief was boundless when his daughter died.

As he made his way up the trail now on this unexpectedly nice summer day, he remembered getting caught in a storm while snowshoeing with Lisa. The snow felt like sand on his face much like it did that morning when he was a boy with his father. Lisa was scared because visibility had gotten poor quickly. Tom turned to Lisa, grabbing her hand, and told her about the snow and why to avoid eating it when it is cold. She had looked at him then like he imagined himself looking at his father all those years before, calmer, stronger, and thankful.

Tom looked at his watch. He had been hiking for almost an hour. It was getting late and close to dinner time. He turned around and started back to his car at the camp. It was quiet, even a bit eerie. The wind was still. All he could hear was the crunching of dirt underneath his boots.

The sun was going down fast and the shadows were long and dark. As he walked through the woods, the silence spoke to him. He felt a presence, a tender voice almost calling to him, like something was about to happen, something that could change the way he felt, lift the emptiness from his heart and make him feel whole again.

CHAPTER 3

The Dedication Ceremony

Nicole walked across the campus to her new office. It was early September, the college coming alive as a new academic calendar year began. The syllabi were printed, the lines at the campus bookstore were long, and suddenly unstructured time transformed into a rigid class schedule. The chairperson of the department showed her the mailroom, where to make copies, and where to get free coffee. Unfortunately, the university coffee was putrid, which prompted her to begin a new morning ritual. Nicole stopped at the local Mini-Mart to pick up a copy of *USA Today*, an occasional box of Pop Tarts, and a cup of French vanilla cappuccino dispensed from a self-serve machine. It wasn't Starbucks but the coffee didn't taste half bad.

Her office was large but lacked a window, which didn't bother her. She was used to sharing a small cubicle with two other graduate students at NYU. The florescent lights bothered her eyes, however, so she purchased two halogen lamps that gave the room a warm glow. She hung her diplomas on the wall behind her desk as reassurance of her accomplishments. She placed a small plant on her desk and organized all of her folders and textbooks. She unpacked all the boxes of books that she had lugged from Manhattan and wondered if she shouldn't have put some in storage. She tacked up a wall calendar of New York scenes in front of her desk so she could count the days until she left Bradford, and she brought in her portable stereo and a selection of CDs. She knew she was investing more time decorating her office than her apartment, but she figured this is where she'd be spending most of her time.

Her teaching load was heavy, five sections a semester: three sections of Introduction to Political Science, a section of Quantitative Political Research, and a section of American Government, her specialty. Nicole would also need to squeeze in time for grant writing and student advising. She began her routine of arriving before the noise of the faculty and students set in. Her morning ritual consisted of crossing off a calendar day, sipping her cappuccino, cracking open her newspaper, and playing a little Billy Joel or the Eagles. As the chatter outside her office grew louder, she turned off her stereo, checked her e-mail, and got down to work.

Her American Government class was on Monday morning, her first class of the new semester in this new place. Nicole was one of those teachers who made all the students introduce themselves, tell where they were from, their major in college, and so on the first day of school. While students hated the exercise, she knew that getting them to talk on the first day broke the ice for the rest of the semester. Her first class went smoothly, and she felt ready for the next.

Teaching was perhaps the only place she revealed her heart. At Citibank, Nicole wanted to feel passion in her work, but deep down, she never felt comfortable in the ruthless world of corporate America. She loved the look of her neatly pressed business suits and the feel of her briefcase as she walked through the bustling streets and into her office building, and waiting with the crowds at the elevators made her feel a part of the fast track. She felt important as she said good morning to her coworkers too, but once she reached her desk, she felt like a complete impostor.

Her confidence was fragile, and throughout the day she tried to please her boss in the same way she had tried to please her mother as a little girl. Once, she confided in Michael that her mother was a critical and bitter woman. Her mother dreamed of going to college, but instead she became pregnant with Nicole and married her father. When Nicole was growing up, her mother acted as if she resented her for all the lost opportunities in her life. Nothing Nicole did was ever good enough. When she was grown up, she envied the relationship her friends had with their mothers, the shopping, luncheons, and girl talk. She especially hated it when another woman described her mother as her best friend. As an adult, Nicole acted poised and confident but continued to feel the insecurity surge inside whenever dealing with an authority figure.

Although she appeared outwardly optimistic, she wrote poetry that reflected an underlying dark and tragic mood. She admired the greats such as Whitman, Emerson, and especially Emily Bronte when she obsessed over doomed relationships. After watching Robin Williams in the movie *The Dead Poets Society*, her career direction changed. The movie struck a deep chord that helped her decide to apply her scholarly achievement to the art of teaching. With the help of her dissertation advisor, who mentored her, she no longer felt like an impostor but like someone who had found her true passion.

The hardest part of her job was the academic bureaucracy, however. As she watched the pettiness of departmental meetings, she thought, "All this education in one room and no one can make a decision."

The next morning, Nicole was running late for class and made a quick stop to get gas. She didn't have time for her daily cappuccino fix. When she got in line to pay the cashier, she spotted Tom Ryan pouring a cup of coffee.

"Hi there," Nicole said as she walked up behind him. "Remember me?"

"Of course," Tom said, turning around, the look of surprise on his face somehow pleasing to Nicole. "From the Crook Farm."

"So you need your caffeine fix, too," she joked, noticing that he was staring at her face, lingering on her eyes the same way he did the day they met at the fair.

"I'll need it for my meeting with the board this morning. We're reviewing the budget." Tom managed a smile, but Nicole thought that a feather could have made him drop. He looked disconcerted to see her again, and she wondered if maybe he was only uncomfortable around women of her age. Maybe he had been married so long he was intimidated by an attractive woman making conversation.

"I need my daily injection," Nicole said, laughing. She decided that, since she was already late, she might as well grab her usual cup of cappuccino. "Funny running into you again," she said as the swishing sound of the cappuccino machine started.

"Hazards of a small town I guess," Tom said over the noise of the machine. Nicole noticed that he seemed to have gathered his wits about him and she assumed he was probably thinking about his day.

Nicole wanted to stay and talk, perhaps have an interesting conversation, but she glanced at the long line that had formed at the checkout counter and then looked at her watch. "I'm sorry, but I'm late for class."

"I'm running late myself," Tom said as he reached for a lid for his coffee cup. "It was nice seeing you again." He smiled and waved goodbye.

A few minutes later, Tom was standing at the counter. Nicole got in line a few customers behind him. She noticed his love handles, which suggested he didn't work out regularly, and although he was dressed in a blue suit, she noted that his attire didn't exactly scream *GQ*. As Nicole paid the cashier, she thought she caught him looking back at her again, but he looked away so fast she was unsure that he looked at her all. Nicole ran to her car, which was still at the gas pump, an irate customer waiting impatiently for his turn.

Her whole day felt rushed, and tonight of all nights she had to go to a cocktail party at school. The university was sponsoring a dedication ceremony for a new clock tower. Nicole wasn't going to attend, but then she talked to Carol, who told her that all the faculty were "encouraged" to attend. After her last class, Nicole called her father to tell him that she would visit that weekend and then hurried to her apartment to dress for the evening.

"This is Bradford, not New York," she said to herself as she stood in front of her closet and combed through her clothes. She settled on a simple yet elegant black dress that clung nicely to her slender figure. She usually hated pantyhose, but for some reason, she needed to feel like she was going to a glamorous city event, even if it was dinky Bradford. As Nicole touched up her hair and her makeup, she decided to wear her string of pearls, which, like her Nikon, was a gift from Michael. She smoked the last of her cigarette, brushed her teeth, put on a light coat of lipstick, and a few minutes later headed out the door.

Already fashionably late, she wasn't in the mood to mingle, and she dreaded arriving alone. As Nicole approached the gathering, she immediately looked for the bar and proceeded to get a glass of merlot, compliments of the university. President Sampson and his wife were greeting the distinguished members of the university advisory board. As Nicole milled around, saying hello to a few of the faculty she knew, she noticed a buffet of finger sandwiches, shrimp cocktail, clams casino, and scallops wrapped in bacon. Dinner without having to cook, she thought, as she loaded a plate and sat down alone at one of the tables set up around the bell tower.

"Hi stranger," a voice said from behind.

Nicole turned. It was Tom.

"We're going to set a record for bumping into one another." She smiled.

"I saw you walk in. I didn't know you'd be here too." He smiled and felt a twinge of shyness seeing Nicole this time. Standing at the bar, he had seen Nicole sitting at a table alone. He debated if he should go over to talk with her. A part of him felt he shouldn't. He didn't want to give the wrong impression being a married man but his body moved uncontrollably, almost without thought, rationalizing that it would not hurt to say hello, giving in to the feeling that he wanted to talk with her.

"I was told faculty should be here. It's sort of a command performance," Nicole said, noticing the plate of food in Tom's hand. "Do you want to sit?" she asked and then wondered if he was alone.

"Sure." He laid his plate on the table, pulled out a chair, and sat down. "Normally, Rose, my wife would be here but she's not feeling well."

"Nothing serious, I hope."

"Nothing serious, just a touch of the flu." Tom placed a napkin on his lap and took a sip of his wine. He looked at Nicole again closely, closer than he had allowed himself to look at any other woman. She had long dark hair that flowed over her shoulders, a petite figure, and warm brown eyes that indicated a depth that went beyond her intellect and classic beauty. She hardly wore any makeup compared to some women he met. She had a natural beauty and especially nice legs. Maybe she was a dancer earlier in her life, he thought. He rationalized that it was harmless to admire her. After all, a woman with her beauty could never be interested in a man like him, he thought: old, pudgy, and gray.

"So how was your day since this morning?" Nicole said. "You seemed a bit distracted."

"It was okay. And your day?"

"Oh, fine." Nicole sighed. "I was already late for class, and then with this thing tonight . . . I would have preferred to have stayed home and rented a movie."

"I know exactly what you mean. I don't much care for these kinds of things." Mingling wasn't what he preferred to do, but it had become ritual. Being involved in the community had meant being invited to numerous cocktail parties and receptions, and he felt obligated to go.

"So, how did your meeting go? The one with your board?" she asked.

"It could have been better, but it could have been worse, too," he said. "We're going through budget cuts. Everyone is a little on edge, wondering what will happen next year. We just hired a new grant writer who has secured a few grants from the National Geriatric Society. These days, it's about finding creative ways to deal with overpopulated facilities and an underpaid staff." Tom paused. It was so easy talking with Nicole. "I hope I'm not boring you with shop talk?" Tom asked.

"You're not boring me at all." Nicole found the conversation quite refreshing compared to dates with men eager to impress her with their incomes. Then she reminded herself this wasn't a date, that this man had no reason to want to impress her. After all, he was married.

"This year seems worse than last. Our annual bus trip to Shea's Theater in Buffalo may even be cancelled."

"Buffalo? I'm from Buffalo."

"I thought you were from New York City."

"No, I just moved there for college. That was almost seventeen years ago, so New York's kind of my home, but I am originally from Buffalo. That's why I'm here now. My dad still lives there with his girlfriend, Jean, or his companion, as he calls her. At his age, I figure that's only fair. Girlfriend sounds too much like high school, and Jean's a grandmother."

"I used to go to the Sabres games all the time," Tom said.

"You're kidding? I love the Sabres," Nicole said. "My dad took us to the games whenever he could. Do you know what my favorite part was?"

"The Zamboni," they said at the same time and laughed.

"I love the way this big machine looks so ungainly yet it pirouettes around the ice so effortlessly," Nicole said.

"My son loves hockey," Tom said, unable to take his eyes off Nicole. "We used to go to the Penguins games when we lived in Pittsburgh. Now we cheer for the Sabres."

"What about Rose?"

"Rose isn't much into hockey, so after Robert reached that age when hanging out with dad was no longer cool, we stopped going." He felt guilty mentioning Rose's name. Not that he had done anything wrong, anything at all. Yet he could still feel the slight twinge of guilt and awkwardness and wondered why he felt this clumsy, almost bashful as he talked to Nicole.

"How old is Robert?" Nicole asked, trying to gauge Tom's age.

"Twenty-three."

"What does he do?"

"He graduated from Pitt last year and works in the city as a financial analyst. He's going to night school to get his MBA. When he was young, he played hockey, but now he mostly works, studies, and flirts with the ladies." Tom paused, and then, like he was fondly remembering his son, he said, "Robert's a great kid."

"You look too young to have a son who has graduated from college." He definitely didn't look older than the mid-forties, she thought, then wondered immediately why she cared how old he might be.

"Rose and I were in college when we started our family. We met at the University of Pittsburgh. She was a nursing major. I majored in health sciences. We took the same biology class and planned on getting married after graduation, until Robert came along. We got married earlier than we planned. After school, I worked days at a hospital in Pittsburgh while Rose worked nights as a nurse. For us, it was sort of tag-team babysitting for a while. Thankfully, Rose's parents are from Pittsburgh and so they were able to help."

"Sounds like you have a nice family," Nicole said, impressed with anyone who could sustain a relationship for so long. She envied the stability of marriage and family. Most of her friends were already working on their second or third marriages. Never married herself and a product of divorce, she thought it must have been nice to have grown up with both parents around.

"I've been blessed," Tom said, and he meant it. In many ways, he was blessed. Despite their distance and their disagreements, he still valued the good things that he and Rose shared over the last twenty-three years. He remembered their first apartment, a tiny little shoebox of a place, and how happy he was the day Robert was born, how they raised him together, taking him to kindergarten and Little League and sharing a thousand little moments that make up a life together.

"So what made you come to Bradford?" Nicole asked.

"I'm from here," Tom replied. "My mother was diagnosed with cancer several years ago. We moved back to take care of her."

"Sort of why I moved here, to be closer to my dad," Nicole said. As she listened, she admired Tom even more. Most people she knew wouldn't even take a day off to visit a sick relative.

"Besides, we were getting tired of the city," he said. "We settled right in, but poor Robert hated Bradford and couldn't wait to leave."

Tom looked out the window over the hillsides surrounding the college.

"Speaking of Bradford," he said. "Have you seen the Kinzua Bridge?"

"Just on the brochures they send from the Chamber." Nicole laughed and jokingly said, "I still only know my way to campus and to the Mini-Mart."

"You should go," he said. "The leaves will be beautiful in a few weeks."

Nicole doubted she would find looking at leaves interesting. To her, a leaf was a leaf.

"The hills get crisp with deep reds and oranges, especially against the hemlock. Did you know leaves that change color in the fall actually have those same colors all year round?" Tom asked.

"No, I didn't know that."

"The green pigment is from the chlorophyll that is so concentrated in the spring and summer, which masks the other colors that are present. As the green disappears, the other colors—red, orange, yellow, and so forth—emerge. The amount of color a tree will show in the fall depends on its ability to enter dormancy, or its winter sleep." Tom continued to explain almost on autopilot. Nicole was intrigued by his passion.

"Actually, I do some photography," Nicole interrupted, surprised by her own excitement. "I took photography classes in college and am pretty much a self-taught amateur. I've got some great shots of St. Patrick's Cathedral and touristy places in the city, but the closest I've come to taking pictures of nature are of Central Park."

"One thing about this area, especially the Kinzua Valley, is that it is breathtaking in the fall."

"Sounds like something I should see," Nicole said as Carol suddenly appeared.

"There you are. I've been looking all over for you," Carol said as she sat down with a drink in hand. "Hi ya, Tom. Keeping our new faculty company?"

"Hello, Carol. How are you?" Tom said. He felt uncomfortable that Carol had seen him talking with Nicole alone twice.

"I would have gotten here sooner, but I couldn't find the right outfit to wear," Carol said. She was dressed in a yellow floral-print sundress with lime-green vines running through it that Nicole thought might have looked better as a kitchen curtain.

By now, Nicole had learned that Carol was constantly late and she wondered how Carol ever got to her classes on time. Then the ceremony began. The president of the university welcomed everyone and introduced several members of the advisory board from among the audience, including Tom Ryan. He thanked the benefactors for their generosity, including the Bronson family, who had donated the money for the new bell tower. Then the chairman of the advisory board spoke, and the program was concluded with a bottle of champagne being cracked over the cement bottom of the bell tower.

Right after the ceremony, some people grabbed their coats to leave while the diehard party types resumed their mingle mode. Before Tom or Nicole had a chance to speak, Carol jumped up from the table. "I've got to go schmooze with the administration," she announced, and she started to walk away but then abruptly turned back to Nicole. "Wait here for me. I'll be just a minute."

Nicole had also learned that Carol's minute equaled an hour. After Carol left, she turned to Tom. "Sounds like the valley is going to be really beautiful in a few weeks," she said.

"I didn't realize the time." Tom stood from the table, not seeming to hear her.

Nicole was about to say goodbye when he turned to her. "If you want a guided tour of the bridge, I'd be glad to take you. There are some great spots that aren't in the brochures." Why he asked, he was not sure. He was not an impulsive man, quite the contrary. In fact, asking Nicole if she was interested in seeing the bridge was the most impulsive thing he had done in a long time. He silently cursed himself. He had been so swept up in his own emotions about the bridge when talking about the leaves and the Kinzua Valley and how much it had meant to him, to his father, to his daughter, that it had made sense to share it with Nicole. At least, it made sense for a split second. He barely knew this woman but she had been on his mind since the day they had met. Now he had asked her to join him in the one place he never would have guessed he would ask a stranger.

Nicole was taken aback, slightly, by the offer. He wasn't like other men she knew. He had a nice family and seemed content with his life, so why then, did he ask her to see the bridge? His eyes, his deep green eyes, seemed so trusting and kind and he didn't seem like a player, far from it. He seemed safe, like nothing he could do would hurt another soul.

"I'd love a tour," she said, recovering quickly. Since she had received the news that her father was dying, she had been trying to live in the moment, to not plan, not obsess, not control everything that happened in her life. She reached inside her purse for a pen and wrote her work number on a napkin.

"I'll give you a call when the leaves have turned." Tom stuffed the napkin in his wallet.

"I'll bring my camera." She smiled.

"Goodnight." Tom extended his hand to shake Nicole's in a rather business-like fashion.

"Drive safely," she instinctively replied.

Nicole tossed out her plate and waited a few minutes for Carol. As the crowd continued to dwindle, her contacts started to bother her eyes and she realized she was exhausted. She scanned the area for Carol and spotted her engrossed in conversation with President Sampson. Not up for more pleasantries, Nicole tossed her purse over her shoulder, walked into the crisp night air and toward the nearly empty parking lot, replaying her conversation with Tom.

Nicole arrived at the Mini-Mart at her usual time wondering if she'd bump into Tom again, but he was nowhere to be seen. She thought it was for the best that she didn't see him. She was not in the mood to start a relationship with anyone, especially someone who was married, and she had found herself thinking a lot about this man she barely knew. She now wondered what she could possibly have been thinking when she accepted his invitation. She bought her usual cappuccino and paper and drove to campus. She settled into her routine, clicking on her stereo and playing Phil Collins. As she glanced over the headlines of the *USA Today*, Carol appeared at her office door.

"Where'd you go last night? I thought we'd go back to my place for some drinks."

"I'm sorry. I was exhausted. I think moving took more out of me than it has in the past."

"It was only ten o'clock. Are you turning into an old lady on me?"

"I guess my stamina to party isn't what it used to be," Nicole said with a laugh.

"Well, I'll forgive you if you go antiquing with me."

"Antiquing?" To Nicole, antiquing wasn't a verb.

"Please, I know some great places."

"I'm more the mall type."

"Oh, come on. Be adventurous," Carol insisted.

Nicole thought about it. The fact was she did owe it to Carol to spend time with her. Carol was her only real friend in Bradford, and she called every day and invited her over for dinner at least once a week. Nicole didn't even knock when she visited Carol anymore; she just came right into the kitchen and checked the refrigerator for snacks and beverages. Carol even came along to visit her father, who loved Carol's accent and her zany stories about England. For Nicole, Carol made the drive back and forth to Buffalo bearable and added levity to a tough situation.

Nicole's routine when she visited her dad was to drive to Buffalo after her classes. She stayed in his guest room and helped Jean with the cooking and the cleaning. They would play cards after dinner—her dad loved gin rummy. Nicole would also drive him when she could to his chemotherapy treatments. That was hard. Nicole always made small talk on their way to the doctor's office, and her dad would reminisce about buildings they passed where he did the electrical work and talk about how much he missed going fishing. He took every treatment like a champ, like he was going to get his hair cut or pick up his dry cleaning, like just another appointment. But Nicole imagined the needles poking his skin as she sat in the waiting room, knowing that toxic chemicals were being pumped into his body. He handled the nausea and vomiting afterwards, the pain and fatigue, but it was like she was suffering along with him. The one thing her father didn't like was the hair loss. He was a proud man and losing the full head of hair that he still had prior to treatment was hard on him, and sometimes Nicole thought it was harder for him than the treatment or even the disease itself.

Once, after a particularly difficult round of chemo, her father was very sick in bed. Her father's hair had been falling out for some time now, but he refused a hairpiece. "Too much pride," he would say. That day, a clump of hair fell out in the bathroom sink. A normally polite and quiet man, he was so upset that he started barking orders. After dinner, Carol was in the kitchen making her famous rhubarb crumble for dessert, Jean was cleaning the bathroom, and Nicole had been tidying up the living room. His hair was a small part of why he was upset. He needed the house to be in order, and he was angry that he could no longer keep the house up himself, that he was dependent on others, that he was weak and tired all the time. He yelled, "I'm balding, damn it."

Carol snapped back, "Oh, it makes you sexier for the women. They'll think you have more testosterone." Her father stopped in his tracks, realizing how silly and childish he was acting and laughed, a good, hearty belly laugh. It was the first time he had laughed in weeks.

"I guess I do need to expand my horizons," Nicole finally said as she wondered just what antiquing might possibly amount to anyway.

"We'll have fun. You'll see." Carol hugged Nicole and they agreed to go in October when the leaves had changed. Carol dashed off to class, late as usual, and Nicole turned to her computer wondering what she had gotten herself into. She did a quick check of her e-mail and found nothing special, just a memo from her chairperson and an e-mail from Allison, who just finished putting the boys to bed. Nicole then clicked on *The Chronicle of Higher Education* site and scanned the job ads, now beginning to get worried that she might not even find a job when her year in Bradford was over.

There were tenure-track positions in Albany, a few in Syracuse, and one in Plattsburgh, north of the Adirondack Mountains.

"Too cold," Nicole said as she narrowed her search to the greater New York Metropolitan area. She found one job at a community college in White Plains, about a thirty-minute train ride from the city. But she wanted to teach at a four-year college and could do without a commute. There was an opening at Pace University, but it was only for a visiting professor. She decided that she desperately needed stability at this point in her life. There was a tenure-track position at Hunter College, but it was in the International Relations Department and her field was American Politics. Then Nicole saw it, her dream job. She read the ad over again and again—a tenure-stream position at Columbia University and exactly in her field. This was not only her chance to teach at an Ivy League school but it was also her chance to be back in Manhattan.

The next several weeks she spent chained to her office. She printed her curriculum vita on white bond paper, triple checked it for typos, and practically lived at the Xerox machine furiously copying all her application materials before the various deadlines.

Nicole sent out a dozen applications, deciding that it was only prudent to apply for several positions, even those in which she wasn't that interested. The job market was tight, she reasoned, and she needed a solid job offer when her visiting professorship in Bradford was over. Most of the jobs she applied for were in Manhattan, a few in Philadelphia, New Jersey, and Boston, places close enough to New York. She even sent one to Hunter College on the off chance they were looking for someone with her background. Unlike all the other applications, she sent her job application to Columbia certified mail.

"Still up for antiquing?" Carol asked, popping her head inside Nicole's office.

"Is it October already?" Nicole looked up at her calendar.

"My dear, where have you been? It's been October for almost two weeks," Carol said, leaning against a bookshelf. "The leaves are simply splendid."

"The leaves?"

"Hadn't you noticed? The hills are aglow."

Nicole had been so swamped with putting together job application packets that she hadn't noticed if it was rainy or sunny outside much less if the leaves had changed. She suddenly thought of Tom Ryan. She hadn't thought of him in weeks, not since the night of the dedication ceremony for the clock tower. Nor had she run into him, even though she stopped at the Mini-Mart every weekday morning. She looked at her calendar again. It was mid-October, exactly when he said he would call.

"Oh my, must dash," Carol said. "I'll pick you up at noon."

Nicole had finished teaching for the day, and she gathered up her book bag, locked up her office, and stopped at the grocery store to pick up a fresh salad for dinner on her way home.

Back at her apartment, she slipped into a pair of sweatpants and a T-shirt and clicked on CNN to watch while she ate. The television merely blared in the background, however, as her mind turned again to Tom. She got up to check her caller ID. Perhaps he had called but hadn't left a message. He hadn't. How silly, she thought, as she walked into the kitchen and poured a glass of wine. She had just sat down in front of the TV when the phone rang. She glanced down at her caller ID momentarily, vaguely hoping it was Tom and vaguely hoping it wasn't. It was Jennifer Miller, her best friend since they were college roommates at Fordham.

"Hey girl, I just got home from work and I am beat." Jennifer sighed. "And the day isn't over yet. I'm getting ready for a hotel premiere in Midtown that we're promoting. I never know what shoes to wear. Should I go with the Guccis or the Botticellis?"

A native New Yorker from an affluent family, it was Jennifer who had taught Nicole how to navigate the subways, the proper way to hail a cab, and the best way to meet eligible bachelors on the train.

"Maybe I'll wear the Manolos?" As Jennifer obsessed over her footwear selection, Nicole craved the city. She pictured Radio City Music Hall, Rockefeller Center, and Times Square, all within walking distance of where Jennifer would be that night.

Nicole always felt more like a "plain Jane" in her Ralph Lauren outlet sweaters compared to Jennifer, who wore revealing dresses and high pumps when they went bar hopping. Nicole had quickly noticed in their relationship that Jennifer was more outgoing and relaxed when meeting men than she was. She merely fidgeted and felt like a failure at flirting. Nicole tried to make conversation with men but always felt like a bore making small talk. After graduation, Jennifer started her own promotions firm and handled some of the trendiest art premieres, elite hotel openings, and celebrity-filled political fundraisers in the city. Nicole tagged along to premieres at the Guggenheim and the Metropolitan Museum of Art. Once, she even met Hillary when Bill Clinton was first running for President.

Jennifer never did understand Nicole's decision to be a college professor, and Nicole never did quite fit into Jennifer's lavish lifestyle, but through the years they had been like sisters. Nicole marveled how they remained so close despite coming from such different worlds.

"I wish I was going with you." Nicole sighed. "The most excitement I have to look forward to this evening is watching the latest episode of ER."

"Remember, you'll be back at Thanksgiving for my fabulously catered feast. I've got about thirty guests coming this year," Jennifer said, who now lived in a roomy two-bedroom brownstone on the Upper East Side, which had become like Nicole's second home when she could get back to the City.

"How could I forget? I booked my flight the same day I rented the moving van."

"Who knows? Maybe you'll meet a cute little professor at Podunk U." Jennifer laughed before declaring succinctly that she had decided upon the Botticelli's.

"Please, after Michael, I can't even think about getting involved."

"Oh, please, Michael was a pompous jerk," Jennifer snapped. "All he wanted was the perfect wife and perfect hostess for his hospital benefits. Ending things with him was the right thing to do."

"Sometimes, I wonder if it was Michael or if it was me."

"Oh, honey, it was him. You didn't want *that* for the rest of your life. He didn't see you when he was looking right at you. He saw himself in your image, big difference. He wanted you to fit into his world. He didn't acknowledge that you had goals too."

Nicole had always questioned the validity of their relationship, the way Michael always picked the restaurant and how he insisted on going to his pretentious country club in Manhattan instead of a quiet night at home. Then he had taken to minimizing her career while talking incessantly about his own. One night over dinner at another one of Michael's fancy restaurants, she had looked at him, looked deeper into his dark brown eyes and Italian features than she had before. While they were a good-on-paper couple, she could never see growing old with him.

"Maybe I'll buy a dog," Nicole said.

"That's cheaper than a divorce." Jennifer laughed. She was recently divorced from Ricardo, an Italian architect from Milan she met while doing PR for his firm. They had been married for only a year when Jennifer discovered he was having an affair with a model from Geneva.

"Maybe I should come visit you in Hooterville?"

"You're kidding? The closest you've come to the rural outdoors is staying at your parents' place in the Hamptons."

"Too true. I don't see visiting Mayberry either. Look, Nic. I'm so sorry but I gotta run." Like Carol, Jennifer had made a career out of always running late. "But remember, November is just around the corner. And we're gonna party our asses off."

"Thanks. Your party gives me something to look forward to." Nicole hung up the phone and took her wine out on her balcony to have a cigarette. Sipping her wine, she thought about the lights of Broadway and remembered the night Michael took her to see *Phantom of the Opera*, the same night she found out that her father had cancer. After the performance, they came back to her apartment.

Allison had left a frantic message on her answering machine, and Michael stayed the night and held Nicole as she cried. In the morning, he had paid for Nicole's plane ticket back to Buffalo and called every day while she was away. She had to admit, he had been there for her when she needed him the most.

Yes, Michael could be a jerk, but he was also the man she had shared her life with for the past two years. While Nicole could never say that she totally loved him with all her heart, she could say that he had been good to her at times, and they did have fun on trips to Cancun and Key West. She remembered meeting his parents last Christmas and how kind they had been to her. When they talked about marriage, his parents were supportive. They had accepted Nicole as part of the family. Michael could be sweet and kind. Once, he had bought her a dozen roses. He had given a beautiful bouquet of eleven real roses and one fake rose. He said, "I will love you until the last flower dies." If only she felt the same way, it might have been a perfect match.

Nicole finished her cigarette and came inside. She wasn't sure if it was the wine or feeling lonely in Bradford, or if she just needed to hear Michael's voice, but she dialed his number.

"Hi Michael. It's me," she blurted out before she had the chance to hang up. Besides, she remembered that he had caller ID, too.

"Nicole?" Michael clearly sounded surprised.

"How are you?" she said, and hated herself for being the first one to call after the breakup.

"Aren't you supposed to be in Bradford?"

"I'm in Bradford." She paused, still unsure why she had called. After an awkward silence she somehow got out the words. "You can't imagine the town. There's not much to do unless you like to hunt or fish. My only real friend is a frumpy old professor who's into antiques."

"Did I tell you about our new office?" Michael asked as if he hadn't heard her at all. "We moved our practice to Park Avenue and we can't keep up with all the new business. It's the best move I've made, and guess what? I just bought a brand new Porsche 911 Cabriolet, cherry red. You gotta see it, Nic. It goes from zero to sixty in a heartbeat and it's fully loaded: automatic climate control, leather seats, cruise, power everything. And it has this electronic convertible top that goes up and down with a click of a button. I'd love to take you for a ride sometime."

The more Michael bragged about his new Porsche, the more Nicole regretted calling.

"You coming back to the city anytime soon?" he asked. "Perhaps we can get together."

"I'm not really sure what I'm doing yet." Nicole didn't want to tell him that she already had plans to stay with Jennifer. "I might be back for Thanksgiving. I haven't decided."

"If you are in town, call me. I'm moving to an apartment with an incredible view of Central Park next weekend. Nic, you've got to check it out."

"Sure. If I am in town, I'll call you. Look, it's late and I have to get up early. I'll let you know about Thanksgiving."

"If not then, perhaps Christmas," Michael said before he hung up.

Nicole lit another cigarette and mentally calculated that Michael now owned a car worth as much as she owed in student loans. And he didn't even need a car in the city. She thought it odd that neither of them brought up the breakup after being together for two years. Then again, they never were very good at talking about their relationship. The phone call reinforced why she broke up with him. She could never see growing old with someone so shallow and so self-absorbed. He never once asked how she was, how she felt about the move, or how her dad was doing. Yes, she had done the right thing in breaking up with Michael, but it was still hard to be on her own. She had clung to Michael like a security blanket that comforted her when she was feeling down and alone. In this town deep in the woods, she never felt more alone, but for the first time that she could remember, she was glad that Michael was not part of her life.

Nicole took her wine and went back to the balcony. Leaning back in a folding chair that was once a part of her kitchen set, she placed her drink on a small white plastic table that she bought at the local Dollar Store. She looked out at the hillside illuminated by the moonlight. The trees reminded her of Tom Ryan. Why hadn't he called? Would he call? Why was she thinking of him, this married man she hardly knew? Was she just feeling lonely without Michael? Was it the woods, the quiet and solitude? Then that voice inside of her started in again. At thirty-five years old, why was she still single? She had seen all of her friends lead semi-permanent relationships—even Jennifer had tried marriage. Nicole couldn't even think about walking down that aisle, and with a surgeon worth more than she would make in a lifetime. Maybe she liked Tom because he seemed to have the life that she wondered about for herself. Not that she wanted the same things he had; she didn't. She had avoided commitment like the plague. Whenever someone got too close she always found a way to push them away. But Tom seemed *so* stable, *so* solidly in his life. She gave up thinking about any of it and just looked at the stars. After another glass of wine, she headed off to bed, slightly tipsy and too exhausted to obsess.

Tom sat in his office, hesitating before he picked up the phone. He hadn't called a woman for any reason besides work in a long time. He wondered for the millionth time since he asked her why he had even thought about taking Nicole to see the bridge. He wondered why he wanted to take her there and why she might want to go. He didn't have a good answer to either question.

Work had gotten busy, and he had spent less time in the woods than he liked. But he still thought about the cabin a lot. He remembered hiking the trails with his father as a boy. How they climbed down through the rocks to the bottom of the bridge. How they fished in the reservoir and how his father taught him to skip rocks on the water. He remembered all the simple things he did with his father.

Tom felt a strange sense of nervous anticipation at hearing her voice again as he dialed the number, something he couldn't quite explain, nor did he want to try. He decided he just liked feeling something again, something that didn't remind him of Lisa.

Nicole was working late. It was midterm at the university, and she had a fresh stack of exams to grade. She had gone downstairs to grab a can of Coke and a bag of chips from the vending machines, and she heard her phone ringing on the way back to her office. She hurried down the hall. It was five o'clock, the time Carol usually called to see if she wanted to come over for dinner.

"Hello, Dr. Benson speaking."

"Hello, this is Tom Ryan." He felt his heart beating when she answered. "I hope I'm not calling at a bad time."

"It's you." Nicole sounded surprised. "I'm sorry. How are you?"

"I'm fine. And you?"

"Oh, I'm fine."

There was a long pause. Tom tried to focus his mind. What was he doing calling this woman?

"It's been a while since the dedication ceremony." He paused again, awkward and a little nervous, even shy. He tried to regroup mentally. "I was calling to see if you were still interested in seeing the bridge?" Tom got out the words all in a rush. He had mixed feelings about the answer and was half hoping Nicole would say no. He was prepared for rejection. He believed that she had forgotten all about meeting him and their conversation and about his invitation.

"Actually, I was just thinking about the leaves," she said.

"I know this one spot," Tom said, now strangely happy that she seemed on the cusp of saying yes. "It's a bit of a walk, but it's the best spot for pictures."

"That sounds great."

"How's Saturday?" Whatever fear he had faded that moment. He couldn't explain why, but it felt natural, comfortable like a warm blanket when she accepted his offer because he realized there was a possibility that she might also have been thinking about him.

"Saturday's good. I was supposed to go antiquing with Carol, but to be honest, I am not that into it."

"Are you sure? We can go another day?"

"No, it's okay. This gives me a reason not to go."

"I'll be working in the morning," he said. "Can we meet around nine?"

"How about ten? Saturday is my day to sleep in." Nicole laughed.

"Ten it is," he said. "We can meet at my office. I can drive us from there." He had lots of men and women meet him in his office, suppliers for the nursing home and potential clients and the adult children of potential clients, and so it would not be unusual. He thought meeting at his office would also seem more businesslike and less like a date. He gave Nicole directions to the nursing home.

"Great," she said. "See you then."

"See you then." As he hung up the phone, Tom reached for his appointment book. Writing down Nicole's name by the date they were to meet, he slowly drew a circle around it. Then the questions started again. What was he thinking? Why had he called? Why had she said yes? He had never done something like this before? Taking anyone to see the bridge much less a woman was so out of character for him. He wasn't sure how else to say it. Was he starting something that could grow into more? If it did, then what? Bradford was too small a town to get involved with a woman and have it stay a secret for very long.

CHAPTER 4

The Kinzua Bridge

Nicole pulled into the nursing home parking lot and decided to leave her camera bag in the car. She made her way up the stairs and entered a long corridor, at the end of which was Tom's office. As she walked down the hallway, she passed an empty recreational room with card tables and chairs. In another lounge, she saw a group of elderly residents watching a big screen television and passed what appeared to be small bedrooms.

Some of the residents were sitting in wheelchairs along the hall, milling around, some with vacant looks, one person drooling. Nicole simply kept her head down and nodded hello. Old people made her uncomfortable. As she hastened her pace, Nicole ran right into an elderly woman wheeling herself down the hallway.

"Oh, excuse me," she said after she banged against the footrest of the wheelchair.

"That's fine, dear." The old woman lifted her hand to take Nicole's. "How are you, dear?"

Reluctantly, Nicole reached down to the take the woman's hand. "I'm looking for Mr. Ryan's office," she said, but the woman said nothing in response and Nicole wondered if she could hear. So she asked again, louder. "Mr. Ryan's office? Do you know where it is?"

"Mr. Ryan's office?"

"Yes, Mr. Ryan's office," she repeated again, wondering now if the old woman was senile rather than deaf. Maybe she didn't even know there was a Tom Ryan. Nicole abruptly pulled her hand away and turned down the hall. "I'm really late for a meeting with him."

"Well then, you're going in the wrong direction," the elderly woman replied, and she pointed toward the other end of the hall. "Mr. Ryan's office is that way."

Nicole froze in mid-step. The woman was right and Nicole felt like an idiot. She turned around, thanked the woman, and walked past her toward Tom's office.

Although her heels clicked against the cracked linoleum floor, Tom didn't hear her enter his office. The phone receiver was cradled between his cheek and his shoulder and he was taking notes as he talked. He finally looked up, smiled, and waved for Nicole to take a seat.

Tom was dressed casually, in a navy shirt and a pair of beige Dockers. Somehow he looked better than Nicole remembered. He seemed thinner and more muscular. She sat down in a chair next to his desk, a battered black metal one like hers. While he finished his telephone conversation, she looked around the office. It was cramped like hers, but at least it had a window. She noticed the wall of file cabinets behind his desk, stacked with folders on top and piles of folders on the floor. "He collects paper, too," she joked to herself.

Then she noticed a picture frame on Tom's desk, a family portrait. Tom had his arms around a woman's waist, Rose she assumed, and they stood behind two children. She studied Tom's face. He looked proud. Rose looked sweet, and the whole family looked happy. As she stared at the picture, she assumed the older boy was Robert but wasn't sure who the little girl was. Tom never mentioned a daughter.

"Sorry to keep you waiting," Tom said as he hung up the phone. "There is a crisis at the Friendship Table."

"The Friendship Table?"

"It's our local soup kitchen. We're getting ready for our annual Thanksgiving dinner and one of our regular volunteers died."

"I'm sorry to hear that."

"He was seventy-eight and had more energy than any of the rest of us," Tom said, and he smiled, apparently remembering this man affectionately for all he had done. "I'm the chairperson for the dinner this year, and he did the work of at least four people, so it'll be hard finding volunteers to replace him." He paused. "So are you ready to see the bridge?"

"Sure am." Nicole stood up, grabbed her purse, and on their way out, Tom grabbed a leather jacket that hung from a coat rack and closed the door behind him. As they walked down the hallway, Nicole noticed that the old woman who helped her find Tom's office was gone.

She gathered up her camera bag and a pair of old flats from her Nova and climbed into the passenger side of Tom's Chevy Tahoe. His SUV felt a bit like riding in a small bus as they drove into the hills of the Kinzua Valley. The drive itself was very scenic, and Tom was careful to point out many of the area's historical points. The farther they got from town, the more wooded the area became. Tom started to point out various tree species.

"Leaf colors are determined by the species of trees. The main ones in Pennsylvania are maples, like the ones over here, which show more of a red and orange. Over there are hickories, which give more of a golden yellow; and those tall ones are oaks, which turn more of a bronze. That's hemlock, which stays green year round." To Nicole, a tree was a tree.

"Here's where we begin," he said as he pulled his SUV along the side of the road and turned off the engine.

"Here?" All Nicole saw was miles upon miles of trees on both sides of the road.

"The state park is a few miles south of here. That's where most people go, but where we are going is the best view of the bridge. There's a clear path to the spot just over there." Tom pointed to a narrow dirt path surrounded by trees and bushes barely visible from the road.

"I see." Not much of a hiker, Nicole had worn her heels and a skirt.

"I'm sorry. I should have told you to wear something more comfortable." Tom smiled. "We can go to the park area. It's paved and would be easier to walk."

"It's my fault. I'm not much of a country girl," Nicole said. "I'll be fine. I brought some flats."

"You sure?"

"I'm sure." Nicole pulled up on the door handle and confidently swung open the door.

"At least let me carry this," Tom said, as he grabbed the strap of her camera bag. They walked just a few steps to the edge of the woods and the start of the dirt path. Though mostly clear, it was surrounded by brush, and periodically they had to climb over a fallen tree. Tom walked in front and pushed away the brush while Nicole followed carefully, stepping gingerly over any obstacles.

As they headed deep into the woods, Nicole took note of the quiet. No noise from the highway penetrated the forest. Except for the sound of their steps, there was absolute silence, and the massive size of the trees dwarfed them. Her gaze followed the trunks into the sky, but she couldn't see the end of the treetops. Then, suddenly, something shook in the bushes behind her. She jumped, picturing a hungry bear ready to eat her. When she turned around, she saw a harmless chipmunk running under a pile of leaves.

She took a couple of depth breaths to settle her nerves then continued to hike, calmer though slightly out of breath. Tom looked unfazed. He told her, "For a city girl, you seem pretty tough. The stones on the trail have got to be difficult to navigate in those shoes."

"Yeah, I'm all grace in action in the wild," Nicole joked as she made a point to step as daintily as possible over a downed tree trunk.

They hiked for what seemed like hours until the trees finally parted revealing a small clearing on the hillside. Her first glimpse of the Kinzua Bridge, glistening tall in the sunlight of the warm autumn morning, made her gasp.

"It's lovely," she said, soaking up the lush view.

She looked out over the valley at the steel girders. The thick steel towers looked grand in the landscape of orange and red hillsides. No one was on the bridge, and the forest around them was quiet except for a slight sound of the wind that made the trees rustle. She saw a hawk in the distance swooping down over the bridge. They stood still taking in the view side by side.

"The Kinzua Bridge was built in 1882, and was once dubbed The Eighth Wonder of the World," Tom said as he pointed to the bridge. "Upon completion, it was the world's tallest and longest railroad bridge, 301 feet high and 2,053 feet long. That's over thirty stories tall and more than a quarter of a mile long. And see way down there?" he asked, and he pointed down to a stream in the center of the valley. "That is the Kinzua creek that runs directly into the Allegheny Reservoir. It's full of trout."

The scene was truly beautiful. Nicole stared at the thick steel beams that comprised the Kinzua Bridge. The structure towered over the deep valley of trees that rolled on for miles. The backdrop of crisp yellow, bronze, red, and orange leaves reminded her of family vacations as a child. Her father would pile everyone into the station wagon and they would head east toward New England to see the leaves in the fall. They'd drive all day and sing songs until her father got tired, and then they would look for a place to stay. Usually, they would stay at a cheap motel along the highway, but on occasion, they'd find a quaint bed and breakfast, complete with old-fashioned porcelain bowls in the room and a fireplace downstairs. They'd eat a hearty breakfast, the kind that never tasted the same if you made it at home, and best of all, they were all together laughing. Even her mother seemed happy back then.

"Here's the best place to sit." Tom pointed to a large rock that protruded from the hillside. Nicole also didn't realize that there would be no benches. She stood looking at the rock and tried to figure out the best way to climb over it wearing a skirt. While long, it was still a skirt.

"Let me help you." Tom motioned for her to take his hand. "On the count of three. One. Two. Three." Tom's strong hands felt good to Nicole as he gently lifted her over a small pile of jagged stone that lay around the foot of the rock. As she wiggled around trying to find a comfortable spot to sit, her skirt rose revealing her lower thighs. She noticed Tom's eyes glance down at her legs when he thought she wasn't looking. Now Nicole was glad that she decided to wear the skirt.

"Actually, in 1977, the Kinzua Bridge was placed on the National Register of Historic Civil Engineering Landmarks," Tom explained as he hoisted himself over the rock. For a large man, Nicole noticed how his body moved gracefully as he took a seat on the rock beside her and handed her the camera.

"I'm impressed. It's hard to believe such a bridge exists out in the middle of nowhere," she said, as she opened her camera bag to pull out two bottles of water. "I picked these up on my way to your office. Thought you might like one."

"Good thinking. Thank you," Tom said, accepting one of the water bottles. "Actually, I've hunted all throughout these woods since I was a little boy, mostly deer and turkey, although my father also liked to hunt bear."

"There are bear around here?" Nicole asked nervously.

"Sure. McKean County has the sixth largest bear harvest in the Commonwealth. Actually bear meat is pretty good. Tastes like chicken," he joked. "Actually, it tastes rather gamey, sort of wild. We have it every year at our game dinner, a big party to which people bring all kinds of wild meat," he said as he took a sip from his water bottle. "Bear generally go into hibernation about October and won't emerge until April, possibly May. Don't worry. We're safe up here."

Nicole felt more settled and began to wonder about Tom. He didn't look like a hunter. She always pictured the stereotypical Grizzly Adams, not a clean-shaven man like Tom.

"When I was a kid, my father took me through the woods to look for deer tracks."

"Is that how you know so much about the area?" she asked, opening her water bottle.

"Yep. We'd walk and he'd explain all the local history as we covered every crevice of these woods. He was a history teacher and loved to tell me about the bridge, or the Kinzua Viaduct as people called it."

"What's so special about it, besides its size and overall majesty, I mean?"

"Well, for one thing, it only took ninety-four days to build."

"To build all that?"

"The real kicker is that a crew of just forty men built that. And at that time, no scaffolding of any type was used."

"How did they put it together then?"

"Preliminary construction began in 1881 when the foundations of the bridge's 110 stone piers were laid. They used a rig called a gin pole to erect the first iron tower and then a wooden crane was built at the top of that one to set the second tower," Tom explained as he pointed to the thick legs of the bridge. "A total of twenty iron towers were placed in the bridge and joined together by sixty foot of lattice. The viaduct was then bolted together." He relished telling her the story like a great historian. "There will never be another bridge like this. It is known as one of the great historic American bridges, and as I said, the Eighth Wonder of the World."

God, it was far different from anything Nicole had seen. Whenever she heard the word bridge, she pictured rush hour traffic on the George Washington out of Manhattan. She looked again at the old steel girders. "Is it still in use?"

"A new bridge was necessary, and in May of 1900, the iron viaduct was closed to traffic. Construction of a new steel bridge soon began. The entire ironworks were torn down and replaced by the sturdier steel structure that you see now. The new structure retained the same height and weight but was heavier so it could handle the heavier trains. As trains were used less in hauling coal, the bridge was closed from 1959 until the mid-80s until a local railroad company started to offer excursion rides. Rose and I took an excursion from Kane one year. From the train, you can see spectacular scenic views. You should take a ride sometime."

"Except for the subway, I'm not much of a train person." Nicole couldn't imagine the inane boredom of being held captive on a train with nothing to look at but trees and more trees.

"The best time to view the bridge is in the winter. My dad and I would come out when the ice crystallized over the barren tree branches. He'd take me through those fields to see the hoof prints of deer in the snow. It was so quiet all we'd hear is the snow crunching under our boots. It was my favorite part of the hike."

Tom's version of winter didn't sound at all like growing up in Buffalo, where winter meant slushy streets, dirty snow, and cold, hard air. Now, Nicole pictured a freshly fallen snow still untouched by man that looked soft and warm, ironic for snow, but that was how it felt when he talked about it. Tom spoke, almost to himself. "Somehow, I always feel closer to God when I'm up here."

Nicole put down her camera bag and inhaled what seemed to be the cleanest air to ever touch her lungs, not a single noxious fume and no exhaust. As they sat silently for a moment, a hard gust of air kicked over her bottle of water that she had rested on the rock.

"It gets pretty windy up here," Tom said as he jumped quickly to recover it. He pointed north into the woods. "I own a hunting camp just a few miles down the road from here. It was my father's. After he died, I took it over, and I have been fixing it up over the years."

"How did he die?" With her own father's inevitable death, she felt compelled to ask. Seeing how much this place meant to Tom, Nicole also wondered why this man had taken her to such a sacred spot.

"A hunting accident," Tom said, and then he became very quiet for a time. He spoke again after inhaling deeply. "My father was turkey hunting when another hunter didn't properly identify his target."

"I'm sorry. That must have been so hard for you."

"He went doing what he loved." Tom paused again, and they sat quietly together for a long while before he said, "Besides, it was a long time ago."

"Do you spend much time at your camp?" Nicole asked, sensing that he wanted to change the subject.

"I try to spend as much time as I can there. When I lived in Pittsburgh, I didn't really visit much, but that's changed since I moved back to Bradford. Although, lately, even my weekends are tied up with work so it's hard to get away as much I'd like. Even this weekend is a work weekend of sorts. Rose went to Pittsburgh to visit Robert, and tonight is our annual bus trip to the Niagara Falls Casino. I go every year with our ladies. They love the slots."

"I know how work can keep you busy. I've got more job applications to finish tonight."

"Job applications?" Tom looked directly at Nicole. He felt an ache, a slight tugging ache. It hadn't occurred to him that she might be leaving. He hoped his face didn't reveal how he was feeling.

She noticed him bristle slightly. Why he would care one way or another, she wasn't sure. They hardly knew one another.

"I'm only here for a year as a visiting professor," Nicole said. Saying the words aloud, seeing his reaction, she suddenly became uneasy. Could it be he liked her? Was something starting to happen that signified more than just becoming friends, if that was even the right word? There was an intensity in his eyes as he looked into hers, and she had to turn away. She started rummaging through her camera bag, looking for her telephoto lens. She didn't want to dwell on her leaving. It was simply a fact. When her year in Bradford was over, she was gone. No need to make more of it than it had to be.

"I've sent out a bunch of applications, but the only place I've heard from is High Point College. I'm not overjoyed or even excited about the interview," she said in a matter-of-fact tone. "It's just my back up school if I don't get a job anywhere else." A flood of guilt suddenly swept through Nicole as she thought about her sister. She pulled out her telephoto lens.

"I only applied on a whim. High Point is near my sister. She lives in Greensboro, which is about fifteen minutes from the school. We were close growing up, but we drifted apart over the years. Ultimately, I see myself living back in New York. But as I get older, I start thinking that it would be nice to be close again to Allison. I know my father would like to see that. He's always reminiscing about when we were young. We all used to go camping every summer. My dad would make his famous chicken BBQ on the grill. Allison and I would swim all day. But that was then—things are different now. It's been hard to find common ground, so to speak. We are just two completely different people. She's focused on her own family. I've been focused on my career. It's been two years since we've seen one another, just after her youngest was born." Then it was Nicole's turn to be silent for a few moments, the wind whistling around them the only sound.

"You know where I really want to teach?" Nicole asked rhetorically after a bit, trying to change the subject. "Columbia." Her inflection hinted at her excitement even saying the name. "Not that I think I have a chance. They haven't even called me for an interview."

"Why Columbia?" he asked. He looked away from Nicole, trying to understand why her leaving bothered him. He didn't want to start anything, anything at all.

He liked her. That is all he knew. She seemed like a breath of fresh air. She wasn't like other people he had met around town with only a limited range of topics for conversation and a limited curiosity for the world. Nicole could talk about places she had traveled, books she had read, and events in the news. Her mind was active, and he could tell she obviously was ambitious. It was only natural that she would desire something more than teaching in a small town like Bradford.

"I always wanted to go to an Ivy League school," Nicole said. "A place like Columbia only takes the cream of the crop, usually those who graduated from Ivy League schools. I wasn't that smart, even when I studied all the time." She laughed. "I was lucky just to get into NYU. That was like a dream come true. I didn't even think I'd get accepted. I was diagnosed with a reading disability when I was younger, and that disability didn't help me in school. My grades at Fordham were shaky. After graduation and before grad school, I did a brief stint in DC working as a political consultant for a senator. He wrote me a letter of recommendation that helped me get in."

Nicole paused, resting her camera on her lap as she remembered all that she loved about Manhattan. The shops, the fashion, and the elegance, the urban rush that made her feel part of the world, the towering buildings that lit up the streets at night, the museums and the culture, and the excitement of her Sunday morning gossip sessions about the weekend at Jennifer's. The city was like one big continuous date and she missed it all.

"Besides," she said. "I would be back in New York with my friends. I do miss them. Bradford's okay, but it's hard adjusting to a small town if you're not from one."

"There's something comforting about living in a small town."

Nicole stopped to consider life from Tom's perspective. She wasn't a half-hour subway ride to work anymore, just a five-minute drive. Actually, it was a five-minute drive to anywhere in town. And Bradford did seem friendlier—she already knew the name of the lady at the bank and the name of the checkout girl at the Mini-Mart. Still, the town was miles from a good mall, a museum, or a real coffee shop.

"Doesn't it get boring?"

"Not really. You just gotta know where to look." Tom smiled, then took another sip from his water bottle. "Where else would you get such a view?"

"Oh yes, the view." She took off her sunglasses and held the camera lens to her eye. She panned the area, then playfully turned the camera on Tom. "Smile and say cheese."

"No," Tom said, quickly putting his head down. "I hate having my picture taken."

"Oh come on," Nicole said, laughing. "Look over here." She didn't take the camera off Tom.

"Nahhh, I don't think so." Tom kept his head turned.

"Must be a guy thing." She could see he wasn't going to turn around. "Okay, you win."

She panned toward the Kinzua Bridge. As she focused, she marveled at its construction through her lens. Then she snapped various picture angles. How did it only take ninety-four days to build all of this? With only forty men to build it, when they didn't even have scaffolding? How was this possible? It would have taken over a year to build a structure that intricate today, even with all the modern technology. To have lasted all these years, carefully preserved, the bridge had to be well constructed too. This bridge kept in a secret nook of the valley with nothing surrounding it except the trees was indeed a marvel. It sprung up from the ground like a sacred monument where people could come to visit and pay tribute to ingenuity and hard work.

Tom watched her work the camera. "You seem to love photography," he said.

"It's just a hobby," Nicole said, focusing the lens. "I used to take long walks at night and lose myself behind the camera. I'd pretend that I was a famous French photographer, but in truth I don't see any art exhibits in my future. I am not talented enough to make a living at it, but God knows, I'll never be rich being a teacher."

"It's not always about money, is it?" Tom asked.

"You're right. I know it's all relative. Still, I constantly compare myself to my friends who are already established in their careers while I'm just starting mine. It's like I put my entire life on hold while I put myself through school," said Nicole as she reached for her water bottle. "You know what I really want to do?"

"What?" Tom gave her his full attention.

"Write a novel." Nicole surprised herself with the admission. She had never told that to anyone, not even Jennifer. "Once," she explained, "when I was eight, I wrote this silly story about a girl named Peg and her dog named Wag, and in my story they went to buy groceries for their sick mother. Then in high school, I wrote short stories that got published in our school magazine, but I haven't written one creative word since. I still read lots of fiction, and I make up story lines sometimes just to see if I can match some of the novels I've read as far as drama is concerned, but my writing life for years has consisted of research for my dissertation and then pumping out drafts, all that academic prose."

"Perhaps you just haven't had the right inspiration." Something in his tone made Nicole feel as if one day it might be true.

Nicole smiled. "I read somewhere that a professional writer is an amateur that didn't quit."

"Richard Bach," Tom said. "He's one of my favorite authors."

"You're kidding. Mine too," Nicole said, surprised that Tom had even heard of Richard Bach. "Did you read . . ."

"*Jonathan Livingston Seagull.*" They both said at the same time.

"Wow," Nicole exclaimed. "I've never met anyone who's read him. I read him in high school when I was going through the dark times with my parents' divorce. Have you read *Illusions?*"

"About the reluctant Messiah," he said. "I have a tattered copy of it by my bed. When I used to go up to my camp more, I read it several times. The pages have even come loose."

"I love one particular quote: 'Perspective—use it or lose it'. Do you remember it?"

"Yes, and I tell myself that all the time," Tom said.

"Speaking of perspective," Nicole said, glancing down at her camera. "Do you want to take some pictures?" She had an eerie feeling; no man she ever met had heard of Richard Bach. Most guys, no matter how educated they seemed, were into watching Jean-Claude Van Damme or Steven Seagal movies and not into reading about an inspirational bird as the central character.

"I'm not sure how to work that thing." He put down his water bottle.

"There's nothing to it. A monkey could do it." Nicole handed Tom the camera.

"So, what you're telling me is, if I shoot this photo, I'm no better than a monkey?" Tom grinned as he put the camera to his face and adjusted it to see the bridge. "Wow, this does have a great zoom lens," he said. "You can see every rivet and bolt with this thing."

"The display lets you customize your settings," Nicole explained as she looked over Tom's shoulder. "That's pretty good. Finish the roll. I've got another roll here somewhere."

Tom snapped several pictures while Nicole reached inside her camera bag to find her second canister of film. Then Tom suddenly pointed the camera at her.

"Hey. No. Don't." She put her hands in front of the lens, but it was too late.

"What did you do that for?"

"It's only fair. You tried to take mine," he said and he smiled.

"Yes, but I never got *your* picture. Someone wouldn't let me."

"You're right. I guess I don't play fair."

"I guess it's okay." Nicole smiled back and wondered why Tom would even want her picture.

"I guess it's a woman thing," he quipped, turning the camera back toward the valley to take more pictures.

To Tom, Nicole thought, this was probably like any other day outside enjoying the peace and quiet of the woods. He seemed to especially enjoy the solitude and the calm it offered. For her, this was a world far away from the crowds and noise of the city. She used to take long walks alone. It was her therapy, a private activity where she could let herself go by taking pictures of anything that caught her fancy. Some came out well. Others were a blur. She played with the camera lens to take different light settings, like today, showing Tom. She had never shared her hobby with anyone. It was nice to share it now, and he seemed to appreciate it.

Nicole sipped the last of her bottled water, watching how his hands gently held the camera, and she found herself wondering if he would be a tender lover. Soft, that was the word that occurred to her. He seemed soft and not like other men she had been with, who all seemed hard, rough romantically and always trying to impress women with their careers. The men she had known were focused only on sex, saying or doing anything to get a woman into bed. Strangely, she didn't feel guilty as she imagined how it would feel to have Tom's hands on her body, but she quickly told herself to stop thinking that way because it was pointless and reached over to show Tom how to adjust the camera's shutter speed.

They had gone through both rolls of film before Tom glanced down at his watch. "It's about that time. I need to get back to the office."

"I didn't realize it had gotten so late." Nicole packed up the film canisters, detached her camera lens, and placed it in her camera bag while Tom gulped the last of his water.

"There aren't any garbage cans around here," Tom said.

"That's fine. Give it to me. I'll toss the bottles out at home." She stuffed her camera and the bottles into her bag as Tom jumped down from the rock.

"Let me get that." He threw the bag over his shoulder and extended his arm to help Nicole off the rock. As they retraced their steps back down the path, Tom forged ahead to push away all the tree branches for her. Was he always this much of a gentleman, she wondered, as he kicked brush off the path? She was grateful because the clearer path allowed her to be decidedly more graceful on the climb down. She only stumbled a few times.

"We got some great shots today," she said as they drove back to town. "I can make doubles if you'd like copies."

"That'd be great," he said as he clicked on the car stereo. He was listening to a Jim Brickman CD. Nicole loved Jim Brickman. Jennifer had gotten them front row tickets to his concert for her birthday last year. The notes seemed even sweeter now as they listened. Tom pulled into the parking lot of the nursing home pavilion and parked next to her Nova.

"The Kinzua Bridge was great. I really enjoyed myself." She grabbed the strap of her camera bag.

"I've never taken anyone there before," Tom said as he stepped out of his Tahoe. He wondered immediately why he told her that.

Never? Not even his wife? What did this mean? Why did he show her? Nicole debated if she should ask the questions out loud.

"None of my ladies from the nursing home could make the climb, you know," he joked self consciously.

Nicole jumped from the Tahoe and decided it was best not to say anything. She climbed into her Nova and waved goodbye.

Tom waved back, shut off the engine to his Tahoe and took one last look at Nicole. His gaze lingered on Nicole's face as she pulled away, much as the first time he saw her at the Crook Farm, her long dark hair rolling over her shoulders, her lips soft and full, and her smile that could light up a room. He did not mean to stare. He worried she would notice the way he looked at her.

It had been years since he had talked to anyone about his father. After his dad died, hiking through the woods was just never the same. The woods seemed empty and lonely, even when he took Robert and Lisa. But he saw the woods differently now. He saw Nicole differently. Drawn to her in a way he hadn't been to a woman in years, he was suddenly afraid. After feeling dead for so long, Nicole made him feel so alive.

CHAPTER 5

The Friendship Table

Monday morning found Nicole scraping a layer of frost off her car with her credit card. It was the first frost of the season. Living in New York City for so long, she had forgotten about the sudden changes of weather common for the region. She hadn't even bought a shovel, an ice scraper, or an insulated pair of mittens.

"Oh, to have a heated garage," she said as she waited for her heater to start putting out warm air. She picked up her morning paper and cappuccino, glancing around to see if Tom's Tahoe was parked in the lot. It wasn't. She paid the cashier and headed for her office.

Today she was giving a quiz in her American Government class, a good way to start a crappy Monday, she thought. She hung up her coat and walked downstairs to the copy machine. As she turned the corner, she saw a big sign posted on the wall: "The Friendship Table Drop Off Box." Underneath it was a large cardboard box to donate canned goods and non-perishables. She thought of Tom. Now she would have a constant reminder of his presence in her life every time she went to get copies, which was at least once a day.

When she returned from class, Carol was waiting outside her door. "My mother had a heart attack last night," Carol sobbed, and Nicole quickly cleared a pile of exams from the chair next to her desk. "My father says it was a bad one. She's downtown at Northwestern Memorial Hospital. They're doing a bypass. I'm booked on a flight to Chicago tomorrow afternoon."

Nicole stayed with Carol that night and helped her pack. Nicole envied Carol's relationship with her mother. Nicole had picked up the telephone a hundred times trying to get the courage to call her own mother over the years. She hated the distance and the sense of abandonment, and she wanted the kind of relationship she saw other women have with their mothers, but she knew she would never have that kind of closeness with her mom no matter what. Everything changed the day her mother left and her bitterness had only grown over time. When her mother sent cards at Christmas, the letters were merely empty reminders that her mother was gone and didn't want any type of relationship at all with her daughters.

The next day, Nicole drove Carol to the Buffalo airport. She was grateful for their friendship. Carol had helped Nicole keep her sanity during such an insane time, the move to Bradford and her dad's illness.

Nicole stayed with her father that night. He was still struggling with the chemotherapy, the hair loss, and the indignity of slowly dying. There wasn't much hope. The doctors were supposedly slowing his deterioration, but the prognosis remained the same, his life measured in months not years. He had lost weight due to the treatments and wasn't eating much, but no matter what came along, no matter what his temperament, whether he was sanguine about his condition or in despair, questioning his strength to go on, Nicole saw each day as a gift. Each time she hugged him goodbye, she never knew if it would be the last time.

The drive to Bradford was quiet without Carol, and the weather had turned to a light snowfall. The snow looked like soft powder covering the trees, and Nicole imagined the Kinzua Bridge in wintertime. Like a flash of light, she wondered, "Just what *did* Tom mean when he said he had never taken anyone to that hillside before?" The question occupied her for the rest of the trip.

Back in Bradford without Carol, she was on her own for the rest of the weekend, and that evening she treated herself to a nice dinner, filet mignon and a good bottle of merlot. For fun, she rented *Sleepless in Seattle* for the fifth or sixth time, and over dinner, she tried to focus on the movie. Somehow, Tom kept popping into her mind.

She washed the dishes and let them dry in the sink. Nothing good was on television, and it was only nine o'clock. She turned on the computer to read more about High Point College, which the website told her was a four-year coed liberal arts university and the Department of History and Political Science offered both a major and a minor. High Point was close to Winston-Salem as well as Greensboro. Were cigarettes any cheaper there, she wondered, chuckling at her own joke? But then, what did she care? She was waiting for Columbia to call.

There was an e-mail from Carol to let her know that her mother's surgery went well. There was an electronic greeting card from Jennifer that read, "Hang in there," under a picture of a cat dangling by its front claws from a tree.

Trees? Nicole remembered her hike with Tom. She had been so busy helping Carol that getting the pictures developed had completely slipped her mind. The pictures and the day were coming back. She glanced down at her computer and wondered if Tom had an e-mail address. At the search prompt, she typed in Bradford, Pennsylvania. She scrolled through the Bradford Area Chamber of Commerce website. Nothing. She typed in the Crook Farm and Landmark Society websites. Still nothing. She finally typed in the name of the nursing home where he worked and scrolled through the staff members. Bingo. There was Thomas J. Ryan and his e-mail address.

Now what? She didn't have the film developed so she couldn't e-mail him about that. But perhaps she could send him a nice "thank you" e-mail. Yes, that's it. "A thank-you e-mail wouldn't hurt," she said out loud. She started to type: "Dear Tom." No, that was too formal. "Hello Tom." Yes, that was more casual. Two hours later, she had finally written four sentences that conveyed just the right tone. Not too obvious. Not too bland. Nothing suggestive. Sincere. Before she had a chance to change her mind, she hit the send button.

She awoke early on Sunday, feeling like a little girl on Christmas morning as she checked her e-mail. She quickly scrolled her Inbox, but there was nothing but junk. Well, it was Sunday. He probably didn't check his e-mail except at work. She puttered around all day cleaning her apartment. She put another load of laundry in the washer downstairs, folded her clothes on the bed, vacuumed the carpet, and washed the dishes, all the while thinking about Tom. She liked him. She didn't know exactly why, except that he seemed comforting. He was the kind of guy who didn't make her feel embarrassed when she spilled powdered sugar on herself. He was the kind of guy who seemed to enjoy the mundane aspects of life, like looking at the leaves, and who didn't need fancy cocktail parties and hospital benefits that she had grown accustomed to while dating Michael. He seemed like the singular person she had met in this small town she could relate to. Yes, there was Carol, and they had grown close, but Tom was the kind of person with whom she could share aspirations. She hadn't thought much about writing her novel for a very long time. So, why did she blurt that out to Tom? She had never even told Michael. Nicole checked her e-mail again that evening, just to see if perhaps Tom had e-mailed during the day. Nothing. But then, what did she expect, she wondered?

On Monday morning, she skipped her usual ritual of reading the paper and went right to the computer. Still nothing. Maybe Tom hadn't gotten to work yet. She kept her e-mail on all day. Several days passed, and she still hadn't received an e-mail reply. Of course, her e-mail to him didn't exactly demand a response, but she hoped that Tom would at least send some acknowledgment. By the end of the week, she realized how silly she was acting.

Friday afternoon, the phone rang while she was finishing grading papers before she left for her interview at High Point College. Nicole thought it was probably Carol calling to update Nicole about her mother's recovery.

"Hello, Dr. Benson," the voice said. "This is Dr. Danforth from Columbia University."

Nicole began to tremble. The chairperson of the search committee had called to invite her for an interview. They discussed the position, her research interests, and then finalized plans for an interview date after Christmas when Nicole would be back in Manhattan. As part of the interview process, he told her, every candidate had to make a formal presentation of their research to the faculty. She couldn't stop trembling as she hung up the phone. This was it. She finally had her chance.

Nicole kept thinking about Columbia and had trouble focusing on work the following week. She decided it would be another quiz day in her Monday morning class and walked downstairs to the copy machine. She stopped dead when she turned the corner. There, hunched over the cardboard box for the

Friendship Table food drive, was Tom Ryan. He had his back to her and was stuffing the contents from the box into a large sack. Nicole quietly walked up behind him.

"Stop stealing the food or I'll call the cops," she said, sticking her finger into his back like a gun.

Tom jumped slightly, obviously startled. "It's you." He smiled. He stood up and gave Nicole a hug as if on instinct, though she wondered if perhaps it was more impulsive than she at first imagined. He seemed to be blushing, and she wondered if the hug was different somehow qualitatively from the hugs he gave to the residents at the nursing home and to female colleagues when he handed out Christmas gifts or bonuses. "How have you been?"

"Fine. What are you doing here?" she asked.

"It's my turn to empty the drop-off boxes," he said. "Thanksgiving is just a week away."

"Did you get my e-mail?" she asked, still wondering why she hadn't heard from him.

"E-mail?" He looked surprised. "Never touch it."

"You don't use e-mail?"

"I'm what you'd call computer illiterate," he said.

Nicole had not stopped to think that universities were among the first to adopt this technology or that many people were altogether intimidated by computers, perhaps especially people Tom's age and older. Nicole felt relieved. This explained why she hadn't heard from him. "I just wanted to let you know the pictures should be back soon," she said.

"I'd still love to see them." Tom glanced down at the sack of food. "If you'll be in town for Thanksgiving, we can always use an extra hand." He seemed shocked that these words came out of his mouth. "It doesn't have to be an all-day commitment," he rambled, now obviously nervous. "Some people just come in the morning to help so they can still get home with their families later. Others just work cleanup."

"I'm not sure what I'm doing yet." Somehow, Nicole couldn't tell Tom that she already had plans. She knew that she had feelings for Tom, and she knew she had to stop those feelings. What would be the point? He was married and not available. Taking the hike was good—she enjoyed his company—but her priorities were now to get back to New York and move on with her life and her career. Yet, she couldn't just tell him that she was going to New York for the holiday. She stopped the words from coming out. She wasn't sure why, if she didn't want to disappoint him or if part of her wanted to keep that offer open in case she changed her mind.

"I've cooked dinner at the shelter for about five, no, six years now," Tom said.

"Isn't that hard with your family?"

"No. Rose spends Thanksgiving with Robert and her parents in Pittsburgh, and I open the camp over the holiday so it works out for everyone."

"I'm late for class," Nicole said, glancing up at the wall clock. Her life was way too complicated to think about giving up Manhattan to volunteer at some shelter. She needed to see Jennifer. She needed to get away from Bradford. "Thanks for the invitation. I'll see."

"We can always use a hand," Tom said as Nicole walked down the hallway.

Tom's heart felt heavy as he watched Nicole walk away. He was confused again, feeling the way he felt after their day at the bridge. He had imagined what it would be like to run into Nicole again. He thought he might see her when he went to the drop box on campus, and he alternately held out hope and tried to pretend to himself that he didn't care. But running into her just now, he had to admit that his feelings for her were strong. He had to admit that he was becoming consumed with thinking about her. Remembering their day at the bridge was how he started each morning. He remembered Nicole's smile as she snapped pictures of the bridge and how happy she seemed going there with him. He imagined conversations with Nicole that never happened—that he never thought would happen. It was a hundred imagined conversations about her day, wondering what she did when she wasn't teaching. He was still surprised at his own openness about his father, something about which he had never even talked with Rose much about. He wasn't sure if it was love or infatuation, all he knew was something he couldn't quite explain was happening to him.

Every year since moving back to Bradford, Tom had wished that Rose would have stayed to go to the camp for Thanksgiving, but like Robert, Rose hated the emptiness and quiet of the woods and craved the excitement of the city, enjoying her trips to Pittsburgh, shopping, going out to eat, and visiting with her family. Tom had never minded because he had the shelter meal to prepare, and he looked forward to his time alone at the cabin. But now he found himself wondering what it would be like to have Nicole around over the holiday. He shook himself out of his reverie and headed for the car.

The following week, Nicole flew into the Piedmont Triad International Airport outside of High Point. Two members from the search committee greeted her. They drove her to a Holiday Inn and offered to take her to dinner, which she declined. Tired from the flight, she ordered room service and turned in early.

The next morning, the chairperson of the search committee escorted her to the campus and stayed with her throughout the day. She met with the entire search committee, whose members were clearly impressed with her credentials and research. In the afternoon, she made her teaching presentation, which was flawless. After a full day of interviews, the chairperson took her for a tour of the campus. He showed her the office she would occupy if she joined the faculty, which was spacious with a large window that overlooked the campus and the rolling hills of North Carolina.

For a small college, the department had state-of-the-art facilities, not to mention the lush grounds and well-manicured gardens of the campus. The search committee took her for an elegant dinner and the chairperson announced that she was their top choice from the pool of candidates. While she liked the looks of High Point College and the faculty seemed very nice, she had no intention of taking the job. No way would she move so far from New York City and her dream of teaching at Columbia.

It was the Wednesday before Thanksgiving, and Nicole woke up early to catch her flight. She packed her new cable knit sweater to wear at Jennifer's holiday party. The weatherman had predicted a blizzard in Buffalo, but she only saw sunshine mixed with a few clouds in Bradford. As she headed north to the Buffalo Niagara International Airport, she listened to weather reports on the radio that said the snow was falling three inches an hour and that the airport had begun canceling flights.

Nicole was determined. She kept driving until she hit a blinding snow squall and had to slow to five miles per hour. Her wipers were on high, but the snow was accumulating too quickly. She had driven in worse growing up in Buffalo, but it had been seventeen years since she had had that experience. Nevertheless, the art of driving in inclement weather came back to her quickly, like riding a proverbial bike, she thought. She inched her way along until the radio reported that the Buffalo airport was officially closed.

She managed to find a place to turn around, and on the way back to Bradford, the weather gradually cleared. It was hard to imagine that, just fifty miles north, lake-effect snow was pounding her hometown. She desperately needed to get to the city. When she got back to her apartment, she called to rebook her flight. The next available flight was Saturday, which didn't help. Jennifer's party would be over.

She called Jennifer to tell her that she couldn't make it. She sat at the kitchen table and lit a cigarette, wondering what she was going to do for Thanksgiving. The weather was so bad that she couldn't make it to her father's, and Carol had already left to visit her mother. There was only one other person she knew in Bradford.

Early on Thanksgiving morning, Nicole read her horoscope in the paper, as she did every morning: *The unknown has a direct impact on the direction of the present. Stifle your fear of change and look to the intuitive voice within for guidance.* She felt an eerie chill as she read it again. She dressed in a pair of black jeans and her well-worn New York University sweatshirt and headed out the door to the Friendship Table. She walked into a large room decorated in orange and yellow crepe paper with tacky little turkey-shaped lights hanging around the room. She glanced over the dozens of metal tables covered with white paper tablecloths with patterns of leaves. Tom must have picked those.

"Hey, glad you could make it," Tom called from behind. He was dressed in denim jeans, a large apron over a work shirt, and a baseball cap. Nicole noted that there was no hug this time. Instead, he introduced Nicole to the other volunteers and showed her around the kitchen, which was decorated with plywood cabinets with fake wood veneer and two large wooden tables full of bowls, plates, plastic silverware, and canned goods. One team stirred pots on a double-wide stove. Another team set the dining tables and another poured milk into pitchers. Nicole heard a television in the background broadcasting the Macy's Thanksgiving Day Parade. As she listened to the announcers, she longed to be at Jennifer's buffet of assorted French cheeses, fresh prosciutto, and her traditional rack of lamb, all served in Jennifer's best china and crystal.

"I've already stuffed the turkeys this morning, but there's still plenty to do," Tom said as he handed Nicole an apron. She poured cans of gravy into steel trays heated with Sterno and emptied cans of yams and cranberry sauce into large bowls. As afternoon approached, lines of people formed at the door and began to take seats in the dining hall. She glanced through the crowd, noticing several families with young children and even some with babies. She saw dozens of elderly couples dressed in ragged clothes and one man with no leg who hopped inside with only one crutch. Nicole felt like an idiot for feeling sorry for herself because she could not partake of an intimate gathering that easily cost more to put on than this entire spread for almost three hundred people.

Tom pulled turkeys from the oven, replacing them with new ones, while Nicole helped serve, working alongside the mayor, a retired naval officer from Bradford, and a Lutheran minister. During dinner, someone needed to refill the coffee. Nicole surprised herself when she volunteered. As she went from table to table pouring coffee, everyone seemed to be so happy. The food was so simple compared to rack of lamb, and none of it was served on fine china, and yet these people really seemed to appreciate their meal. When one little boy hugged her before he left, Nicole caught herself fighting back a tear.

It was late and the dining hall was nearly empty. Nicole was ready to collapse. She was dumping garbage bags on the outside porch when she saw Tom washing dishes by the sink tubs—alone. She quickly tossed the last of the garbage bags out the door and walked over to him.

"Need any help?"

"Always. Grab a towel," Tom replied as he pointed to a kitchen drawer.

She pulled out a towel and started to wipe off the excess water from the pots and pans. A team of volunteers threw away the paper tablecloths and plastic dishes, while another team broke down tables and folding chairs. Soon everything, including those turkey-shaped lights, were taken down and put away.

"Don't forget to lock up," one of the volunteers said to Tom as she placed a thick set of keys on the kitchen counter.

"Sure. No problem. Goodnight," he said as he washed the last of the pots.

As the door slammed behind the woman, Nicole was acutely aware that she was completely alone with Tom. They hadn't been alone together since their day of taking photographs of the bridge. Being alone with him now seemed different than that first time, however. After his hug in the hallway, she wondered if Tom had feelings for her. His body did feel warm and soft, but getting involved was the last thing on her mind, especially with a married man. But after the e-mail "incident" and obsessing about a response from Tom, she had to wonder what she was starting to feel for him.

They finished the dishes, and Nicole wiped down the kitchen table while Tom took one last walk through the hall to make sure everything was put away.

"It looks like we're officially done here." Tom walked back into the kitchen.

Nicole was sitting at the table. She hadn't sat down all day.

"This is hard work." Nicole stretched in the chair. "Every muscle in my body aches." Tom sat down in a chair across the table.

"I was supposed to be in New York visiting my friends, but the storm closed the airport," Nicole explained. "So you won by default." She laughed and looked at her watch. It was nine-thirty. Nicole thought about Jennifer's party. The teetotalers were just leaving and the heavy drinkers were just getting started. She told him about her attempt to get to the airport.

"I'm sorry you had such a terrible drive," Tom said. "But I'm glad you ended up here."

He could feel the question bubbling up. He was going to the camp that weekend. Would she like to join him? They could hike the trails. She could bring her camera to take pictures. Tom stopped himself. No, he shouldn't. He couldn't. The camp was too personal and too private. What about Rose? What was he doing thinking about this other woman? What was he doing even considering asking her to the cabin? He had no good answer.

"It's perhaps the most charitable thing I've done." Nicole laughed. "I've never even given blood."

"You underestimate yourself," Tom said, pulling out a can of Copenhagen snuff from his pants pocket. "I started in high school. Not many people know. I mainly do it at home."

Tom didn't look the type to chew snuff, Nicole thought, but if he chewed then he wouldn't mind if she smoked. She had hidden her habit for nearly three months from Michael, who distained smokers, before he discovered a pack of Marlboro Ultra-Lights in her purse.

"Actually, I smoke." Nicole felt comforted that Tom kept his addiction a secret too.

"Funny, you don't look like a smoker," Tom said.

"Funny, you don't like a chewer." Nicole smiled.

"You can smoke here," he said, stuffing his Copenhagen into his back pocket.

"I didn't bring my cigarettes with me," she replied.

"We can fix that," Tom said as he stood up and opened a drawer of one of the cupboards to pull out a pack of Salem Lights. He bent down to retrieve an ashtray from under the kitchen sink. Even though they weren't the brand Nicole smoked, she lit up.

"I'll be going to the camp this weekend for the opening of deer season," Tom said, the words tumbling out. "It's got some great hiking trails. There's a small pond where I used to fish in the summer."

Why didn't he stop himself? Why didn't he have better self-control? Sitting at the table across from Nicole, he remembered the last time he was at camp with Lisa. She colored in her coloring books in front of the woodstove. He made fresh venison steaks, and after dinner they played cards in the living room. It was a simple night like any other night at camp.

"Would you be interested in going for a hike on Saturday?" The question surprised Tom as it came out of his mouth. A part of him wanted to show Nicole the camp, while another part, somewhere deeper in his heart, was frightened by the idea of sharing it with anyone again.

"A hike?" Nicole couldn't imagine another hike like the last one out to the hillside. Then again she didn't have any better offers. She had finished all her grading before break, and Carol was in Chicago. With the snow, she couldn't even visit her father. "Sure, why not."

"It's just over the hill." Tom started to draw a map on the back of a napkin. "You make the first right, but it's not marked." The more he told her about the camp, the more he wanted Nicole to see it, to share it with her. By the time he was through with the driving instructions, he was looking forward to spending time with her again and all doubts about asking her were gone. "There's a curve in the road about a quarter of a mile in, then you turn left on a small road that isn't marked either. Go about another half mile, then make a sharp right down a dirt path."

Nicole looked confused.

"Maybe it'd be easier if I just picked you up?"

"Yeah, I think that would be better. I have no idea where you mean."

"I can pick you up about ten?" Tom asked.

"How about noon? It's my only day to sleep in and get errands done."

Tom locked up the shelter and waved goodbye as he said, "Until Saturday."

The next morning, Tom went to the camp to cut firewood and get the camp ready for deer season as he did every Friday after Thanksgiving, his ritual. But this year was different. Nicole was coming. Was he getting it ready for her? He hadn't thought about the implications when he asked her to join him, but now, having time alone to think, he wondered anew why he had invited her. He did not think he should be alone with a woman he was attracted to and someone he had started to care about, not when he had Rose. Did Nicole think he was trying to put the moves on her? Why did Nicole agree to come? Was she attracted to him too? Impossible, he thought. There was no way a beautiful woman like Nicole could be attracted to him. She was younger than he was, more worldly and better educated; it didn't seem likely.

He heaved the ax down to crack another log. He studied the wood, noting the knots and limbs. It was part of what he did. He tried to split in between those areas, as it was much harder to split across the knots, which held the wood together like nails.

He balanced another piece of wood on the chopping block. When he was younger, he used to cut three full cords of wood in a day. Now he was lucky to get in one or two. Balancing himself, he drove the ax downward and split another log.

He remembered trying to teach Rose how to split wood when they were dating in college. He had brought her home to meet his parents for the first time almost twenty-four years ago. He took her to the camp. Rose didn't like the camp then and she didn't like it now. She wasn't a rustic sort of woman, but then neither was Nicole.

Why had he invited Nicole to camp? What about Rose? The questions came at him again like snapping dogs. Twenty-three years was a long time to be with someone. He would never want to do anything to hurt Rose. Then what was he doing with another woman? He'd had opportunities to stray before, a few instances when he ignored the signs of a woman being interested in him. He would never want to risk the life he had made with Rose. Yes, they had their differences. Yes, emotionally he felt estranged from her, but he never had allowed himself to get this close to another woman.

Tom slid one hand up near the head of the ax, then let it slide down the long handle toward the other hand as he swung downward. This helped maintain control and delivered a more powerful blow. He swung again. The wood cracked open but not enough. Anchoring another log on the chopping block, he swung again, harder, the release of emotions flooding through him with each blow.

Why had he invited Nicole to camp? He did not know what to do. Was she interested in him? Why was she coming to see him at his cabin—alone? He hadn't been alone with another woman in years. The only time he could remember was going to a conference in Harrisburg with Betsy, a colleague from work. They had dinner together one night. Betsy was also twice his age and the trip was far from romantic. But Nicole was an attractive, younger woman. Now, once again, Tom felt nervous about seeing Nicole. He felt like he was on an emotional seesaw.

He had been curious about Nicole since the day they first met. Somehow her image constantly seemed to pop into his mind: when he would wake in the morning, when he was driving to work, when he was going to sleep at night. He had not been curious about a woman in a long time, not since Rose. He fell in love with Rose instantly, from across the classroom when he first saw her in college. The following week, he had worked up enough courage to ask her on a date. She instantly said yes and he knew he loved her. It was easy to be curious about a woman then, before he had any commitments, when the world was open and his life was still ahead of him; but at forty-four and entrenched in the structure of the day-to-day grind, life seemed to be passing him by.

He couldn't remember a time without Rose in his life. He had dated a few women before Rose, but he was young and could hardly remember any of them. He figured the number of women he had been with was low compared to other men, but most men were not married so young. It was just what you did back then, the path he chose. Grow up, go to college, get married, and start a family. It was what everyone did.

Balancing another log on the chopping block, Tom remembered how happy he was the day Robert was born. Tom rushed out of a meeting at work to reach Rose, who was already at the hospital. Her water broke earlier than the doctor expected, and there were worries that Robert was going to be okay. Tom had to wait outside the delivery room. He paced all night long it seemed; his heart pounding as he waited for the baby to be born. His parents were there, and Rose's parents too. When the nurse came out to tell him he had a healthy seven-pound boy, Tom had never felt so relieved.

He felt so young at the time, like a child himself, the first time he held his new son. He was only twenty-one and Rose only twenty. They had no clue how to raise a child, and they lived in a one-bedroom apartment—they had nothing but were happy. Tom was working at his first job out of college, and yet, as he held his son, his whole life seemed to be set, his path predestined.

Tom's shoulder was hurting him and so he decided to stop for the day. He put the ax back into the shed and started stacking the wood up on the porch. He had always wished that Rose loved the camp and the woods like he did. Rose came to the camp twice with Lisa when their daughter was young, but she never felt comfortable staying over night in the cabin. Tom felt okay about that for the most part. He didn't expect Rose to love it the way he did, but after meeting Nicole, he was excited at the prospect of spending time with someone who might share his passion for the woods. Despite being a sexy and sophisticated woman from the city, Nicole agreed to take that hike the day at the bridge and she came down to the homeless shelter to fix dinners for the poor and forgotten. Tom was now wondering if she only came because he asked or if she had such interests, such compassion, and would have come no matter who asked.

He remembered that it was hard on Rose when they moved to Bradford, the adjustment to life in a small town after growing up in Pittsburgh. Nicole would probably feel the same way, he reminded himself, and so maybe she was interested in him. Although she had helped him at The Friendship Table, she admitted that she was not prone to giving of her time for charity. That was the first time it seemed fun to wash dishes, he thought.

He stacked another layer of wood alongside the porch wall. His gloves were thick and the baseball cap he wore kept his head warm, but he felt the wind pick up and the air turn cold. He grabbed another log to stack and wondered what he should do when Nicole arrived. What would they do to pass the time? This wasn't like The Friendship Table with other people around and tasks to complete. This wasn't like being alone when they were at the bridge. Then he didn't know Nicole very well and didn't think about her all the time. Then he didn't have feelings for her. What was he doing? Like a shot through his heart, he felt fear. Again, the question: what was he doing? The panic bubbled up and he couldn't stop it. The feelings kept flooding over him. He wasn't sure if he was infatuated. He hadn't really felt like this before. Was he falling in love with Nicole?

He shuddered at the implications. What about Rose? The guilt swept over him like a tidal wave. How could he even have feelings for another woman? He loved Rose and they had a good life together. They had gone through so much together. What could he possibly be thinking? He could never hurt Rose like that. But he was getting ahead of himself. Nicole could be coming just to get away, just to go on a hike, to get away from the academic grind. Maybe what he was feeling had nothing to do with her, and yet, he had an intuition that it had everything to do with her. She was beautiful and smart, and she had made him feel alive again.

He stacked the last of the wood. He wondered what a young, attractive woman like Nicole could possibly see in him, and he decided it was probably safe to have her come for a hike. They would talk and that would be about all. There was no way anything more could happen. Nicole could never be interested in him, not in any romantic way. She had too many other choices in her life. Yet, for a moment, just a moment, Tom wondered what he would do if she had feelings for him too.

CHAPTER 6

The Unspoken Rule

Tom arrived promptly at noon. Nicole met him downstairs so he couldn't see how messy her apartment was. She climbed into his Tahoe, and this time she came prepared to hike. She was dressed in blue jeans, her extra thick NYU sweatshirt with a turtleneck, and a pair of L.L. Bean Gore-Tex boots and a pair of thick wool gloves that she bought.

Tom drove toward the Allegheny National Forest. The trees had lost most of their leaves, and their density and height made the drive feel ominous and eerie to Nicole. The light snowfall from the night before made the roads slick, and she feared that the Tahoe would end up at the bottom of a ditch. Just past a large curve, Tom turned onto a paved road that gradually climbed a steep hill and forked into two paths at the top. The road eventually turned to gravel and quickly narrowed. The road was so narrow that Tom had to pull over to let a Ford pickup going in the opposite direction pass. As they approached the top of a steep ravine, a deer ran in front of the truck. Tom was calm as he slammed on the brakes, but Nicole held on tight to the handlebar above the passenger window, imagining herself dying in this wilderness obstacle course.

At the top of the hill, Tom turned into a long dirt driveway and a small house nestled in the woods suddenly appeared. The exterior was built from pine, and the house had a large wooden porch with a green awning. They climbed out of the SUV and Tom said, "Well, this is it," as they made their way up a gravel walkway. The porch steps were steep, and as Nicole lifted her leg up to reach the first one, she stopped to look at an antique rocking chair in the corner.

"I refinished that last summer," Tom said as he unlocked the front door and pushed it open. Before he walked into the camp, he paused. "Turn around and take it in. That's the main reason my father bought this property."

"It's just lovely," Nicole said as she looked back at a breathtaking view of the entire valley. There were miles of dips and curves of rolling hills and an unobstructed view of the Kinzua Bridge in the distance.

As she stepped inside the camp, she immediately smelled the knotty pine and the pungent odor of wood smoke from previous fires in a large black potbelly stove that sat on the left side of the camp's main living room. Even though the place had electricity and was heated with oil, Tom told her he preferred to read by a fire in the wood stove in the evenings. Next to the iron stove was a small stereo system that sat on top of a television with the old-style turn knobs. Not even a remote.

"That's such a relic," Nicole said.

"It only gets two channels."

"No cable? Have I just entered some kind of time warp?"

In the center of the living room, Nicole spotted a set of narrow wooden stairs leading to a loft. To the right of the stairs was a large couch upholstered with a print of deer running through fields interspersed with trees. Two brown sofa pillows were tossed on top. In place of a coffee table, Tom used an old army chest, with a few copies of *Field & Stream* on top. Instead of normal end tables, Tom's had wooden tops with deer antlers for legs.

"My dad made those." Tom smiled as he walked toward the kitchen. Nicole followed slowly behind, still looking around. Why did he spend so much time in a place like this, she wondered?

The cabin was larger than it looked from the outside. There were two spare bedrooms and a large kitchen, circa 1950s. The kitchen was modestly furnished with a Formica table with four straight-backed wood chairs around it in the middle of the room, white metal cabinets with black hinges, and a large pantry to the right of the refrigerator.

"This is where I do most of my cooking," Tom said as he showed Nicole through a back door that led onto a small outside porch, which sported a fairly new looking gas grill. He finished the tour of the cabin with a peek into the bathroom located down the hallway. A mirrored medicine cabinet hung over a white porcelain sink with his razor on the vanity. There was no tub in the bathroom, just a steel shower stall about three feet square.

Tom guided her upstairs to the loft, an area he used as his main bedroom. The loft overlooked the living room and had a view out the front window. There was a double bed covered in a green wool blanket with three beige-colored pillow cases. Across from the bed was an antique chest of drawers, and wooden nightstands stood on each side of the bed. The nightstand to the right had a small reading lamp on it and a stack of books, most by John Grisham, Tom Clancy, and Zane Grey.

As they walked downstairs, Nicole pulled up the collar on her turtleneck. The walls of his dank camp were decorated like a man would decorate them, empty except for one wall hanging, which was large and took up most of the wall. It was a framed drawing that, when she looked closer, turned out to be a set of blueprints done on thick paper and in black ink. As she looked yet closer, she noticed the date: May 1882.

"These are the original drawings for the Kinzua Bridge," Tom said from behind Nicole. She studied the details.

"See the signature in the corner," he said. "That's the signature of Oliver Barnes, the chief engineer for the bridge. General Kane commissioned the construction of the viaduct to get across the Kinzua Valley, and Anthony Bonzano of the Phoenixville Bridge Company developed this design with Barnes. The plans were drawn up in less than a week. We had the sketches treated and framed into this lithograph."

"It's remarkable," Nicole said. The lithograph captured every piece of the bridge construction and detailed the placements of each tower, rivet, and bolt. The print was well preserved for its age, the paper only slightly yellowed and creased. The lines in ink were perfectly clear.

"My father was close friends with a retired Army officer from Mount Jewett who lived just a few miles south of the bridge. Everyone just called him Colonel, although his real name was Wilber. The Colonel and my dad were hunting partners for decades. When the Colonel died, his daughters weren't interested in the drawings and he didn't have any sons, so they gave the drawings to my father. More interestingly, the Colonel inherited the prints from his father, who inherited them from his father, who was one of the original forty men who built the Kinzua Bridge."

"The lithograph is certainly rare, something worthy of the Smithsonian or the Museum of American History."

"It's my most cherished possession." Tom looked hard at the lithograph. "I could never part with it."

Nicole glanced around the living room. She noticed a framed picture sitting on top of one of his antler-legged end tables.

"Who's this?" she asked as she studied the photograph more closely.

"That's me and my dad. I must be seven, maybe eight."

Nicole stared at the picture of a young boy wearing an orange hunting cap. The boy was standing next to an older man on the front porch of this hunting camp. Tom had inherited his father's build and had that same sweet smile, even back then.

"So are you ready for a hike?" Tom asked. She noticed that he held a thermos in his hand.

As they made their way into the trees, Nicole felt apprehensive about being so far out in the wilderness, but something about Tom made her feel completely safe. As they trudged through mounds of snow at least a foot deep in most places and almost knee high in some, Nicole remembered their day at the bridge and how Tom told her that he loved to hear the crunching snow underneath his boots.

Tom dressed in a thick down-filled jacket and hiking boots led the way down the path. How virile he looked, she thought, as he forged through the untouched snow. As they walked in silence, Nicole was surprised at how well she kept up and how comfortable it was just to be with Tom. No conversation was necessary. Suddenly, Tom stopped and turned back to her with his finger held to his lips even though Nicole hadn't said a word. Tom pointed through the trees toward a doe eating a leaf from a tree branch. The doe suddenly popped her head up.

Nicole stood completely still as the doe with her large brown eyes appeared to stare right back at her. The deer's nose twitched and her ears fluttered. Nicole remained ever so still, and several minutes passed. Hearing the echo of a tree branch snapping, the doe turned her ears this way and that, listening intently. Then, in a single bound, the deer landed at least ten feet away, and with two more bounds, she was gone from sight, disappearing deep into the woods.

"Amazing," Nicole whispered. "I've never been so close except at the petting zoo."

"The deer are just beautiful. I can walk for hours just to see them."

"So how can you hurt little Bambi?"

"I cried the first time I shot one," Tom said, remembering how his father only hunted for food and not so much for sport. "My father showed me how to smoke the meat and cut steaks. Now, I go less for the hunting and more for being out in the woods."

"You always come up here alone?" Nicole asked as she sat down on a large tree trunk, clearly out of breath. No doubt from too many cigarettes, she thought.

"These days I usually come alone." He took out his thermos and poured a cup of hot cocoa. "Rose never liked the camp or the woods much, but I used to take the kids here."

"Kids?" Nicole suddenly remembered the girl in the picture.

"Robert hated coming to camp. It was too far away from civilization for him. But then we had Lisa. Lisa loved the woods and loved hiking up here before she died."

Nicole was stunned. How terrible to lose a child.

"I'm so sorry," she whispered.

"We tried to have another child after Robert, but Rose miscarried, twice. We had given up until Lisa. Lisa was our miracle baby when she was finally born, which made it all the harder when she was diagnosed with leukemia. She would be fourteen now. We went to specialists from Erie to Pittsburgh to the Roswell Cancer Center in Buffalo, but there wasn't much that the doctors could do." He looked out at the woods as he spoke.

"After the funeral, Rose was devastated. We both were. She became very protective of Robert while I withdrew up here where Lisa and I had some special time together." Tom paused, and Nicole knew he was probably remembering Lisa's face, how she loved the woods, how she loved the camp. "Even talking about happy memories of Lisa was too hard for us. We really never dealt with her death."

He took a small sip of cocoa. "You look tired," he said a bit abruptly as if he wanted to change the subject. "Want to head back?"

"I'd love to. My feet are killing me." Nicole finished the last of her cocoa and Tom stuffed the thermos back into his jacket pocket. The snow started to fall on the hike back, and the wind picked up as they arrived at the camp. Tom offered to make fresh hot chocolate and disappeared in the kitchen. Nicole admired the lithograph again, noticing every detail of the drawings, imagining how impressive the Kinzua Bridge must have been when it was first built.

"You want some marshmallows in that?" Tom shouted from the kitchen.

"Yes, please."

Tom carried two mugs into the living room, a bag of pretzels tucked under his arm.

"Thought you might want a snack."

"Thank you." Nicole immediately opened the bag and joined Tom on the couch.

"My father bought the property from an old farmer's estate," Tom explained. "My dad renovated the cabin and put on a new roof, but it wasn't until I inherited it that I got a new oil heater and sewer system."

The camp suddenly seemed cozy.

"This would be a great place to write," Nicole said, leaning back in the couch. As she looked around the room, she pictured a roll-top desk in front of the window overlooking the valley and the Kinzua Bridge. She imagined waking up in the loft and fixing a cup of coffee and taking a cup to the desk with a blanket over her shoulders and opening up her laptop. No cell phone. No Internet. Nothing but quiet. It was hard to imagine a place like this existed. But it was real! She thought about how she filled her days with constant stimulation, like a mouse running on a wheel. The image did not make her happy, but it was apt:

she was running like mad but never getting any further, never making the time to focus on her creative writing, just research. Something about the cabin drew her in deeper and deeper.

"There'd be no distractions here except for the squirrels," Tom said, disrupting her train of thought. "They like to run around on the roof." He then looked at the empty bag of pretzels in her hand. "You hungry for something more to eat?"

"Oh, I'm so sorry." Nicole hadn't even realized that she never offered any to Tom.

"Come on, let's see what we've got," he said and they walked to the kitchen. Tom pulled a can of beef stew from the pantry and then looked inside the refrigerator. "You want a beer?"

He handed her a can of Coors Light and a glass. Without her asking for it, Tom placed an ashtray on the Formica tabletop, and with his unspoken permission, Nicole took out a pack from her purse and lit a cigarette. She offered to help cook but Tom insisted that he was a master chef.

"You're just a little Betty Crocker, aren't you?" She said as she sipped her beer, while watching Tom move about the kitchen, obviously comfortable in this element. She remembered the meals that her father had cooked for her and thought how nice it was to have a man cook for her again, even if it was just grilled cheese sandwiches and beef stew. She insisted that she help.

"Just relax." Tom dismissed her request and opened the cupboard to pull out two plates. The old stoneware fit the antiquated look of the kitchen. From a drawer, he unearthed two forks, two spoons, and two knives from a jumble of silverware. He opened a beer for himself and set it next to the stove as he stirred the pot of stew. She watched him and wondered if he ever cooked for his wife.

"Here we go." Tom slid a freshly made grilled cheese sandwich onto her plate from an iron skillet. Then he served up a bowl of stew. He took two more beers from the refrigerator and sat down. He grabbed her hand and Nicole felt shocked when he said grace. Saying grace before dinner wasn't what she was accustomed to; moreover, men usually did not try to bring religion into the picture, at least never so soon. Tom was definitely different. He had a way of making her feel at peace despite her chaotic and driven existence. Michael would never have taken a moment to say grace much less cook for her and serve her dinner. She suppressed a laugh knowing that Michael would have ordered out instead. Holding Tom's hand, she remembered her father grabbing her hand to say grace, even after her mother left. Grace was the one thing that they did as a family, her father's attempt to help Allison and Nicole strengthen their spirituality. Church was every Sunday, even though he was a divorced man. It was important to him to blend religion into their routine. Nicole wondered, ironically, if it was the kind of thing Tom did with Rose and his family.

She usually limited her conversations with men to work, school, and her research, but with Tom she felt comfortable talking about anything. The hours passed quickly as they talked over dinner, then over their empty dishes. Nicole learned that Tom was the older of two brothers. Shawn, his younger brother, was married with two children and lived in Houston, where he worked as a civil engineer.

"It was difficult for him to move back when our mother became sick. Shawn didn't like small towns or the woods, and so there wasn't much for him to come back to here," Tom explained, offering Nicole more stew.

"I'm good," she declined.

"It's just your dad and sister?" he asked, spooning the last of the stew on his plate.

"Yeah, pretty much."

"What happened to your mother?"

Nicole bristled in her familiar way. She had told Jennifer bits and pieces about her childhood and how she had watched her parents drift completely apart, but she had never really told anyone about her mother leaving. Nicole took a swig of beer.

"I really don't talk much about her." She paused, trying to remember her mother's face, her hair, what she looked like. "My memories of her have faded so much over the years."

Nicole spoke slowly, carefully, thinking about her words.

"I was so ashamed growing up without a mother that I couldn't bring myself to talk about her. I would always talk about my dad and how close we were. I think most people just assumed she died. I always thought that would have been easier. It's not easy for people to wrap their head around a mother who disowned not just one but two daughters."

"I'm sure that's been hard on you."

"Don't get me wrong. I don't go around feeling sorry for myself. It became a fact of life for me, but it's just that I feel ashamed talking about it. It isn't easy to admit that she left us."

Nicole was quiet again, concentrating on the last time she saw her mother.

"I was fifteen and she was leaving for work. She worked as a waitress, and she was dressed in a brown uniform and a white apron, getting ready for the breakfast rush. It seemed like every other morning, except that morning, she hugged Allison and me goodbye. She left a note on the kitchen table, something about her leaving being for the best, that she fell in love with an insurance salesman from Detroit. The night my father told me, he was crying. He had found the note first. They weren't happy, that much I knew, but none of us expected her to simply leave."

"At least you had your father."

"If it wasn't for him, I don't think I could have survived."

Nicole felt a lump in her throat. "That's why I'm here. I think that, after she left, I tried to run away from it all, to bury myself in my work and career. I moved to New York City for school, worked on Wall Street, went to graduate school. I didn't leave much time for my dad."

Tom was attentive as Nicole spoke. Now he took out two more beers.

"Have you ever been married?" he asked. Instead of handing her the can, he took the liberty of pouring it for her.

"Married?" Nicole said. That was a big question. How could she explain the ghosts of all her past relationships to a man who had been married for twenty-three years?

"I was engaged once," she said, deciding Peter was safe to talk about. The relationship was long gone and the closest to marriage that she had come. "We met in college. Peter was an ambitious young business major. He didn't drink, didn't smoke, and would have made a good provider. We planned on getting married after graduation, but every time Peter started talking about setting a wedding date, I felt like I couldn't breathe."

"Did you love him?" Tom asked.

"I guess so, but it was so long ago that Peter seems like a faint memory now."

"What happened?"

"Peter wanted to settle down and start a family while I wanted to travel and wasn't sure that I wanted to be a mother. I broke off our engagement a few months later."

Nicole thought about the men who had been in her life. Peter was the start of a series of relationships with the same ending. She ran away from many of them, some for good reasons and some because she was afraid of commitment. She wasn't sure anymore what love was, why she hadn't found the right man. Was it her or was it them? She turned to Tom feeling the need to explain, not so much to help him understand but to help herself understand her feelings.

"I didn't want to be like my mother," she said. "I thought that, if I picked someone and got married, I would fall into the same pattern. I thought that I would become unhappy, feel tied down, or that I would screw it up like she did. I think I could have had a husband and kids with the white picket fence, but I just didn't want it that badly enough. There are days it seems like it would have been easier, as I don't feel that far along at all. I scrimped and saved, and for what? I certainly didn't pick a lucrative profession. I think I was afraid of getting close to anyone, close in a needy, dependent sort of way. The worst part is that, the older I get, the more I worry that I am turning into my mother, distant and guarded. Not just with boyfriends but with friends, with my sister, and even with my father."

"You don't seem that way now," Tom said.

Nicole turned, and looking into his deep green eyes, she said, "I feel safe talking with you."

Nicole looked down at the dirty dishes. This time, she was the one who wanted to change the subject. She got up to clear the table. Tom tried to grab the plates from her hand, but she insisted. Tom washed and she dried, and it felt like being back at the Friendship Table. She and Tom did not speak of Peter or of her past again.

After the dishes, Tom made a pot of decaf coffee and they retired to the living room. He disappeared back into the kitchen and returned with a bottle of Bailey's Irish Cream. "Thought you might like a little in your coffee."

"Yes, please," she said as she poured some into her cup and watched the dark liquid turn an almond color. All at once, the sound of the wind gusts swirled outside the camp, beating the shutters against the windows. Tom got up to turn on the radio to get the forecast.

Reports indicated that the snow advisories were in effect for the surrounding counties. Ice and heavy snow had closed all the major roads and a travel ban was in effect for McKean County.

Tom peered out the window. "Looks like the snow is starting to accumulate. We could get off the hill, but it sounds like the main road into town would be closed. We could try it," Tom said, still looking out the window. Nicole noted that he did not turn toward her and wondered if he might be afraid of the implications.

"The storm system must have come earlier than they expected. They didn't expect it to get bad until tomorrow," Nicole said, unsure what she was feeling herself, her thoughts racing. Could they drive off the hill? Maybe the main road wasn't closed. She didn't know what to say next as she hadn't planned a sleep over.

"No, the weather service called for only a light snow." Tom kept his eye focused on the window, snow falling quickly over the valley, visibility poor. He said, "I have the spare room for you if we need to stay for the night." He hadn't expected a sleep over either.

An awkward silence filled the room as they both stared out the front window, not sure what to do.

"We could try to drive back to town—that truck is pretty good in the snow," Tom finally said.

"You know, I really wouldn't want to chance it. It is a steep incline. I would imagine that even a little snow makes it slick, much less this stuff."

"You sure?" Tom asked, now looking away from the window and at Nicole.

"That's fine." Nicole tried to remain calm as she thought of the unspoken rule. At the bars, she was used to seeing married men flirting. She usually ignored them while her friends would flirt back, especially if they thought it would get them free drinks. However, at the end of the evening, most people understood the unspoken rule and went their separate ways, never crossing the invisible line.

But Tom Ryan was completely different. He wasn't the type to be at the bar with the boys in the first place. Nor was he the type to even flirt. He was more sincere than that, which made him exactly the type of man that she would break the rule for.

Tom stoked the wood stove, which pushed dust and smoke into the room. Her contacts started to itch. Luckily, Nicole had brought her glasses, something she had become used to carrying from her bar hopping days, as the smoke always bothered her eyes. On her way back from the bathroom, she looked outside at the darkness. Nicole wasn't used to being anywhere that didn't have streetlights and realized just how completely alone with Tom she was.

"Much better," she said as she slid her boots off and relaxed back on the couch. She looked at Tom, who looked so good in his flannel shirt. She suddenly remembered her horoscope from Thanksgiving morning: *Stifle your fear of change and look to the intuitive voice within for guidance.* But just what was her inner voice trying to tell her? Her heart pounded as they sat there quietly watching the fire.

The warmth felt good as she faced the wood stove, and she turned her body slightly toward Tom with her arm extended on the back of the couch. Tom's hand slowly moved over hers and sat there, as if questioning if he should move closer. Without a word or sound, he caressed the back of her hand with his fingertips. Chills shot up her spine. No man had touched her like that before. Her body quivered as she fell naturally into his arms. She lifted her head to reach his kiss. His lips were softer than she imagined. Her hand rested on his chest as her mouth remained on his. She melted into his body as he kissed her more passionately. His lips, his body, everything about him felt so good. They stayed pressed together until she gently broke away.

"We shouldn't be doing this," Nicole whispered and looked into his deep green eyes. It was as if Tom saw right into her heart, as if he saw the soft part of herself that she thought had died years ago, a part of her that she didn't even know existed. Mixed with happiness and sadness, tears began to swell in her eyes. "For so many reasons we shouldn't be doing this," she whispered again.

"Please don't cry," Tom said, drawing her body close into his chest. She felt warm and soft in his arms as he took a deep breath. "Don't you know from the moment I saw you I couldn't take my eyes off you?"

"Really," she said softly as she looked up at Tom and used the sleeve of her sweatshirt to dry her tears. "The first time you saw me?"

For some reason, she trusted Tom in a way that she didn't usually trust a man. She couldn't explain why, but she took him at his word that this wasn't all some fancy line to get her into bed.

"Yes. That day at the Crook Farm, I noticed you walking around with Carol, and I followed you. I was trying to figure out how to say hello, and I thought it was an act of God when that mother ran into you with the stroller," Tom said as he gently stroked her hair. "Your smile is contagious. Once I saw it, I just had to meet you," Tom continued, and then his voice became soft. "Please don't misunderstand. I've never done this before."

Somehow Nicole already knew that Tom Ryan was not the type to stray. It was in the way he looked and in the way he acted. He was a faithful man.

She smiled as Tom tenderly rubbed her lips with his finger. "There's that infectious smile." Tom paused and then looked into her eyes. "You're simply radiant."

How was that possible? She was in jeans. She didn't have makeup on. Her hair was a mess. She didn't have her contacts in. In fact, this was the grubbiest she'd ever been in front of a man. Her teeth weren't even brushed. Well, not since morning anyway. Without waiting for her response, Tom whispered, "You are absolutely the most beautiful woman I have ever seen."

Beautiful? She never saw herself as beautiful. Cute maybe, but never beautiful. At parties, men always fell all over themselves at the sight of Jennifer's blonde hair and long legs while Nicole stood alone at the buffet table. Inevitably, at the bars, men liked "good conversation" with her but went home with the women in slinky dresses. But here, now, with Tom, all that didn't matter. With him, she felt like the most desirable woman in the world.

"This is all new for me," he said, obviously struggling to put words to what he was feeling. "I've not been alone with another woman since I met Rose. Nothing has surprised me more than meeting you and how I feel." He paused, carefully trying to find the next words. "I haven't done anything like this before. Inviting you to the camp is the craziest thing I've done, at least in a long while. I haven't reacted to another woman the way I have to you. After Lisa died, there was one woman I worked with. Her name was Maggie. I could tell she liked me. She brought me cookies and pies. She always asked if I wanted to go for a drink after work. She was an attractive woman, single and available. Even though Rose and I were having a hard time dealing with the loss of Lisa, I wasn't remotely interested. I thought how easily I could have been, but that's not what I wanted. I wasn't that guy. I never thought about another woman the way I feel about you. You are like a breath of fresh air. I haven't felt this good in a long time. I get up in the mornings and now look forward to the day. I haven't looked forward to anything in a long time. I hope I will run into you. I realized that you have become important to me. After Lisa, I learned that life is short. Remembering that one day, I decided to invite you here to the camp. This place means the world to me and I wanted to share it with you. Please understand. I didn't plan on making love to you, or even kissing you, or even having a sleepover with the two of us in separate rooms."

Nicole was quiet, listening intently. Instinctively, she trusted him. She wanted to believe him. He wasn't some Casanova with an agenda; he wasn't some guy on the prowl. He wasn't trying to use her for sex.

"All I can say is that sharing the bridge with you was amazing. I've gone back since that day, thinking about you, reliving the moments. Being with you here, now, sharing the lithograph, cooking for you, holding you, all I know is that I haven't felt this good in a long time. Just to have this moment, right now, I thank you for that." Tom then inhaled deeply. "I love you for that."

The words sent chills up her spine even more than Tom's touch. Love? Her heart pounded so loudly she thought Tom might hear it. Thoughts raced in her head. How could he love her? He didn't even know her. Maybe it was just infatuation? How did he really know? How does anyone know? Then, suddenly, like a dart hitting her heart, a pang of pain ripped through her, the internal panic that she was accustomed to feeling at the beginning of any new relationship.

"How can you possibly say you love me? You hardly know me?"

"You're right. I don't know you. I came here yesterday to cut wood for the fire. I spent the whole day cutting wood. I had so much energy. The cabin was a mess but I was excited to have you here. I haven't had anyone here since Lisa. Not even Rose."

"Not even Robert?"

"Robert doesn't stay here. When he visits, he stays at the house."

Nicole sensed that this was a big thing for Tom to have her at the cabin. In some strange emotional way, not a sexual way, the feelings she sensed threw her off her guard. It was abnormal almost to be alone with a guy that she was attracted to and not have sex.

"So why me?" she asked.

"You're not like the other women around here. You're smart, funny, and you make me laugh—and you're sweet."

"Sweet? Now, I know you don't know me well."

"You underestimate yourself, again and again."

Something in Tom's voice eased her fear. Why, she wasn't sure. She could tell his feelings for her were strong, even if this was just infatuation. She still didn't know what she was feeling or how to respond, but she relaxed into his arms again, completely at peace. As she leaned against his chest, they talked about books, family, and wherever else the conversation led until they drifted off to sleep.

Nicole awoke the next morning to the smell of bacon. As she looked around the room, she discovered she was lying on the sofa. She was still in her sweatshirt and jeans, but her glasses were on the old army chest. There was a pillow under her head and a green wool blanket covered her body. From the kitchen, she heard pans clink and felt happy to know that Tom was in the next room.

"Good morning," Tom said when he saw Nicole standing in the doorway of the kitchen. He was at the counter and dressed in the same clothes from the night before, except his shirt was unbuttoned and hung open. Nicole glanced at his chest and quickly remembered how good it felt to be held in his arms. She wasn't sure if she should kiss him, but before she had a chance to think, Tom put down the chopping knife, wiped his hand on a towel, and walked over to kiss her lips. He released her body slightly, just enough to see her face. "Did you sleep okay?"

"I don't remember taking my glasses off," she mumbled.

"We fell asleep in front of the stove," Tom said. "I woke up when the room got cold and took your glasses off for you. I rekindled the fire and covered you up with a blanket."

Unlike Nicole, Tom loved mornings, especially at camp. He told her that that was the reason he was up early and started to make breakfast. Tom turned and grabbed a mug from the cupboard. "Want some coffee?"

Nicole drank her coffee at the kitchen table as Tom placed a glass full of orange juice, a large plate of crisp bacon, and a plate of scrambled eggs sprinkled with green peppers in front of her. He told her he had already listened to the weather. The sun had melted the snow and the roads were clear. As they ate, Nicole stared out the kitchen window at the ice melting off the trees and decided to enjoy the time she had left with Tom. She could over-analyze and obsess later.

After breakfast, he cleared away the dishes. "I laid some fresh towels in the bathroom for you. All I had was a spare toothbrush from when Lisa used to come out here. It's a little old but unused. I hope you don't mind."

"That'll be fine." Fully alert now, Nicole washed her face in the bathroom sink.

Tom shoveled the steps of the porch while she bundled up in her newly purchased gloves and boots. As she looked around the room, she saw the cabin differently than the previous day. It now seemed sweet and inviting. She saw Tom differently too. She wasn't sure if his loneliness had gotten the best of him, if he was having a mid-life crisis, or if he really loved her. Even if she couldn't explain her own emotions when she was around him, he made her feel special and that was a feeling she hadn't had in a long time.

Nicole waited inside the Tahoe while Tom packed the last of his belongings in the back. The roads were plowed and cleared as they made their way back to town. Apart from making small talk about the weather and how much snow had fallen during the night, the drive back was generally quiet. Tom pulled into her driveway. As if they were instinctively following another unspoken rule, there was no kiss and there was no hug. But before Nicole jumped out of the Tahoe, Tom turned to her and his deep green eyes spoke volumes as he said, "You've been a ray of sunshine in my life."

CHAPTER 7

New York

Even work couldn't distract Nicole that Monday as she continually replayed the feel of Tom's kiss. While a part of her enjoyed the delicious feeling of a new romance, another part was locked in obsessive fear. She remembered Peter's wedding proposal, the way he looked in his leather bomber jacket when they went to their favorite Chinese place to celebrate and back to her dorm room to make love. At twenty, falling in love was so easy, so simple. The whole concept of love seemed so simple then. Now, it was the epitome of confusion.

After her last class, she packed up her books and briefcase and decided to go straight home, but as she was walking out the front door, she bumped right into Carol.

"I was just going to your office," Carol said, hugging Nicole. "You've got to come over for dinner. I want to hear all about your Thanksgiving."

What could she tell Carol? Bradford was a fishbowl of a town. Nicole couldn't tell her about Tom, but she knew she was obligated to tell Carol something. Nicole promised to come to dinner, then made her way to her car and drove home.

At Carol's that evening, Nicole was careful as she spoke about the weekend. She told Carol about the snow storm and the airport being closed. That part was easy to explain, but how she ended up at The Friendship Table meant bringing up Tom's name. She was honest and told Carol that she had bumped into him when he collected food at the drop box on campus and had invited her to volunteer if she was around for Thanksgiving. Carol seemed satisfied that things had merely gone as she indicated, though Nicole noted a slight twinkle in her friend's eye that made her think Carol was suspicious. Nicole convinced herself that she was just being paranoid, part of her own sense of guilt. She decided to make it an early night at Carol's and went home to bed.

That night, the phone rang at half past midnight. Nicole jolted upright in bed and knew there was only one person it could be.

"Hey, girl, it's me. I just got back from the most incredible date. Dennis something. He's Asian American and a network engineer," Jennifer shouted into the phone, clearly after one too many martinis. "We met at an art exhibit last week. He took me to LeCirque, and Gwyneth Paltrow even sat at a table near us. After dinner, we went back to his place for dessert. And let me tell you honey, Asian men are so, how shall I say, grateful." Divorce had liberated Jennifer, and she had developed an insatiable appetite for rich attractive men.

"The best part is that he has this great friend, Tony. He's a computer guru at some new software company. He's hot and single and only thirty-two. I invited Tony over for Thanksgiving and he is dying to meet you. When you come home at Christmas, we'll all go out and you can meet him."

"I'm not interested in any fix-ups," Nicole said now fully awake.

"Why? Did you meet someone fuckable in Mayberry?" Jennifer shouted again into the phone.

"There's not much here except factory workers and retirees." Nicole was in no mood to tell Jennifer about Tom, and Jennifer was in no condition to listen. "It's late and I have to get up early. Can I call you tomorrow?"

Nicole rushed her friend off the phone. Her thoughts immediately turned to Tom. Unable to fall back to sleep, she got up from bed to smoke a cigarette. At her kitchen table, she looked down at her hand and imagined Tom's fingers intertwined with hers. A chill went up her spine. Then she began to cry. She knew they had to end things while they still could.

The following week, Nicole picked up the photographs from their day at the bridge. The bridge looked exquisite against the blue sky, and the rich colors of the leaves were captured in every image. Tom had taken several close-ups with the zoom lens that even made the railroad ties visible. In the photo he took of her face, her hair was slightly windblown but her smile was perfectly captured. She felt a tear well up and wanted to hear his voice.

Each morning before school, she stopped at the Mini-Mart for her paper and cappuccino, almost praying to bump into Tom Ryan, but he was never there. She went through the motions of the day and then headed straight home, the routine of a hermit. She avoided Carol, hardly went out, and sat alone in her apartment trying to sort out her life. Where was she going at thirty-five? She wasn't getting any younger, and yet she didn't seem to have much direction. Everything in her life that once made sense no longer did. What did Tom mean when he said he loved her? How could he love her? He didn't know her. She didn't know him. She had always remained distant and aloof from people, and sitting there, looking again at her picture from their day at the bridge, she realized that she had let Tom in. She was impervious to love, or so she assumed, but now she was falling for this man. But to what end? Nicole knew she needed to stop thinking about Tom. She needed to move on, to move past this feeling and concentrate on her future, her father. She needed to stay focused on what she was going to do about her job and where she would live when her year in Bradford was over.

The week before Christmas, Michael left two messages on her voice mail. He wanted to see her when she was back in New York for the holiday. Nicole had purposely put off returning his calls, but the more she thought about Michael, the more she realized she had always put off dealing with their relationship.

Nicole started to call Michael. She needed some sense of closure. They had been back and forth in their relationship for far too long. She didn't know what she wanted. Could she see a future with Michael? Could she see marrying him? Was she just settling? Did she ever love him? The questions were swirling in her head as she heard his voice answer the phone.

"Nicole?" Michael sounded surprised.

As they talked more about New York, Michael was particularly attentive and sounded excited to hear about her interview at Columbia.

"I'll take you out to celebrate," Michael promised before he hung up the phone. For the first time in weeks, she was looking forward to seeing him again.

In fact, as her plane flew over the city skyline, Manhattan looked like the face of an old friend and Bradford seemed a million miles away. She caught a cab to Jennifer's apartment and used her spare key to get in. She immediately took off her shoes and poured herself a large glass of merlot. It felt good to be back. She called Jennifer at work, who wanted to treat her to the Gramercy Tavern—her favorite restaurant in the city.

It felt good to walk into the Gramercy again. Jennifer ordered a bottle of 1995 Plumpjack Cabernet Sauvignon at $65 a bottle. Nicole had forgotten how much she adored their sautéed sea bass. It was the best meal that she'd had in months. For a moment, she allowed herself to believe that these touches of her old life, the wine and her friends and the noisy city, not to mention the sea bass were almost good enough to make her forget about Tom Ryan—but it only lasted that moment.

"What's going on with you? You're awfully quiet. Not even the chocolate soufflé is putting a smile on your face," Jennifer asked toward the end of dinner. There was no faking it with her.

"I met someone," Nicole blurted out.

"That much I had already figured out," Jennifer said.

The emotional floodgates opened as Nicole began to explain every detail of Tom Ryan, from meeting him at Crook Farm to kissing him at the camp.

"Why didn't you tell me all this before?" Jennifer asked, and then she ordered another bottle of wine for them. "Don't you know by now that you can tell me anything?"

"I know. I know," Nicole said. "I'm just trying to figure out how I feel."

"Do you love him?"

"I don't know, maybe. I even worked at a food shelter to spend time with him. Me!"

"Does he love you?"

"He said he does."

"Do you believe him?"

"Yeah, I do," Nicole said without hesitation. "Something in how he said it made me really believe him."

They drank and talked, and then Jennifer revealed that she too had an affair with a married man.

"We kept bumping into each other at the same Starbucks, and one thing led to another," she said. "But it was more lust than love, and so I ended it after a few weeks."

"That's the strange part." Nicole felt confused about the whole night with Tom. "If it was just lust with Tom, we would have done it at the cabin. We had plenty of opportunity. We spent all night together with nothing more than a kiss. And what about him? If all he wanted was sex, he could have tried harder. He could have pushed me more in that direction, but he didn't. Hardly anything happened, and yet this feels like the most emotional relationship I've ever been in."

"Look, Nic. All I know is that I've never seen you react to a guy like this before."

It was late and Jennifer had to get up early for work. Nicole needed to sleep off the wine. They didn't say another word about Tom Ryan until New Year's Eve when Jennifer had a small party to celebrate. As they watched the ball drop in Times Square, all the guests gathered in front of the television to do the final countdown: Three. Two. One. Happy New Year! Everyone kissed and hugged. As Jennifer reached to hug Nicole, she whispered into her ear, "I'm sure he's thinking of you right now," and Nicole privately wished Tom a Happy New Year.

Nicole took an extra hour to primp the morning of her interview at Columbia. She was up early—too early—and she had time to kill before she needed to dress. It had been a week since she had checked her e-mail, so she set up her laptop. There was nothing but junk e-mail that she deleted. Then she checked her horoscope: *Don't let tension with a partner spoil your fun right now. Life is too short to let the opportunity for good times slip by.* What did that mean? What partner? Tom? Was life too short to pass up being with him? Or was it about the tension she felt about her date with Michael that evening?

On the cab ride to the Columbia campus, she triple-checked her briefcase to make sure all her notes were in order. She couldn't lose her place during her presentation, which had to be flawless. Even though she arrived promptly for the interview, Dr. Danforth, the search committee chairperson, kept her waiting for nearly half an hour, which was okay with Nicole. It gave her another chance to check how she looked. In the bathroom, her hair looked good as did her dark blue Anne Taylor pantsuit. The outfit was the best Nicole owned, and her new shoes matched perfectly.

Dr. Danforth looked ominous as he walked out of his office, his suit neatly pressed, his beard meticulously trimmed, and his shoes newly buffed. This was far different than the interview at High Point when the search chairman greeted her in a pair of faded jeans and a cardigan. After a few pleasantries, Dr. Danforth provided a quick tour of the department and explained that junior faculty didn't have windows in their office; only tenured faculty had windows. He seated her in a large paneled conference room where Nicole was joined by five other members of the search committee, who collectively spent the rest of the afternoon conducting an intensive examination of her credentials and aptitude.

Nothing about the day was relaxed. Even during lunch, the panel grilled her on the merits of her research and her ability to raise external grants to fund her projects. In the afternoon came her presentation to the faculty. Public speaking rarely rattled her, but this time she had to run to the bathroom twice before she spoke. It wasn't until she started her lecture that she went on autopilot and entered that zone where the words poured confidently from her mouth with grace and ease. The presentation was a success, Nicole thought, until the audience started to pick apart her research methodology like hungry wolves devouring a doe.

The more they probed, the more nervous she got. When the grilling finally ceased, all she felt was relief. On her way out, Dr. Danforth made no attempt to suggest that she was a top candidate or even being seriously considered. Apparently, the day had been an unmitigated disaster, she thought. On the cab ride back to Jennifer's apartment, Nicole had to fight back tears.

As she dressed for her date with Michael, Nicole tried to put the experience back into perspective. "Use it or lose it" is what Richard Bach would say. Perhaps she was overreacting. After all, she usually overreacted to any type of criticism, so why would this experience, the biggest job interview of her life, be different. Besides, she had no time to dwell on it—Michael was due to arrive any minute and she still needed to fix her hair. He was taking her to the Gotham Bar and Grill, repeatedly ranked by Zagat's guide as one of New Yorkers' favorite restaurants. She wore her favorite black cocktail dress and the sapphire earrings that Michael had bought for her birthday. She was refreshing her lipstick when the buzzer rang.

Michael's dark Italian features were indeed inviting, and his thick, well-groomed mustache tickled her as he kissed her hello. When he gave her a bouquet of yellow roses, she couldn't help but notice his tall muscular physique. Michael helped with her coat as he asked, "Ready for the best automotive experience of your life?"

Nicole slid inside the black leather interior of Michael's new Porsche, and he sped away from the curb. As he drove through Manhattan and explained the car's aerodynamics, she finally relaxed. Nicole enjoyed seeing pedestrians notice Michael's car as it stopped at the traffic lights, and she especially loved stepping out of his Porsche in front of the restaurant.

The Gotham Bar and Grill was packed, and even though they had reservations, they had to wait for a table. As they had a drink at the bar, Nicole opened her purse to pull out her Marlboros and her new Zippo lighter. As she lit a cigarette, her mind flashed to Tom Ryan. No, she told herself. She wasn't going to think of him. He's home with his wife and she was out with an eligible bachelor.

Her dinner with Michael was like old times. He shared his smoked duck breast while she shared her roasted Maine lobster tail, and they split a piece of the chocolate cake served with espresso ice cream for dessert. Michael had created another one of his perfect dates, and by the end of the meal she felt close to him again. They talked about his parents and his sister who was an attorney for a healthcare firm in California, and Michael asked about her father. Talking with him again felt like old times as Michael helped her on with her coat and they walked hand in hand out of the restaurant. She felt good knowing that he was hers—or at least he had been.

Michael helped her into his car and insisted that she see the view from his new apartment.

"I don't think that's a good idea," Nicole said, resistant to the possibilities.

"Nic, it's a great place, the kind of place we always talked about getting for ourselves." He always had a way of convincing her to do things against her better judgment, and she agreed to see the apartment.

Michael parked the car in the garage. Walking inside, his hand slipped around her waist, and it stayed there as they rode the elevator upstairs. He took her coat off and hung it in the closet as she marveled at the apartment. His marble floors looked stunning in the entranceway, and the living room was decorated in black Italian leather with chrome lamps and a large Nagel framed over the fireplace. It was just the way they had imagined their apartment if she had agreed to move in with him.

He showed her the custom built bookshelves in his den, and on her way out, Nicole noticed a photograph of the two of them in Key West on his desk. She took the picture on their vacation just after he bought her the Nikon camera. It was her favorite photo of them together. She thought of asking him why it was on his desk, but then she thought of her horoscope—she didn't want tension with a partner to spoil her fun.

"Isn't it a great view?" Michael said as they stood in front of his large bay window to behold a panoramic view of Central Park, one of the most coveted views in the city.

"It's wonderful," Nicole replied, and indeed she was impressed. But then the view from Tom's camp of the Kinzua Bridge popped inside her head. No, she scolded herself. She wasn't going to think about that. Not tonight. Not now.

She concentrated on how good she and Michael looked together in the reflection in the window. On paper, they *were* perfect. They were both well educated, never married, and had the same tastes; and they both loved New York. Maybe she had been too hard on him, she thought.

"The view looks almost as good as you do," Michael said, slipping his arms around her waist. It felt good to be held by Michael, but Nicole wasn't sure if she was ready to slip back into bed with him.

"Do you have any wine?" she asked. Michael disappeared into the kitchen. When he returned, he carried two crystal wine glasses and a newly opened bottle of merlot. He placed them on his glass coffee table and sat down next to her. With a remote, he dimmed the light and clicked on his stereo, which played light jazz.

Over wine, Michael reminisced about their vacation to the Pocono's the previous winter when he tried to teach her to ski, and about the time they went snorkeling in Key West. Michael talked on and on about the past, and suddenly, without warning, he took the glass from her hand and kissed her. It was a soft, short kiss. "I think it's time we consider something more permanent," he said.

"Permanent?"

"Look Nic, I've been doing a lot of thinking," Michael said as he took her hand. "You've put all this distance between us, and it's only made me realize how much I need you. I make enough to support you even if you don't get the job at Columbia. I'm sure you can always get something part-time, but if you want to take some time off, that's okay too. What I'm trying to say is," he paused. "I think we should get married."

"Married?" Before Nicole could say anymore, Michael pulled her close and kissed her again. This time his lips pressed tighter and his hands rolled down her shoulders to the small of her back. She pretended to kiss him back, but his proposal had slapped her back into reality and the enchantment of the evening was broken. All he ever talked about was taking care of her, but how could she marry someone who so easily dismissed her career? How could she marry someone so self-absorbed? Most of all, how could she marry someone she could never love? She remembered Tom's touch, how right it felt to kiss Tom's lips.

"This is all wrong!" Nicole abruptly broke away from Michael. She desperately needed fresh air. Before Michael had a chance to say another word, Nicole grabbed her coat and bolted out the door. She reached the safety of the elevator before he could stop her, or perhaps he didn't try. Perhaps he knew it was over and that she would never marry him. Perhaps he thought with his money and his looks that he would find someone who would. As she raced from the lobby door and hit the sidewalk, she knew it was the last time she would ever see Michael.

Nicole was scheduled to take a direct flight from LaGuardia to Buffalo the next day, and Jennifer went into work late that morning and waited with Nicole until her cab arrived. The driver honked and Nicole hugged Jennifer goodbye. Jennifer whispered, "It's all going to be okay."

"Thanks, I guess that would cover everything," Nicole said before she got into the cab.

Her plane was delayed, and she read through magazines at the airport newsstand. She hadn't paid attention to the news in weeks and bought a copy of *USA Today* to take back to the gate. She was reading the paper when she noticed an elderly couple across the aisle doing a crossword puzzle together. As she watched them from behind her paper, she imagined that they had celebrated their golden wedding anniversary and were returning home after a visit with their grandchildren. Her heart ached for Tom. She imagined being married to Tom—even pushing a stroller in the park. Her thoughts terrified her. She had never felt this way about a man. She thought about Rose, about Tom being married, and how her entire existence didn't compute to settling down with anyone, much less having any kind of real future with someone who was already in a relationship with someone else, and who had been for half a lifetime. Watching the elderly couple, imagining doing crossword puzzles with Tom in their old age, knowing they never would, she could feel the emotion fill her. That's when Nicole knew, without a doubt, someplace deep in her heart, she had fallen in love with Tom.

After an uneventful airplane ride, Nicole drove to her father's apartment. She desperately needed to spend more time with him. He was looking weaker, and he now needed help getting up from a chair or getting into bed. Jean and Nicole talked while they made soup and sandwiches for lunch. Her father enjoyed the pleasure of a simple meal. He was holding down his food better and said his stomach must be getting used to the chemo. Nicole had bought carrot cake, his favorite. He had a thick slice, and after lunch, he fell asleep in his recliner. Jean said that he was holding up well but that the chemotherapy treatments were taking their toll. He was more fatigued and sick after each one. Nicole told Jean, who had been working hard taking care of him, to go home and rest. Jean grabbed her coat and gave Nicole a hug. They had gotten very close throughout her father's illness.

After Jean left, Nicole watched her father sleep. He looked worn out and his skin seemed thin and pasty. She could tell it was a matter of weeks before the end. Nicole did the dishes, then made a pot of coffee and set up her laptop. She hadn't checked her e-mail since the morning of her interview with Columbia.

As she read down the list of her Inbox, chills went up her spine. There, in between an e-mail from Carol and one from Allison, was an e-mail from Thomas J. Ryan.

The icy roads and snowy weather made for a long drive back to Bradford. "It's all going to be okay," Jennifer had said. But how would it ever be okay? Her interview at Columbia was horrible. Michael was gone. Her father was still dying. And Tom was still married.

It was a quiet drive. Nicole didn't feel like turning on the radio. She reflected. She needed the quiet. She needed to think about how she would learn to live without her father, her anchor. There was no easy answer. His impending death made getting the job at Columbia that much more important. Her career had been the one pillar of her life, but then, suddenly that seemed empty too. Any hope she had for getting an offer at Columbia seemed like a distant possibility after the interview anyway. No matter how prepared she thought she was for the interview process, she wasn't prepared for the grilling, the intensity of it all. She turned off the highway. As she headed through Springville, the snow thickened. Driving south, she drove through Ellicottville, a prime ski area with upscale shopping. The fashionable restaurants she passed reminded her of Michael. She felt relieved that he was gone for good, but she also felt emotionally unsettled, like she had hung on so she could feel that option was still open when, in reality, it was never an option. Then there was Tom, someone she couldn't have, someone she shouldn't have, someone who also was never really an option. By the time she pulled into the parking space outside of her apartment, she was depressed.

As usual, she dumped her bags in the living room. Before taking her coat off, she checked her answering machine. Carol had called to invite her over for dinner when she got back, and Allison had called to wish her a Merry Christmas. There was also a message from the chairperson from the search committee at High Point College. He wanted to speak to her right away about the position.

She had really liked the chairperson and how he organized softball games, potluck dinners, and brown bag lunches for the faculty. Quite a contrast to Dr. Danforth, she thought. Nicole wrote down his phone number and would call him back first thing the next morning.

She unpacked her suitcase and hung up her pantsuit, remembering how awful her interview went at Columbia. Maybe she would never get any other job offers and would be forced to go to High Point College. No, she decided, she shouldn't shut the door on High Point just yet.

As she unpacked her laptop, she reread every word of Tom's e-mail in her mind. Normally, she deleted all her e-mail, but she had saved his. She pulled up her Inbox and scrolled down to reread his message. She looked at the date. He sent it the same day as her interview at Columbia, shortly after she checked for new messages that morning. As she started to read, she thought it strange that he wrote then—she never told him the exact date of her interview.

> *Dear Nicole,*
>
> *Well, you'll probably expect the sky to fall in the near future, eh? I'm actually checking my e-mail and I am going one step further by responding to it. I wanted to wish you luck on your interview with Columbia. I'm sure you'll knock them dead. You are extremely talented, and did I mention, beautiful?*
>
> *I hope your holidays were happy and safe and the city was all it could be. I played Santa Claus for the residents, and no,*

I didn't need a pillow. I went hunting and got a six-point buck.
Not bad. The camp isn't the same without you.

Miss you—Tom

She lit a cigarette. Should she write back? Should she call? Maybe it was best to ignore the message? She hit the respond button and started to type: "Dear Tom." No that seemed too formal now. "My dearest Tom." No, that seemed too mushy. She put out the last of her cigarette and typed a few sentences. Then she stopped. She was just making excuses to talk to him again. She turned off the laptop, and again, tried to put Tom out of her mind.

The next morning was the first day of the spring semester, and as usual, she went through her normal routine looking for signs of Tom Ryan while she picked up her paper and cappuccino. That morning, she took extra time inside the store, so much time that she worried that the clerk thought she was casing the joint. Despite her patience, Tom never showed.

After her morning class, the department chair called a meeting to welcome everyone back for the semester. It was almost lunchtime before she had a chance to call High Point College. After the meeting, Nicole headed straight for her office and picked up the phone. She had to know for sure what High Point wanted. The chairperson seemed pleased to hear back from her so soon, and after some pleasantries, he made the job offer.

She would start off as an Assistant Professor of Political Science and the department would count her prior research, which would speed up applying for her tenure by one year, maybe two. As she spoke on the phone, she looked around her windowless office and pictured herself in her new office with a window that overlooked the High Point campus. And High Point would be closer to her sister. No, she decided. She couldn't say yes. She was waiting for Columbia to call.

"May I have time to think about the offer?" she asked. The chairperson graciously allowed her to take as much time as she needed. The call to High Point made her realize that she hadn't called Allison. Her sister was home resting a few minutes before the kids came home from preschool and was bubbling over with excitement that her husband had bought her a new washer and dryer for

Christmas. Nicole would have preferred diamond earrings, but she thought, to each her own. The kids got new toys and clothes for school. Allison had bought her husband a dremel tool that he wanted for his woodcarving. Nicole wasn't quite sure what a dremel was but she didn't have time to ask.

"How's dad?" Allison asked.

"He didn't look good. He lost a lot of weight in the last month."

Allison couldn't afford to come up for the holiday because her husband was laid off from the construction job he had been working for the past few years. She was saving the money for when they'd have to fly home to Buffalo for the funeral, which they both knew could be any day.

For lunch, Nicole grabbed a package of graham crackers and a can of Coke from the vending machines. As she ate, she checked her e-mail. Not that she expected anything, but she had to look at Tom's e-mail once more. After her class, she called Carol to see about dinner. Carol was tired and not in the mood to cook, and so they planned to meet at Beefeaters, a restaurant in downtown Bradford. It was still only three-thirty, which gave Nicole a few hours to review her class preps. After a moment, she impulsively picked up the phone, but then she hesitated to dial, sitting there with the receiver to her ear. She rehearsed what she would say, "Hi Tom." No, that was way too casual. "Hello, this is Nicole." She cleared her throat. She took a deep breath.

"Hello, Mr. Ryan's office," a secretary answered.

"Hello. Nicole Benson calling for Mr. Ryan, please."

"I'm sorry he's in a meeting. Would you like to leave a message?"

"No. No. That's all right. I'll just try back. Thanks," Nicole replied, and as soon as she hung up the phone, she felt relieved that he wasn't there. Perhaps that was a sign that it was a mistake to call. She read his e-mail one last time and then buried herself in lecture outlines.

As usual, Carol arrived late while Nicole waited at the bar sipping on a glass of wine. Over dinner, Carol rambled on about her mother and the cold weather in Chicago. Nicole told Carol about her interview at Columbia. Carol was one of the few people who would understand the torture of having one's research completely dissected. It wasn't until the coffee and dessert came that Nicole told her about her job offer at High Point College.

"Why didn't you tell me this afternoon?" Carol said as she reached over to hug Nicole. For the first time, Nicole felt happy about the job offer.

"At least I'll have somewhere to go when this year is over." Nicole laughed. Carol called the waitress over to order two shots of Bailey's to mix in their coffees and insisted on paying for dinner to celebrate. As the brown liquid turned almond, Nicole remembered her night at the camp and now wished Tom had been at his desk when she called.

The next morning, early into work, she tried to get back into her routine. She put on Bob Seger's *Greatest Hits* and was reading *USA Today* when the phone rang.

"Hello, Professor Benson," she answered.

"Nicole?"

She sat up in her chair.

"Tom?" she said.

"I hope I'm not calling at a bad time. My secretary mentioned you called."

Damn that woman, Nicole thought as she cringed, but she was so happy Tom called that she forgave the woman immediately.

"I didn't realize she would tell you," Nicole said.

"I'm glad she did."

They spoke like old friends as she rattled on about her trip to New York and her time with Jennifer and her interview at Columbia. She told him about her job offer at High Point College, and Tom seemed genuinely happy for her. He told her about Robert's new apartment in Pittsburgh and their trip to the Carnegie Science Museum together. Tom had gone up to the camp and told her all about the six-point buck he shot. Nicole mentioned everything about her trip except her date with Michael, and he mentioned everything except for Christmas with his family. Then Tom started to talk about a surprise party for one of his residents.

"Mildred's turning eighty, and we wanted to do something special for her. The staff planned a 'This is your Life' type of thing for her birthday, and we've coordinated it with her family so they can all come in for the celebration. Mildred came to the home the year I started. She's one of my special ladies."

Nicole didn't understand what Mildred's party had to do with her until he said, "We'd like someone to take pictures for her new scrapbook. I was thinking you could be our photographer for the party."

"Take pictures?" He sounded so business-like.

"We could pay you something," Tom added.

"Pay?" Nicole erupted. "Did our weekend together mean nothing to you?"

"I'm sorry. I wasn't sure if I should call. I didn't know what to say. When my secretary said you called, I realized that I wanted to hear your voice."

Nicole fell silent for a moment. "I'm sorry," she said, her voice softer. "It's a defense mechanism to self-protect. I overreacted. I am sorry. I wanted to hear your voice too."

"Honestly, I was thrilled when my secretary mentioned you had called. I'm sorry I wasn't in. I was trying to find a way to see you without saying I missed you, in case it wasn't reciprocal."

"I got your e-mail," Nicole said.

"I thought you'd be impressed." Tom laughed.

"That's what made me call your office. I missed you too."

The more they spoke, the more Nicole needed to see him again. She agreed to take pictures for the birthday party for free. What could that hurt? They would never be alone. It was a safe place to meet. The party was Saturday at the nursing home.

Nicole looked up at her wall calendar. Now, instead of counting the days before she left Bradford, she would start counting the days until she got to see Tom Ryan.

On Saturday morning Nicole awoke at six-thirty, too excited about seeing Tom to sleep in. She made a pot of coffee, showered, and dressed in black jeans and a new gray cashmere sweater that Jennifer bought her for Christmas. She threw her photography bag in the back of her Nova and used her new shovel to dig out her car from the snow that had fallen the night before. As she drove to the nursing home, she felt like a child on her way to the circus.

As she walked inside the nursing home and made her way to the Activity Center, she felt more relaxed than the last time she was there. She immediately spotted Tom with his back to the door. He was talking with a woman holding a baby. Nicole stood in the entranceway and immediately noticed how pink the room looked: pink streamers, pink plates, and pink paper tablecloths. She watched as people rushed around to set up tables and wheel other residents into the room. Tom still had his back to her. She spotted a woman with an identification badge standing near the door. Nicole walked over to her.

"Hello. I'm Nicole Benson. I'm supposed to be here to take the photographs."

"Oh, yes. Hi. I'm Betsy, one of the social workers helping with the party today. We've been expecting you. You can put your things over there." The woman pointed to a coat rack full of jackets, hats, and boots. As Nicole hung her overcoat, Tom came up behind her.

"It's so good to see you again," he said as he hugged her. It was a deep hug that said more than friendship. Although no one else seemed to notice, a part of her felt exposed. Being in a small town with so many people watching, remembering the kiss they shared, feeling that everyone would have known what happened between them by his hug, and certainly, some of these people knowing Rose, she feared what they would think of her.

As his body pulled away, Nicole couldn't help but notice how handsome he looked in his suit. It made his shoulders look even broader. His green eyes lingered on her face until he broke away—almost by an invisible force—and turned toward the center of the room.

"Pink is Mildred's favorite color," he said.

"So I see," Nicole said. Tom checked the room one last time as she unpacked her camera bag.

"Everyone ready for the guest of honor?" Tom asked in front of the small crowd. They dimmed the lights and a hush came over the room. All the guests and staff hid underneath the tables except for Nicole, who stood in the back of the room adjusting her camera. She aimed her camera toward the doorway with her finger ready to capture Mildred's face as she entered. The echoes of a wheelchair squeaking against the linoleum grew louder and louder. Then the doors swung open and light flooded the room. Like a well-rehearsed play, everyone yelled, "Surprise!" in unison.

"Oh my goodness," Mildred cried out.

Nicole fixed her camera on the old woman as she trembled in her wheelchair. Her two daughters ran up first to hug her, then came their spouses, and then several grandchildren and great-grandchildren. Nicole had snapped several pictures before she recognized the old woman. It was Mildred's wheelchair that she bumped into that Saturday morning when she was looking for Tom's office.

Tom wheeled Mildred to the center table of the room to show her a large scrapbook of names and places from her life that her family had put together as a surprise. There was a picture of her wedding day with Frank. They had been together forty-five years before he died from congestive heart failure. There was another photograph with her family at the historic 1960 World Series when the Pirates beat the Yankees with a game-winning hit by Bill Mazeroski, and one of her with her two daughters in the family's brand new DeSoto. There was a photo of her oldest daughter's graduation from Vassar and another of Mildred holding her first grandson. There were pictures of holidays, birthdays, weddings, and all the other ceremonial events that make up a life.

Mildred had a story for each photograph as she flipped through the pages. How could Nicole have ever thought Mildred was senile? There was nothing demented about *her,* she thought now. Nicole moved about the room with her camera to capture every nuance of the woman. The staff started to sing Happy Birthday as they brought out a large cake, of course with "pink" frosting, and Mildred blew out a single candle shaped like the number eighty. Mildred cried tears of joy as people huddled around her. Nicole noticed how proud she looked of her family. People were already on their second helpings when Tom stepped to the middle of the room with a microphone.

"Mildred, I need to see you up here," he said, and one of the aides wheeled her chair toward him. He acted as the master of ceremonies while the staff paraded out her nephew from California, a long-lost cousin from Florida, and her oldest great-grandson, whom Mildred hadn't seen since he enrolled at West Point three years ago. As Tom introduced each person, Nicole noticed his confidence and charm. It would be easy to fall in love with such a man.

Tom announced more of Mildred's special guests. Nicole could tell that he was unaware that he was being watched through the lens of her camera. She focused the lens in closer and adjusted the shutter speed. The minute she heard the camera snap, she knew that she had taken a perfect picture of Tom Ryan. He radiated. His smile flowed. His deep green eyes shined. Since he wouldn't let her take his picture, this was the only way—and the picture was perfect.

Mildred's oldest daughter got up, took the microphone from Tom, and presented her mother with a large box wrapped in pink paper and white bows. Mildred's hands shook when she saw it was a framed picture of her and Frank on their twenty-fifth wedding anniversary. It had been Mildred's favorite picture, and her oldest daughter had it framed and engraved with their wedding date. She hugged Mildred as she said, "We only wish Dad could have been here today."

Then her youngest daughter got up to take the microphone and handed Mildred another box as she said, "This is to help your game." Everyone chuckled as Mildred, a notorious bridge player, opened a box of extra large print playing cards. As her youngest hugged her mother, Nicole imagined Mildred when her daughters were little. She looked like the type of mom who was their best friend. Nicole flashed on her own mother. Again, she wished that things had been different. She had often wished that her mother was still around. Once, Nicole had mustered the courage to call her mother, but her mother was distant and aloof over the phone. The conversation felt stilted. There was no talk about seeing one another again. Somehow, it had been easier for Allison to overcome the sense of abandonment, to settle down and start a family. Their mother's vanishing act didn't scare her away from relationships, from opening her heart, the way it did Nicole.

The afternoon wore on and Mildred's arms trembled, partly from age and partly from joy, as she hugged each of her guest's goodbye. When all the guests had gone, Tom helped Mildred back to her room while a small crew threw away cups and tablecloths. Nicole dismantled her camera and packed it away in her bag.

"Did you get a piece of cake?" a voice said from behind. By now, she easily recognized Tom's voice. She turned to see him holding a pink plate with a thick piece of cake. "Thought you might be hungry."

"That's nice of you." Nicole smiled. "Actually, what I need right now is a bathroom."

"It's all the way down the hall to the right," Tom said, pointing toward the restrooms. As Nicole walked out of the ladies room, she ran right into Mildred and had a feeling of déjà vu.

"Hello, dear. Could you help me?" Mildred asked as she reached for Nicole's hand. "I need some help in my room. It's just around the corner."

Nicole wheeled Mildred back into her room. As soon as she opened the door, Nicole couldn't help but notice the pink curtains, pink bedspread, and pink floor covering. Maybe Mildred was a flamingo in another life.

"I'd like to put my scrapbook in the dresser, but I can't reach the top drawer," Mildred said as she handed Nicole her new scrapbook. Nicole opened the drawer and placed the scrapbook gently inside. Closing the drawer, she noticed a prominently displayed photograph of a man dressed in combat fatigues on top of the dresser.

"Is this Frank?" Nicole asked.

"No, dear. That's Jeffery. He was my fiancée." Mildred reached up for the photograph. Nicole placed it in her hand and Mildred caressed the frame as if taking herself back to another period of time. "Lieutenant Jeffery Alan Ross was the love of my life. It's the only picture I have of him. We met in high school, and from the moment I saw his face across the room at a dance, I was smitten. He was an Army Ranger Pathfinder—one of the elite. We were supposed to get married after he came back from the war, but he was killed on D-Day at Saint Mere-Eglise. God, that was 1944 and I still remember the day as if it were yesterday."

Mildred caressed the frame even harder as she spoke. "We were so in love. He took me to our prom. He picked me up in his father's Studebaker. My parents loved him too. He was such a gentleman. He asked my father if he could marry me when he came back from the army. We were both so foolish but we were in love. It feels odd to look at his picture now, to look at him at that age, and still feel such profound love for him but to also wonder who he might be now if he hadn't died so long ago. Then again, I am sure he would have grown into his idea of himself, but he looks so young there and I can't even imagine myself at that age anymore."

Mildred paused and the old woman softly whispered almost to herself as if Nicole wasn't there, "Time mutes the pain but true love never dies."

Nicole realized that, after wedding anniversaries and family vacations with someone else, Mildred still loved Jeffery Alan Ross, in the purest way a person can love. Nicole had so many questions and wanted to ask more, but before she could say a word, a knock came at the door.

"There you are." Tom stood in the doorway of Mildred's room holding a plate wrapped in aluminum foil, Nicole's camera bag over his shoulder. "You forgot this," he said as he entered the room.

"Well, hello Mr. Ryan. Your lady friend was just helping me put away my new scrapbook," Mildred said.

"Was she now?" Tom smiled as he turned to Nicole. "If you're done here, we've finished cleaning up. I wanted to show you something in my office if you have a moment."

It was as if he read her mind. Nicole hoped they would have time to talk alone.

She looked down again at Mildred, who was still holding the frame, and loved her for sharing Jeffery with her. While there were still questions to ask, Nicole simply whispered, "Thank you," as she bent down to hug Mildred goodbye.

Nicole followed Tom into his office and he closed the door behind them. He sat down behind his desk and pulled a chair closer for her. He seemed careful not to look too friendly in case someone walked by. Nicole understood.

"It's so good to see you," Tom said again and thanked her for taking the pictures. He offered to pay for the film, but Nicole wouldn't accept any money. In that moment, she didn't care about the pictures, the money, or Mildred's party, as she stared at his lips. It took every ounce of willpower for her not to climb over his desk to kiss him.

"It was a great day. It seems like you made a good impression on Mildred."

"She's a great lady," Nicole said, still unable to take her eyes off his lips.

"There's something I wanted to . . . to ask you." His voice turned serious. "I've been doing a great deal of thinking about us. I realize all the implications, but I can't get you out of my mind. I miss you so much. I keep thinking about our time at camp together. How much we talked. How good you felt." Tom then fell silent for what seemed an eternity. Her eyes fixed on his and she remained still, waiting anxiously for his next words.

"I'm going to camp next weekend. The hiking trails are really great this time of year because of the snow, and I've got some great venison steaks." Tom paused again and then leaned forward in his chair to look directly into her eyes. "I thought you'd like to join me."

Nicole instantly knew what he meant.

CHAPTER 8

In The Depth Of Winter

It was the depth of winter in Bradford, with ten inches of snowfall over the previous week, but the drive to the camp was more peaceful to Nicole than the last time. The icicles glistened and the glare from the sunset between the clouds beamed off the snowdrifts, making the deep blanket of winter look even whiter. The trees looked safe instead of ominous, and the dirt road spoke to her like an old friend. Even when a deer ran in front of Tom's Tahoe, Nicole remained calm. As they pulled up the driveway, she marveled at the orange haze in the background that fell over the entire Kinzua Valley.

She had been anticipating this moment all week. Every night she came home to pack for the weekend, adding a little each time. Unlike packing for a vacation with Michael, which usually entailed cocktail dresses and bathing suits, she was packing winter sweaters and long underwear. But still, what she took with her had to be just right.

Nicole laid out all her sweaters, mostly wool, and cotton crews from Land's End plus one fluorescent orange sweater her father bought for her last Christmas that she didn't have the nerve to say she hated. She packed one black wool sweater and her old NYU sweatshirt, because it was the warmest, and her new gray cashmere, because it was the nicest. She threw into her suitcase two pairs of jeans, two turtlenecks, and a pair of thermal pants. She decided to wear her new Ralph Lauren navy pullover, her white turtleneck, and her beige khakis. She wore her L.L. Bean boots and threw in a pair of sneakers and her slippers because the floor at the cabin wasn't carpeted. She dug through her dresser drawers for underwear, hating the fact that she only had white underwire bras and white Hanes cotton bikini briefs.

She slept in oversized T-shirts, so she didn't have much in terms of sexy sleep attire or any formal sleepwear to speak of. Then she remembered her lingerie from Victoria's Secret—three were gifts from Michael that she never got around to wearing. Three she bought on sale because they were beautiful and she kept them for a special occasion. They all still had the tags on. As she looked for a pair of scissors, she debated whether to take the two black ones, the ivory one, the red one, or the two white ones. She was only going away for two nights and didn't want to appear too presumptuous. She thought Tom looked more like an ivory man, but black always seemed a popular color. Oh hell, she thought. She decided she would just take them all. She then debated taking her long terrycloth robe, which wasn't exactly sexy either, but then she figured she might need it for warmth and threw it into the suitcase.

Her last class ended at noon, so on Friday afternoon before Tom came to pick her up, she went to the store to buy some salad from the salad bar, milk, juice for the morning, and a couple of loaves of bread. She figured he would have already stocked the camp with beer, but she stopped at the liquor store to buy some wine and a bottle of Bailey's Irish Cream. She put in a second bottle of Bailey's in the cart, just in case.

She arrived back at her apartment and still had another hour before he was to arrive. A cigarette on the balcony killed part of the time. Then, as she brushed her teeth, she saw the bottle of Opium, her favorite perfume, sitting on the sink next to the toothpaste. Nicole shoved the bottle into her already over-stuffed suitcase and quadruple-checked her bag. Why, she wasn't sure—nothing else would fit.

As she waited for the door buzzer, she felt like a racehorse before the bell. She heard Tom's Tahoe pull into the drive and grabbed her purse and suitcase before he ever got to the door. As she made her way down the stairwell, she beamed at Tom walking toward her. He helped her into the front seat, opened the cab of the Tahoe, and tossed her suitcase in the back.

"How was your day?" Tom asked as he slammed his door and started the engine.

"It was good, but I felt very distracted." Nicole laughed.

"You did? Now, what could have distracted you? Could it be the same thing that's been distracting me all week?"

"You could say that," she said, smiling.

The rest of the world disappeared as they drove farther and farther out of town and deeper into the woods. Like a young couple on their honeymoon, they held hands.

The camp looked the same from the outside. Tom carried in her suitcase as she took off her boots at the front entrance. The camp smelled of Pine-Sol and looked cleaner than before, and Tom had moved his rocking chair from the porch into the living room. Nicole threw her coat over the chair. The air felt toasty from the wood stove. There were fresh towels in the bathroom, and when she entered the kitchen, she immediately noticed a Mason jar filled with a bouquet of pine sprigs in the center of the table, which Tom had obviously gathered on a hike.

"Everything looks great. Especially these pine sprigs. They're really nice," Nicole shouted up to Tom, who had taken her suitcase upstairs.

She feared the milk would spoil, so she unpacked the groceries. As she put the wine in his cupboard, she noticed that Tom had two full bottles of Bailey's already stocked in the liquor cabinet. She added her own two bottles. They'd have plenty to drink for the weekend. She took out a can of beer for him, set it on the kitchen table, and uncorked a bottle of wine. Before she had a chance to pour, she heard Tom climb down the stairs.

"Everything looks really great," Nicole repeated. She knew Tom had put so much effort into fixing up the place just for her.

"I even put fresh linens on the bed." He smiled as he unzipped his jacket and tossed it over a chair in the kitchen. As he walked toward her, she couldn't help but notice Tom's broad shoulders under his flannel shirt. He placed his bifocals on the table and his deep green eyes looked right into her soul. Without another word, he bent down to kiss her. Nicole melted into his arms. Her legs almost gave way from his touch. His lips pressed softly as his hands moved over her back. She smelled his musty scent of wood smoke and English Leather as she lost herself in the entire experience of Tom Ryan.

Nicole started to unbutton his shirt. He bent down to kiss her again as his hands removed her navy pullover to reveal her neatly tucked in white turtleneck. He unearthed the bottom of her turtleneck to expose an entrance to her bare skin. She pulled open his flannel shirt to reveal his undershirt and softly kissed his neck. "Should we go upstairs?" Tom whispered in her ear.

The stairwell was too narrow for two people to climb at once, so Tom took her hand as he led the way. Once in the loft, Nicole glanced around the room and noticed two pewter candlesticks, one on each nightstand. Freshly lit candles burned and softly illuminated the room. Their future, the consequences, the bottle of wine she left open on the kitchen counter, none of that mattered now as Tom pulled off her turtleneck and glanced down at her body. She dreaded not having something sexier to flaunt than her plain white bra, but his eyes were filled with hunger for her just the same.

She was always nervous the first time with a new lover, but with Tom, she felt completely natural as she undressed. His hands instinctively knew where to touch her and how to apply just the right pressure. Her body quivered with every stroke of his fingers and tongue. While he was a gentle lover, he commanded every part of her.

As she looked into his eyes, her passion grew more intense until a wave of pleasure flooded every muscle in her body. Her body shook. She couldn't help but say Tom's name and invoke God with each contraction. Then they lay together, quietly, just holding one another.

Her body trembled as Nicole squeezed him tight. She had never felt happier as his hands rolled over every inch of her. His body felt soft as she twirled the hair on his chest. She could feel the muscles in his shoulder and his legs against hers. She moved her cheek away from his shoulder, looked up into his deep green eyes. Tom lifted her slender body up to reach his lips. She fell into him as she kissed him. His hands traced her waist and then pulled her close, firmly against him.

Slowly, their passion escalated again as Tom rolled her over on her back. As he moved with such grace and skill over her, the crescendo was nothing like she had known before. She felt the warmth of his body over her as they moved together; then pulling away, slowly, he looked into her face. Looking up, she ran her hand through his hair. Loving him was . . . it seemed wrong to say even in her mind, given their situation, given the fact that he wasn't hers to have, but loving him seemed so right, so tender, and so powerful as their bodies intertwined for hours.

With labored breath, he curled her ever closer. "You're too far away," he whispered. She rested her head on his chest and they lay together quietly, his soft touch a constant presence over her body. As she remembered each movement, it was everything she had imagined.

Nicole was suddenly dying for a cigarette but didn't want to break the moment. She also remembered the wine and started to wonder about dinner. She was relieved when Tom finally asked, "Are you hungry?" He chuckled. "For food?"

"God—yes!" She smiled as she reached up to kiss his lips. "How did you know?"

"Because I'm starving," Tom said as he looked out the window at the moonlight, "and I think it's pretty much past dinner time."

Nicole lifted the covers and walked across the room toward her suitcase. With her back to the room, she bent down to look for her slippers in the side pocket. As she unzipped the suitcase to dig for her robe that was buried somewhere at the bottom, she felt his eyes upon her and turned her head to see Tom staring at her from the bed.

"Did you purposely put this thing on the other side of the room?" she asked.

"No, but I'm sure glad I did." Tom's eyes never moved from her naked body.

"Show's over," she said, covering her body with her terrycloth robe.

"Not in my mind it isn't." Tom grinned as he lifted himself from the bed to find his clothes. She grabbed her toiletry bag to put in the bathroom along with her shampoo and blow dryer while he slid on his jeans. As she watched him, she felt completely content to be with Tom Ryan. She tossed her things on the bed and turned to Tom. She hugged him, feeling the warmth from his chest one more time before leaving their love nest.

He threw on his undershirt and headed downstairs to grill two venison steaks, the best cuts he had. She walked over to the bottle of wine still open on the counter and poured a glass. Tom's beer was warm, so he placed it back in the refrigerator and grabbed a fresh one. Then he reached inside his jeans to pull out his Copenhagen and put in a chew while he prepared dinner.

"Just relax for a while," Tom said as he took out an ashtray from the cupboard.

"You sure you don't want me to help?"

"Maybe later, but just relax for now," Tom said as he pulled a chair out from under the Formica table.

Her slippers shuffled against the floor as she wandered into the living room to retrieve her purse with her cigarettes and lighter inside. Nicole sat at the table bundled in her robe and smoked her first cigarette of the evening. Tom marinated the steaks before putting them on the grill, opened a can of corn, and dished portions of her salad on two plates he pulled from the cupboard. As he cooked, he reassured her that it was fine for her to just sit and drink her wine. She made him promise to at least let her help with the dishes.

Nicole felt completely relaxed, perhaps more relaxed than she had been since moving to Bradford. And in fact she felt more relaxed than she had ever felt with any man. As she watched Tom move about the kitchen, it felt nice to have him take care of her. With Michael, the same thought frightened her to death. But with Tom, it made her feel so comforted, so loved. Nicole knew now, without a doubt, she was in love with this man; and she knew that it was not just about feeling special but the kind of intimacy she had missed her entire life by constantly running away from relationships. This time, she was giving of herself so openly.

He fixed two plates and placed them on the table along with utensils before he grabbed another beer from the refrigerator. After he sat down, he grabbed her hand to say grace. She loved that about Tom. He didn't appear to feel guilty or ashamed or anything except happy to be alone with her. Every action said he loved her.

They cleared the table when the meal ended, and like an old habit, Tom instinctively grabbed the sponge on the sink to wash and Nicole instinctively took the towel from the drawer to dry. As Tom put away the last pot under the sink, he said, "We've got enough Bailey's to serve Coxey's Army. Think we should make some decaf to go with it?"

"That'd be nice," Nicole said and put a filter in the coffee pot while Tom set two coffee mugs on the table and opened one of the new bottles of Bailey's. She lit another cigarette to have with her coffee. As they talked at the kitchen table, she couldn't take her eyes off Tom's broad shoulders. She loved his neck and how strong it looked. Her body ached for him again as she hurried to finish her coffee. She got up to put her mug in the sink.

"I want to freshen up."

"You don't need to freshen up." Tom bent down to kiss her. His lips were tender and warm. Her legs almost crumbled at his touch.

"I need to at least brush my teeth." She was always paranoid about personal hygiene, especially her breath. In fact, she often brushed six times a day.

"You're perfect. Trust me." Tom kissed her again and opened her robe. Without another word, he slid his hands along the warmth of her skin as his tongue encircled her ear, only to move ever so slowly down her neck, then to each breast, and then back up to her neck.

"You're perfect," he whispered again as he closed the robe and took her hand and led her upstairs to the loft. Nicole forgot all her insecurities as Tom completely devoured her body.

It was sometime in the middle of the night when she awoke. It was hard to tell the exact time but she could see the brightness of the moonlight as it came cascading in the front window. Nicole tossed and turned until she realized that she couldn't fall back to sleep. She looked over at Tom and watched him sleep. He looked so peaceful, or maybe exhausted. She laughed as she remembered his energy at lovemaking.

Her hands searched in vain for her robe, which was lost somewhere in the blankets on the bed. Screw it, she thought. She didn't need it. Tom had turned up the oil heater and the camp was very cozy and warm. She quietly got out of bed and started down the stairs without her robe. Her cigarettes were still on the kitchen table. She grabbed the pack and an ashtray and stood in the front window. Nicole had never seen the moon look so powerful. It lit the snow-covered hills for miles. And in the distance, the steel towers of the Kinzua Bridge pierced through the wilderness to transform that old railroad bridge into a magnificent structure that soared over the valley like an eagle. It truly is the Eighth Wonder of the World, she thought as she lit a cigarette.

"You are the most beautiful thing I've ever seen," Tom said, standing at the bottom of the stairs staring at her naked silhouette in the moonlight.

"You don't have your glasses on. How do you know?"

"Then you need to come closer so I can get a better view." He walked toward her wrapped in a large green wool blanket from the loft. He placed it over her shoulders as he hugged her close.

"I love you, you know?" his voice softly asked like it was a question. As if Nicole didn't know. This man loved her like no other man.

"I love you too." Finally, all her fears subsided. She turned to kiss him, then grabbed his hand. "Come here. You've got to see this view." She faced the front window as Tom stood behind her and wrapped them both in his wool blanket.

"Not as good as my view of you."

"I'm serious. Did you see this view? It's spectacular," she said as Tom held her from behind. As she saw their reflection in the front window, she compared Michael to the way Tom felt against her. She compared the way they looked together in their reflection. That's when Nicole realized that, for the first time in her life, somewhere in the wilderness of northwestern Pennsylvania, she was finally in the right place with the right man. Of all the men she knew, Tom Ryan understood her heart. He knew her ambitions and still loved her. He knew her fears and still loved her. She closed her eyes, feeling the tears well up. He wasn't hers to have. He had an entire life with another person. Whatever they shared in that moment, that reality didn't change.

"I must have stood here a thousand times, but this is the most brilliant I've ever seen the valley," Tom said, interrupting her drifting thoughts. He hugged her as if to thank her for showing him the view. "Did you know that the bridge was once used as a weather barometer?"

"How?" Nicole asked. It was their moment. She was not going to ruin it. "Did its knee start to ache whenever it was about to rain?" she said, jokingly.

"No, silly. Actually, through vibration. Instruments placed on the bridge are said to record meteorological waves that indicate what the weather conditions will be in the near future. The bridge won scientific acclaim for its accuracy."

"You're just a plethora of useless facts," Nicole said, constantly amazed at all the trivia that he knew. She, on the other hand, could barely figure out a crossword puzzle.

His intelligence was an aphrodisiac. She turned her body around to press against his warmth and kissed him hard. She then reached for Tom's hand and guided him toward the loft, and this time, she led the way.

Tom was up early and already cooking breakfast when Nicole awoke. He poured her a cup of coffee as she shuffled into the kitchen. He kissed her good morning, and having already learned that she was not much of a morning person, he left her alone. He scrambled the eggs for several minutes, waiting for her caffeine injection to finally kick in.

"What do you want to do this morning?" Nicole uttered her first complete sentence of the day.

Tom looked at his watch. "You mean this afternoon. It's about twelve-thirty. I thought we'd go for a hike, if you're up for it."

"You're kidding?" She laughed, astonished by Tom's perpetual energy. "I barely have the strength to walk to the bathroom and you're ready for a five-mile hike in the snow."

In spite of her complaint, after breakfast, she showered and was ready to begin the day by half past two. She tied her L.L. Beans and grabbed her down jacket as Tom shoveled the steps of the porch. As they trudged through the thick snow, Tom showed her how to track deer and explained how whitetail deer are frequently spotted in this area—two of which they saw on their hike.

"Deer thrive on shrubs, evergreens, and hard and soft fruits," he explained as they walked. "Herds usually feed along the edges of the forest at dawn and at dusk. They have a keen sense of smell, so hunters can't stay in one place too long."

"Is there anything you don't know?" She turned to kiss Tom.

"I guess I'm an inquisitive little boy."

"I guess so," she said as they continued to hike. They covered several miles enjoying the quiet of the woods, the snow crunching underfoot the only sound. Tom's agility and knowledge of the woods allowed him to walk farther ahead while she dawdled slightly behind, breathless too easily from too many cigarettes. She rested on a fallen tree as Tom plodded through the woods. The snowdrifts were beautiful as Nicole looked around. She watched Tom as he looked up at the trees and imagined what he looked like twenty years ago, before the gray, before the love handles, before the bifocals.

"You want to head back?" Tom asked as he walked toward her. He could see Nicole was tired and cold. He helped her up and held her hand as they headed back to the camp. When they entered, he took off his boots and jacket and went directly to the wood stove. The camp was chilly. She removed her boots and jacket and sat on the couch while Tom got a strong fire burning. Nicole took off her socks, tossed them in front of the stove, and sat back.

"Here, let me rub your feet." Tom sat on one end of the couch as she laid back farther. His hands felt good no matter what part of her body he touched. Nicole moaned with every caress. Her body relaxed and the warmth of the fire felt good, so good that she took off her NYU sweatshirt and used it as a pillow. Tom had her roll over on her stomach so he could massage her back. He rubbed the tension from her shoulders, then slid his hands underneath her turtleneck. Her muscles went into a deep coma. His hand slowly unclasped her bra and he leaned down to kiss the small of her back. His tongue flickered up her spine as his hand moved to fondle the back of her thighs.

"What? Do you take vitamins or something?" she asked in honest amazement.

"Relax, honey. You don't have to do a thing," he whispered.

After they made love, Nicole drifted off to sleep. A few hours later, she awoke on the couch wrapped in two large blankets and completely naked underneath. She lay there thinking of Tom. When she heard him clang a pan in the kitchen, she sat up and noticed her terrycloth robe on the coffee table and knew he must have put it there.

She wandered into the kitchen and Tom kissed her hello. He had just started to grill two venison steaks and chop some broccoli to steam. Nicole grabbed a new bottle of wine from the cabinet and poured a glass. She tried to refrain from having a cigarette, but like her addiction to Tom, she eventually gave into the craving. She still had time to take a shower before dinner was ready, so she headed for the bathroom with her wine.

After they said grace, she looked around the kitchen and pictured Tom in the camp alone. She liked her solitude, but there was always the telephone, Internet, and television to keep her company.

"So what do you do here by yourself?" Nicole asked.

"Read mostly, listen to the news on the radio. When I was younger, my dad and I spent a great deal of time here. I hunted with some friends on and off, and when Robert was younger, we'd come up here a lot, but like I said, he never really liked it. Lisa was the only one who really loved it up here."

"Sounds like you and Lisa were close."

"We were."

"I have to tell you something. My father has cancer," Nicole blurted out. She had to tell Tom. There was never going to be a good time. Tom put down his fork and reached over to take her hand as she spoke. "There's not much they can do for him now," she said, holding his hand tight. "It's been a long battle. He looks so drained. I'm not sure why I hadn't told you before. I guess I've just gotten numb to it. It seemed the easiest way for me to deal."

"I understand about not wanting to deal," he said. "I coped with Lisa's death pretty badly. After she died, I became a complete drunk and it took everything in me just to get out of bed in the morning."

"I know what I've been going through with my dad. I can't even imagine how hard it must have been to lose a child. I don't think I realized what an awful burden that must have been until now, the grief that you and Rose must have experienced."

"As I said, we didn't deal with it. And I was a big part of it. At the time, the only person I talked to was Mildred. I used to stay late at the office when the place is the quietest. I'd just check in on Mildred. I think she knew that I wanted to talk. She had just lost Frank and she somehow understood how I felt. And even though I never mentioned the drinking, I think she knew that too. Then one day when I stopped by, she handed me a piece of paper, just a piece of plain, lined, white paper with a quote written on it. Here, let me get it."

Tom got up from the table, went upstairs to the loft, and brought down a folded piece of paper that he kept in his dresser drawer.

"I didn't think I'd get it right if I tried to do it from memory," he said as he handed her the paper. Nicole carefully unfolded it and read it out loud:

In the depth of winter, I finally learned that within me there lay an invincible summer. Albert Camus

"That's a beautiful thought. I guess we all need to hear that," Nicole said as she read the quote again to herself.

"Yes, and I certainly needed to hear it. It was like a cold glass of water in my face the day I read it the first time. It hit me, what I was doing to myself, to Rose, my family, my job. Slowly, I started to put my life back together. That's why Mildred is one of my special ladies."

"That's very sweet." She squeezed his hand.

"Speaking of sweet, I think it's time for the Bailey's," Tom replied, as he leaned over to give her a kiss. Nicole folded the paper back up and he stuffed it in the pocket of his jeans. They had finished dinner and Nicole brewed a pot of decaf. Tom cleared the dishes and they fell into their normal wash routine. Nicole imagined that this is what it would be like if they were married. A wave of sadness washed over her. It would never be. It could never be. Had he been like this with Rose? Why was she here with Tom? Why was Tom here with her? He knew she was leaving someday, after her year of teaching in Bradford was over. He was married, and she found herself wondering if he was really willing to give it all up for her. Did she even want that? Falling in love wasn't at all what she expected. For a moment, she was angry. What did Tom expect? Did he even realize the pain he was causing to her and Rose? Was he just blindly moving forward without any goal?

Tom carried the Bailey's and she balanced two full mugs in her hands as they went into the living room to drink their coffees. He stoked the wood stove once more before he got comfortable on the couch. He took a sip of his coffee and then got up to tune the radio to NPR's classical music broadcast. He sat back down and put his feet up on the old army chest. Watching him, how caring he was, almost nurturing, her momentary anger quickly subsided. She knew the answers to her questions would have to wait. They would both need time to talk, to process, to sort through it all, but not now. Now, his body felt like a warm blanket that made her feel safe as she curled up in his arms. They talked until they were too tired to get up for more coffee and opted to drink the Bailey's straight. As she rested her head on his shoulder, she started to move her hand down his chest to the top of his thigh and down to his knee. She gently rubbed his knee, then slid her hand on the inside of his thigh and brought it slowly back up.

"Are you flirting with me, young lady?"

"I tried to control myself all night. I didn't want you to think that I was just using you for sex." Nicole smiled and looked up into his eyes.

"You can use me for sex anytime." Tom kissed her lips as she unbuttoned his shirt. After a few minutes they retreated upstairs to the loft.

The next morning, when she awoke, Tom was still in bed. He must have overslept or she must have awakened early. She wasn't sure which.

"Good morning." Tom smiled as his arm rolled over her shoulder to bring her closer. He looked at his watch and realized the time. "What are you doing awake so early?"

Nicole wasn't sure if she should tell him why, that in a few hours their weekend together would be over. That she was confused about their future and its uncertainty.

"Just anxious to start the day with you," she said, leaning over to kiss him.

Tom got up to start breakfast. Nicole stumbled to the bathroom to brush her teeth. He had already poured her a cup of coffee when she returned to the kitchen and bacon sizzled on the stove. For the first time all weekend, there was an awkward silence. They both knew they had to go back home—separately.

"Where do we go from here?" The question erupted from her mouth like a volcano that she could no longer contain.

Tom said nothing at first. He just looked out the kitchen window. He put down the iron skillet full of bacon and turned off the burner. He rested his hands on the counter and looked down. Still, not a word came from him. Nicole lit a cigarette—she knew she'd need it for this conversation. Tom turned around to pull out the chair next to her and took her hand with both of his.

"Please understand that . . ." Tom stopped.

Nicole noticed that it was the first time all weekend that he didn't look into her eyes when he spoke. She feared his next words—the big dump she assumed. She had been expecting it but didn't want to admit it to herself.

Tom began again. "Please understand that I love you. I really do. I wouldn't be here with you like this if I didn't really love you. But it's just that . . . I'm not sure how to say this. It's just that I have so much responsibility at home. I've agonized so much about this. Things were lonely between Rose and me, that's true, but that's not why I'm here. I wanted to show you this place before I even knew you. It feels different loving someone at this point in my life after all that has happened. In some ways, it is more intense than when I was younger. There is more at risk at this age, and yet it feels easy to love you. I'm not sure what to say." Tom was struggling to find the right words, but she already knew what he was trying to say. Rose was as much a part of his life as anyone could be, and surprisingly, Nicole understood this. In many ways, she felt like it wasn't right to ask more from Tom, and that it was not right to hurt a woman she never met and ruin a marriage that had struggled through so much. It was not right to break the comfortable balance of a family and the fortitude that comes with having spent so many years together.

"I love you too. That's the hard part," Nicole said and hugged Tom as she started to cry.

Tom held her, and this time, he didn't tell her to stop crying. He knew that it was appropriate. He wished he could join her, but his tears wouldn't come.

They had a quiet breakfast together. Then Nicole showered while Tom cleared the table and washed the dishes alone. When she returned from the bathroom, Tom was outside shoveling the porch. He had stacked a fresh load of firewood, dug out the Tahoe, cleared the path, and was now shoveling the entire porch. Nicole felt that he needed to keep busy because he was unable to deal with the consequences of their situation.

Nicole carried her suitcase down from the loft and was in the kitchen packing the groceries when Tom came back inside. It was early afternoon, and it was mutually understood that it was time to leave. Unlike the rest of the weekend, they didn't make love that day, as if it was also mutually understood that it would only make returning to reality that much harder.

Tom started the Tahoe to warm it for her and loaded the back cab. He climbed inside. Before he pulled away from the camp, he leaned over to kiss Nicole. "I love you, you know." He paused and then added, "Bunches and bunches," as he rubbed her nose with his.

"I love you too." Nicole was quiet on the drive back to town. Tom made small talk about the snowfall, saying something about nearly a foot had accumulated, but she wasn't listening. As she watched him speak, she started to miss the lifetime that they would never have together. At that moment, she learned what Mildred knew all too well—love isn't always fair.

CHAPTER 9

Where Do We Go From Here?

Tom slowed down as he started home after his weekend with Nicole. He was trying to absorb all that happened between them. He never imagined a woman like her loving him. Bright, sophisticated, and kind, Nicole was something out of a novel. She had depth, an intellect, and unparalleled beauty. Hell, he thought, he never imagined he would ever meet that kind of woman let alone that she would be interested in him. The intimacy they shared was unbelievable, something he hadn't imagined with another person.

He had not been with another woman since he and Rose were married, so why this time? His mind was racing. Would his relationship with Rose change? Of course it would, he realized. It already had. Did he want it to change? It had been so long since they were close. On those rare occasions that he and Rose did make love, the act felt distant and mechanical. All he seemed to have were the questions and very few of the answers.

As he pulled into the driveway, Rose's car was already in the garage. She was home from her weekend in Pittsburgh. He grabbed his backpack out of the back of the Tahoe and headed into the house. He found Rose in the kitchen unpacking groceries she had bought at the market on her way home.

"How was your trip?" he asked. He didn't know if the guilt he felt in the pit of his stomach was also apparent on his face. He felt overwhelmed.

"Good. Had a little snow on the way home but I didn't have a problem," she said.

"How is Robert?" Tom asked trying to suppress his guilt, trying to talk about something positive and something that might help him reconnect to Rose.

"Robert has a new girlfriend, and this one may be a keeper. She is all that a mother could want for her son. She's soft spoken, attractive, has a good education and a job," she said, putting away a fresh gallon of milk in the refrigerator.

He watched Rose put away the milk and bread, restocking the refrigerator as she always did, and appreciated how well she took care of the house. She made it a home. She did, he thought. Even though he was lonely, he did appreciate how attentive she was to details, details that he suspected Nicole would not be focused on. With her career, Nicole would probably be the kind of person who would have little time to devote to mundane tasks such as the grocery shopping, dusting, and vacuuming. Nicole was a free spirit. She did not want to be owned, that much Tom understood. While she loved him, could she settle down with him? What if he did leave Rose? Would Nicole become bored with him? Was losing Rose and the life that they had made together something he could risk?

"If he comes home in the spring, he may bring her with him." Rose was still talking while putting away the groceries, breaking Tom's trance. "I think Robert will stay in Pittsburgh after he finishes his MBA. He thinks the bank will offer him a promotion when he graduates, and he really seems to be making his home there."

It had been a long time since Tom had seen Rose this animated.

"You obviously had a good time on this visit."

"Yes, my parents and I went to the Strip District and I brought home some of that chili sauce you like."

This small fact made Tom feel even worse. The guilt, the indecision, all of it was starting to sink in. Rose had been kind to him. Despite their emotional distance, she was kind. He didn't want to hurt her. He agonized. The guilt kept sweeping over him. He wanted to believe that if he saw Nicole again that he would not do it again. That he would be faithful. He couldn't. He knew he was in love with Nicole. Now, he didn't know how to act in front of Rose. His heart was pounding. He didn't know what to say. It would crush Rose if she knew about Nicole. Tom felt so torn, like his insides would explode.

At this point, Rose hadn't asked him how his weekend went.

"I think I'll take a shower." He thought a shower would help clear his head.

"Okay. Do you want me to start dinner?"

"I'm not hungry. I'll have a bowl of cereal if I get hungry later."

He disappeared upstairs, turned on the water in the shower, and looked in the mirror. He remembered how good Nicole felt in his arms. He thought of how happy he felt as they sat by the woodstove together, talking into the night. How happy he was sipping on coffee and Bailey's, which wasn't something he remembered ever sharing with Rose. It was a simple thing. It was a new ritual and could be part of his new life if he chose to have one.

Where do we go from here? He could still hear Nicole's voice asking him the question. What was he even thinking in starting this relationship? He didn't think about the consequences to this woman he loves, the hurt he would be causing her, the implications of her falling in love with him. It didn't occur to him. It was an idea too remote. How could she love a simple man like him, especially when she could get better looking men, richer men, more educated men?

The shower did little to clear his head. He tossed on a pair of pajama pants and pulled out his old grey flannel shirt from his suitcase. He could smell Nicole. He remembered how soft her skin felt and how good her body felt. It was closeness that he missed feeling with Rose.

He walked past Lisa's room. Again, he opened the door and stared inside. He walked inside, reached his hand out, and felt the hand painted mural of fish and the fish peel-and-stick wall decals. For the time he was with Nicole, he forgot the pain of losing Lisa.

He heard Rose's footsteps.

"What are you doing in here?" she asked, sticking her head inside. "I usually keep this door closed, you know that."

"I know." Tom hesitated before speaking. "Come in here."

"Don't be silly. I'm just going to get ready for bed."

"Please, Rose. Come in here," he begged.

Rose stepped inside.

"You haven't been in here in years."

Rose was quiet.

"I've been coming in here more lately," Tom said. "I miss her, too. It is hard to think of life without her, but I think it is time to move on. Maybe we should think about changing this room. You said that you always wanted a spot in the house to use as your sewing room."

"A sewing room?" Rose's tone was angry. "Lisa's room? How can you think about using her room as my sewing room?"

"That's my point, Rose. This isn't Lisa's room anymore. It has been six years." Tom got up from the bed. "We've been ignoring what really happened. She died. We keep this like some kind of shrine. I can understand that. I wanted to keep her memory alive. I did. We can't keep her alive like this, by not moving on. A few months ago, I never thought about changing the room, but when I look at it now, it is a sad reminder of her. We need to be happy again. We stopped being happy, like we thought we shouldn't go on without her."

"You are talking nonsense. I don't need a sewing room."

"That's not the point." Tom felt frustrated and angry. The feelings he had kept bottled for years flowed through him. "I know you don't need a sewing room. I can't keep doing this. I don't think we can keep doing this. We never talk about Lisa. It's my fault too. I know I didn't handle her death well. I wanted to preserve everything about her. Now, I think it's time to move on. I don't know how else to say it. We can make this room anything we want. We just can't leave it as her bedroom."

"Why are you doing this?" Rose was as upset as he had seen her in years.

"I don't know," Tom said, and he couldn't explain what had come over him. He wasn't sure if it was being with Nicole, loving her, his guilt, talking about Lisa to her, but something triggered all these feelings. He knew in his heart it was time to have this conversation with Rose. "Rose, don't you see this conversation between us is long overdue."

"No, I don't. I really don't, Tom," she said, walking out of the room.

Tom didn't go after her. He knew she needed time to process their conversation. They both did. Tom went downstairs to get a beer from the refrigerator. He went into the living room and turned on the TV. There wasn't much on except Sunday afternoon football games. He clicked around. The Buffalo Bills were playing. He tried to focus on the game but couldn't. He kept thinking about Nicole. Being from Buffalo, he suspected she was a fan. He thought about their weekend together, how happy he had been, and how easy it was to talk with Nicole. He thought about how much they had in common emotionally and intellectually, and how she seemed to bring out the warmest part of him, the most vulnerable part.

He sipped his beer, wondering again about Nicole's question: *Where do we go from here?* What did she possibly see in him? He was old, pudgy, and gray, he had joked. What did she see in him? Would her feelings for him last? He wondered and he worried, and yet he could envision spending the rest of his life with Nicole. The prospect was not far-fetched anymore. It was no longer just a fantasy as it had been before this past weekend. He spent most of their relationship in disbelief that she could ever be attracted to him and that she could love him. But she did. What now? It was a legitimate question.

He could move to North Carolina with Nicole. They could start fresh together. It felt so natural with Nicole. He had never felt at so much peace. He could get away from the constant reminders of his old life. But what about Rose? What would she do? She could never understand. What would he tell her? He loved her too but in a completely different way than he loved Nicole. How would Rose get along without him? What would she do when her parents grew older, more frail, and died? She would be alone. He couldn't live with that. What about Robert? He could never get his head around his father seeing another woman. Robert could never see the kind of love Tom felt for Nicole as a good thing. He might never forgive Tom for leaving his mother.

The feelings tumbled down on Tom like an avalanche. He went from feeling like the happiest man on earth thinking about a new life with Nicole to feeling torn and distraught with all the consequences. What would he do about Nicole? He loved her with all his heart and knew he couldn't stop loving her. It was too late for that. He had loved her the moment he saw her. He knew it in his bones. Every part of him tried to resist the feeling, but he loved her. Her mind, her body, and her spirit brought to him a peace he hadn't felt in a long time, if ever. He couldn't remember anymore. He remembered those moments in a man's life like the day he got married and the first time he held his children, and he felt happy to be settled with Rose when they were younger. He felt the joy of becoming a father. But the kind of happiness he felt then was not the same as the happiness he felt when he was with Nicole, a feeling of peace and contentment, a feeling deep in his soul. It was a comfortable feeling. He could just be himself with her. He was at ease and relaxed with her in a way that he had never experienced.

His mind churned for hours. Evening had set in as he drifted off to sleep in the recliner.

The room felt cold when Tom awoke the next morning. His neck was stiff from sleeping upright all night. The TV was still on, and he got up and turned it off. His first thought of the morning was about Nicole. He pictured her face and wondered how she was feeling. Did she survive their weekend together? Had she wanted a future together? Could he build a future with her? As he gathered himself up from the recliner, he poured himself a glass of orange juice in the kitchen. He thought it strange, even after an emotional night with Rose, talking about their daughter who died, that he was thinking about Nicole. Tom could not understand his own emotions.

He went upstairs to shower before work. As he climbed the stairs, he realized that Rose had never come back downstairs the previous night. She would have turned off the television and the living room light if she had. Tom feared that Rose would never forgive him for talking about Lisa. For Rose, the conversation probably seemed completely out of the blue. Why would he bring up Lisa after not talking about her after all these years? She could not know that Tom had been thinking about it for a long time, that he had wanted to talk about it but never knew what to say. Ironically, despite the moral implications of his relationship with Nicole, in some strange way that he couldn't explain, she had helped him find the words.

Tom reached the top of the stairwell. Lisa's bedroom door was ajar. He heard movement inside. He slowly opened the door. Much to his surprise, he found Rose. Rose had her back to the door. She was taking down the large cork bulletin board next to Lisa's bed. Tom didn't say a word. He stood there watching. Rose was carefully boxing up Lisa's pictures, ribbons, and awards.

Rose still didn't notice Tom, and he didn't want to startle her. He cleared his throat.

Rose turned. "I didn't know you were there."

Tom did not say a word. Tom walked over to Rose and looked into her eyes. They were red from crying. His eyes welled up, and then he hugged her, a deep warm hug, the kind that said he loved her for all that she had meant to him for the past twenty three years and all that she had meant to him in that moment, for being willing to take down Lisa's belongings, for letting him move on, for letting them move on.

Then he started to help Rose take down Lisa's things. He helped her pack up Lisa's belongings and boxes. Eventually, they emptied the room together.

Tom had called work on Monday to say he would not be in, and together he and Rose had found storage space for all of Lisa's things. The next morning, Tom got up early, showered, and got ready for work as usual, and he was thinking about the life he had built with Rose. He was thinking about how they finally managed to deal with Lisa's death, how it was only after meeting Nicole that he had found the strength to confront Lisa's death.

He grabbed his briefcase, put his wallet in his back pocket, and headed downstairs. Rose was making breakfast.

"How are you this morning?" Tom asked Rose as he poured a cup of coffee.

"Still adjusting," she replied as she served up two plates of scrambled eggs and put them on the kitchen table.

"Me too," Tom said as he sat down at his place at the table. He looked up at Rose as she set a cup of coffee before him.

They had a quiet breakfast together. This time the feeling was not of emptiness, but of a new kind of closeness that they shared after taking down things from Lisa's room. They needed time to process what had happened. It was a big step for both of them, and yet they both understood it was also a small step toward resolving all the lost intimacy that had occurred between them over six years of growing apart.

After breakfast, Tom gave Rose a kiss on the cheek.

"So, a sewing room?" Tom smiled at Rose.

"I'm still deciding. It might be a good place to move all my yarn baskets and set up my machine." She smiled back as he headed out the door.

His body was on autopilot as he drove through the town, knowing which way to turn left and right, as his mind focused again on Nicole.

Breakfast had been so different with her at the cabin. He didn't mean to compare, but the experience was so fresh on his mind, especially how they talked for hours and how good it felt to look across the table to see Nicole's smile. Loving a woman and being prepared to make a commitment to a woman were two different things, that much Tom understood. He couldn't help how he felt. He couldn't stop loving Nicole. At first, he wanted to stop. He had tried for months to stop. Now he wished in some childish way that the situation and their circumstances were different—that he could simply dive into the feeling of loving this woman and making her as happy as he felt.

As he entered the building, he said hello to coworkers trying to act like nothing had happened when something so big had. He reached his desk, took off his suit jacket and hung it on the back of his chair. His secretary gave him some papers to sign and disappeared back to her office.

Tom sat at his desk, wondering if he would ever hear from Nicole again. He couldn't call her. It wasn't fair. He wanted so much to hear her voice, to feel her skin again, and to see her smile across the table. But he wasn't prepared to offer her more. *Where do we go from here?* Her question echoed through him, but he was no closer to an answer. No, when he had an answer he'd call.

He looked over the budget for next year and reviewed the Medicare insurance forms that he had to approve, two dozen or more. Then he read over files of new residents. He thought about checking in on Mildred, anything to get his mind off Nicole, her face and how good she looked standing in front of the window, the curve of her body in silhouette.

He looked at the picture of his family on his desk. He remembered that Rose had spent hours fixing Lisa's hair and how cranky Lisa was because she didn't want her picture taken. It was a simpler time. He wasn't prepared at all to change everything he knew to be true in his life, and yet he could not deny the feelings he had for Nicole. The buzzer from his intercom went off.

"Yes." Tom wasn't in the mood to talk with anyone.

"You have a phone call," his secretary said.

"Who is it?"

"Nicole Benson. She said she is with the university."

"Yes, I'll take it." He hesitated as his heart skipped a beat before picking up the phone. He wasn't sure if he would ever hear from her again.

"Hello?" Tom said, unsure of why she had called.

"I am sorry to bother you. I didn't know if I should call," Nicole said. "It's my father . . ."

CHAPTER 10

Bittersweet Endings

As Nicole unpacked, she smelled Tom on her clothes. Nicole laughed when she realized that she had spent the entire weekend in her robe and never needed her Victoria's Secret attire.

She walked over to her answering machine, blinking with new messages. There was a message from Carol asking about her weekend. She would have to tell Carol something or else be asked several awkward questions, but not this evening. Jennifer called to ask about the weekend with Tom, but Nicole didn't have the emotional strength or energy to relive the weekend with Jennifer. They'd talk, but not tonight. The third message was a frantic call from Allison—her father was in the hospital and Allison was staying at the Red Roof Inn in Buffalo.

"What happened?" Nicole asked when she heard Allison's voice.

"Dad collapsed on Friday." Allison sounded tired. "I got in this morning, after Jean called. Dad's fine now. Stable. He's alert but very weak. The doctor said he can't go home. We've got an appointment tomorrow to talk with a hospice worker about possible placements."

"Hospice?" Nicole's numbness turned into raw pain as she exploded with a loud cry, and she barely got out the question: "Should I come up tonight?"

"Look, we're all fine. Jean's back at their apartment and I'm here with John and the boys. There's nothing you can do now. Stay there. We'll talk more tomorrow, once I know more. There's nothing we can do tonight." Nicole realized that this was the first time Allison was the calm one.

Nicole tossed and turned most of the night. She dragged herself to campus and tried to get into her normal routine, but there was nothing normal about her life. She couldn't get her father out of her mind. She kept questioning what to do about Tom. It was all too much for her to handle. She wanted to run away and fantasized about moving back to New York, where she could walk aimlessly to lose herself in the crowds of people, where all of this heartache seemed so far away. The city, like a drug, had become another way to escape the problems of her life.

That afternoon, she met Allison at the hospice center.

"It's so good to see you," Allison said, hugging Nicole tight.

"You too, Ally." It was the first time that Nicole didn't let go first. "How is he?"

"Prepare yourself. He's pretty bad."

The room smelled of sickness as Nicole stood at the side of his bed. Her father looked peaceful as he lay there, but then she moved closer and realized that he was unable to move. His body was paralyzed from the neck down. His eyes were open. He slowly turned his head toward her and let out a loud incoherent grunt.

"They call it the death rattle," Allison said, tears welling in her eyes.

"The death rattle?"

"That's what the doctor called it. At this stage, they say it's normal. He can't talk anymore but he can still hear us."

Nicole bent over the bed. "I love you."

He made four short grunting sounds and Nicole needed to believe that he muttered the words "I love you too."

"How could this happen so quickly?" Nicole asked. "I just talked to him yesterday."

"The doctor said his body is just giving out. His organs are shutting down one by one. At this point, it could be a few days or a few hours." They stood there silently.

Allison rested her hand on Nicole's shoulder. "Come on, let's get some coffee."

They walked down the hall to the vending machines and sat in two lounge chairs.

"John took the boys back to the motel. I wanted to be here when you arrived."

"Do the boys know what's going on?"

"They know grandpa is sick but we didn't want them to see him like this."

"Where's Jean?"

"She had to go to work, but she'll be back later. Jean gave me this before she left." Allison handed Nicole an envelope.

"Wow, he planned everything." Nicole read down the list. "What type of casket he wanted. What music to play. What hymns to sing. What prayers to read."

Allison put down her coffee cup on the table next to Nicole. "How are you holding up?"

"Not sure. It's worse than I imagined."

"Maybe when this is over, you can come down for a visit," Allison said. "We miss you."

"I'm sorry that it's been so long." Nicole turned, feeling as if a lifetime had gone by since she had seen Allison. "I miss you too."

In the evening, Allison left to check on the boys while Nicole stayed with her father. He drifted in and out of consciousness, and when he was alert enough, she fed him ice chips, the only thing he was allowed to eat.

Nicole kept herself going on coffee and potato chips from the vending machine. It was almost midnight. Too exhausted to drive back to Bradford, she stayed at the hotel with Allison.

The next morning she returned to campus. She hadn't thought about Tom until now. There was just too much to deal with emotionally with her father and her family. Now, sitting alone in her office, she had to hear Tom's voice. She called his office. As the phone rang, Nicole wasn't thinking about the weekend they shared, about making love, about their future, about where their relationship was going, or about the consequences. She just needed to hear his voice. It was the most vulnerable she had felt with a man.

"It's my father," she said and felt relieved to be talking with him. She told Tom about her father being in hospice. "It won't be long now."

"Is there anything I can do?" he asked.

154

"No, just being there for me helps. There isn't anything anyone can do now. I'm heading back to Buffalo this evening. I'll call you as soon as I can. I'll keep you posted."

"Please do. Remember, if you need anything, I'm here for you."

"I know. Thanks."

They didn't say "I love you" before they got off the phone. It didn't feel like the right time or place to bring up their relationship. Nicole needed support and felt comforted in knowing that Tom was there for her just to listen, and just being there for her was what she needed the most to get through the day.

She hung up the phone and tried to remain functional, going about teaching her classes and getting through some paperwork. She had to get back up to her dad. She finished grading and cancelled a few appointments with students so she could get on the road early. She grabbed her purse and keys and turned off her light. She was just about to lock the door when her phone rang. She was worried it was Allison.

"Hello, Dr. Benson. This is Dr. Danforth." Nicole almost dropped the phone. Columbia University was extending her an offer. "We'll need an official transcript to complete the hiring process. We'd like you to start as soon as possible, preferably to teach one of our introductory courses for the summer." Dr. Danforth spoke as if Nicole had already accepted the job.

"Can I have time to consider the offer?" Nicole explained the situation with her father.

There was a long pause before Dr. Danforth replied. "Well, Dr. Benson, this is most unusual. We normally don't run into such delays, but of course, we understand. I can give you until next Friday to decide."

"Well, perhaps a little longer than a week? I'm not sure how things will go with my father," she said. If she emphasized the point, surely Dr. Danforth would be more flexible.

"I regret your situation, but we do have other candidates to consider. You understand."

"Of course." Her fear of authority figures reared its ugly head and Nicole acquiesced to his demands without a fight. She stewed for hours about his call as she drove to Buffalo. How could Dr. Danforth be so insensitive? He acted more interested in filling a job vacancy than her situation. She was fuming until it hit her. Why didn't she jump at the offer? This was Columbia University! She would be on the faculty of an Ivy League school. This was everything she wanted. And she'd be in Manhattan again to walk in the lights of Times Square and eat at the Gramercy and see her friends whenever she wanted. What did she need to think about? Why didn't she just accept Dr. Danforth's offer? The more she obsessed, the more confused she became.

The following week, she slept in lounge chairs at the hospice center and had little time to deliberate over Columbia's offer. She taught in the mornings, stayed with her dad in the afternoons and came back to Bradford late in the evenings. She called Tom when she could in between classes and hospice visits. She gave him brief status reports, which weren't much as her father's condition didn't change. If anything, he only seemed to be getting weaker. Still, Nicole felt good calling Tom, even though he couldn't do much except listen. Having his support comforted her just the same. Throughout the week, she kept up the hectic pace until the night her father died. She was asleep in her own bed when Allison called at exactly 3:32 a.m.

Nicole didn't cry. She got up from the bed, had a cigarette, and blamed herself for not being there in the final moments.

At the funeral home, she felt sick as the director reviewed the paperwork to make the final arrangements. On the day they buried her father, she managed to politely greet guests at his viewing and remained composed at the church for the memorial service as she walked with Allison down the aisle behind the casket. She sat in the front pew, between Jennifer, who flew in for the funeral, and Allison. Behind them, John watched the boys as they played with their Matchbox cars and still didn't comprehend that Grandpa was gone. Carol sat next to the boys. She came up for emotional support, but she had also gotten to know Nicole's father these past few months, difficult but intimate months when he was dying of the cancer. Jean sat next to Allison. Nicole stood to give the eulogy.

"My father was an inspiration to all of us," she began, stoic and controlled as she spoke. "In the face of his own mortality, he maintained an optimistic outlook despite his illness. He embraced life and still loved to fish and loved to watch the birds. He noticed the change in the trees and how strong the wind was blowing, constantly drawn to the beauty of nature. He valued every moment and reflected on all the gifts that God had given to him, and he was at peace with his death because of a life well lived."

Somehow Nicole got through the memorial service and rode to the burial service in the funeral procession. She and the others stood around the casket as the priest recited scripture. Her father had served as a Master Sergeant in the Korean War. When they contacted the VA, they had sent an honor squad and drummer to give him a military salute at the funeral. The squad commander presented the flag to Jean. Afterwards, the family held a reception in the church hall. Through the day, Nicole envied how openly Allison could cry. Nicole could not shed a tear.

When she finally returned to Bradford, she had two messages waiting from Dr. Danforth. It had been exactly one week since he made the offer. He sounded annoyed that she hadn't already given him an answer and insisted she contact him as soon as possible. But after all the events of the past week, Nicole thought for sure he'd understand why she hadn't returned his phone calls.

She canceled her classes, locked the door to her office, and her only thought was of seeing Tom Ryan that evening. She had asked him if they could meet at the cabin and he had agreed. She needed to see him, even if their future was unclear. As she drove to the camp, she felt emotionally raw. Her insides ached from everything she had been through. Her father was now dead and she wasn't sure how to cope with a life that didn't have him in it. The loss of her father was starting to sink in as she flashed back on the funeral, and yet she still couldn't shed a tear.

Tom was waiting for Nicole on the porch in his flannel shirt and jeans as she pulled into the driveway. Nicole jumped from her car, not even worrying about her suitcase. As his arms held her tight, she momentarily forgot the ordeal she had just gone through.

"You feel so good," she said as he bent down to kiss her.

He carried her suitcase inside. The heat from the wood stove felt good as she took off her boots and jacket. She unpacked her groceries and opened a bottle of wine. She pulled the ashtray from the cupboard and took her usual seat at the kitchen table, noticing again the centerpiece of fresh pine sprigs in a Mason jar that Tom had picked. Nicole was quiet as she sipped her wine. She didn't mention a word about her father or the funeral. Tom drank a beer as he puttered around the kitchen.

"Would you like to lie down and get some rest?"

"No, I can't. I'm still on emotional overload. I haven't slept for days, though I am exhausted."

"I understand. Are you hungry? I can make something if you are," Tom said as he looked inside the pantry.

"You know, I am hungry," Nicole started to say, than stood up from the table and walked over to Tom. "But not for food." She pulled his head down toward her lips and then guided him up to the loft.

After they made love, Nicole drifted off to sleep. Tom let her rest while he threw on his clothes and went downstairs to start dinner. Several hours later, Nicole entered the living room dressed in her terrycloth robe. Tom was lying on the couch reading a book and listening to NPR.

"Why didn't you wake me?" she asked, slightly irritated that she had slept so long.

"You needed your sleep. I kept dinner warm." He moved to make room for her on the couch. Nicole curled up in his arms and still couldn't think about food. She wanted to shower first and then try to eat. Tom served a venison steak, a baked potato, and a side dish of green beans. She picked at her plate but still couldn't muster the energy to chew.

He had already brewed a pot of decaf and, as part of their routine he carried the Bailey's while she carried the mugs of coffee into the living room. He felt warm from the fire and took off his shirt as Nicole cuddled beside him on the couch, with her head on his bare shoulder and her robe slightly open. His hand massaged her leg while they sat there quietly. Again, Nicole marveled at how they didn't need conversation to be together. Suddenly like an uncontrollable urge, she began to cry. And for the first time since Allison's call, Nicole wept.

Tom held her close, somehow knowing that she had kept these tears bottled inside and needed to let them out.

"It's all going to be okay," he whispered. It was only after she relaxed, exhausted from the tears, that she felt a weight lifted from her and she was finally ready to talk. She relived every event to the moment from when she saw her father at hospice to the funeral procession to packing his clothes in garbage bags to drop off at Goodwill. Tom listened intently as he held her.

"I understand what it is like to lose a parent."

"Oh gosh. I know. You've lost both," she said, wiping her eyes with her sleeve.

"It's alright. You had your mother leave, and that is like a death."

"Yeah, it feels that way. You're one of the few people to understand that."

"I also know how close you were with your father."

"Yeah, he felt like the only family I had." She looked at Tom, curious about his father's death. "I'm not sure if I should ask, but you never did tell me what happened with your dad."

"No, I don't really talk about it. It was a long time ago."

"It's okay. You don't have to now. It was wrong for me to ask."

"No, it's okay. It's just that mother never wanted to talk about it."

He paused before he spoke, almost as if he was collecting his thoughts.

"It happened on a Saturday, just two weeks before I was about to leave for college," he began. "He left that morning with the Colonel to go turkey hunting. He was just a few miles from camp. They weren't having much luck in their usual spot, so my father wandered deep into the woods alone to travel a new path. No one could say for sure, but my father had a little red in his scarf. It's believed another hunter mistook him for a turkey. He bled to death in the snow. After the funeral, my mother insisted I leave for college. I didn't want to go. I thought I should stay with her, but she made me leave for school. I tried to talk with my mom about him several times, but she always changed the subject. Then one day, she told me straight out that she could not talk about him, not ever again. Even when she was close to dying herself, she couldn't bring herself to talk about him." The tears welled in Tom's eyes.

His story put her father's death into perspective. Nicole was thirty-five. Tom had been only eighteen. How hard it must have been for Tom to lose his father at such a very young age, how much harder than for her, when she got to say goodbye. Besides, she thought, this is nothing like losing a daughter.

159

"You must think me a real wimp, weeping and carrying on, given what you have lost, especially Lisa."

He pulled her closer. "The loss of anyone is hard."

"It's like the words of Albert Camus," Nicole said, sniffling through the last of her tears. "Somehow, you were able to find your invincible summer after your father's death."

"I hadn't thought about it that way until now." He smiled as he looked down at Nicole.

She knew that she would always grieve for her father, but eventually, she too would find *her* invincible summer.

They held each other, talking for hours as Nicole reminisced about happier times with her father and Tom about happier times with his.

"One night, when I was about four or five, a bat got into the camp. My father didn't know what to do with me. I hid under the bed. I was so scared it took him hours to get me out."

"There are bats around here? I think I'd join you under the bed." Nicole laughed. As he spoke, Nicole found herself wanting to ask the forbidden question again—where do they go from here? She wasn't sure what she expected. She knew she loved Tom. She knew that being with him in that moment was exactly what she needed after going through her father's death. She wanted it to last forever. She felt so good curled up in his arms, but was she prepared to stay with him in Bradford? Was he prepared to move with her? She didn't even know where she was going. She hadn't even told him about the job offer at Columbia. At first, she wanted the position so badly. Now, the offer seemed so unimportant, so irrelevant after her father's death. She had to make a decision. She had to tell Tom.

"I was offered the job at Columbia," Nicole blurted out.

"What?"

"I got the job at Columbia. I didn't have time to tell you about it with everything going on with my dad."

"That's great news. I'm genuinely happy for you. I know you wanted that so bad."

"That's the thing. I didn't accept the offer yet."

"How come?" Tom looked perplexed.

"At first, it seemed that there was so much confusion with my dad going in hospice and then the funeral. I didn't have time to think. Now, I don't know why. Things just feel different after my father's death, like I'm not sure where I am going in life—everything feels confusing."

"I understand. I feel that same way."

"I don't have the energy to process this all now. I just wanted you to know. Can we just go to sleep?" Nicole asked. "I'm exhausted."

"Yeah, that sounds good. I'm exhausted too."

The next morning, Nicole awoke to the sound of a door slamming. Tom was bringing in more wood for the stove. She slid on her robe and shuffled into the kitchen to pour some coffee. They kissed good morning and Tom asked what she felt like doing that day. Nicole wasn't in the mood for a hike. Besides, she had exams to finish grading. Tom made a light lunch, and then they listened to NPR as he read and she graded. In the evening, Tom opened a can of beef stew and reheated the green beans from the night before. Nicole fixed a salad and relived her conversation with Dr. Danforth.

"He was so smug," she said, as she shredded the lettuce. "I mean, he wouldn't even give me more time to decide. *Hello?* My father was dying, and the man didn't seem the least bit concerned." Nicole was visibly annoyed and became outright angry the more she spoke about Dr. Danforth and her interview at Columbia. "And the other faculty members were just as arrogant. One woman actually said my research topic was trite. How dare she? The concentration of political power in the United States and its influence on the law is not trite."

Tom let her vent throughout dinner, and afterwards, he grabbed her hand.

"It will all be okay," he said. Like he had a cosmic connection to Jennifer, he had echoed her words. But this time, instead of feeling doubt, Tom's voice made the words seem real. Everything really was going to be okay. She just needed to have faith.

While Tom washed the dishes and Nicole dried, he finally asked, "Have you considered accepting the job at High Point?"

"I really loved the campus and the faculty. My new office would be awesome instead of the dank little closet they called an office at Columbia University. And

Columbia isn't going to allow me to transfer any of my prior research while High Point included my research in the hiring package, saving me at least a year to reach tenure. But it isn't Columbia."

"You said it yourself—the faculty members seem nicer."

"I told you High Point is just my backup school, a no name place in North Carolina."

"Maybe you'd be happier there."

"But they are not the same caliber as Columbia. A few weeks ago, I would have killed for an offer. I don't know why I'm even hesitating now."

"It's not always about ambition," he said.

"What?"

"School, your Ph.D., Columbia. It just seems like you're constantly focused on the next goal."

"How can you say that? This is my chance. I worked with all the right professors. I did extra research so I could get published. I spent six months coding data for a professor I hated because he was friends with the chair at Columbia. This is everything I worked for."

"I used to be that way, much more driven," Tom said. "But after Lisa, everything changed. I started getting involved in the community and volunteering. It made me feel a part of something and gave me some sense of purpose after she died."

"But this isn't just about my career," Nicole insisted. "Greensboro is hundreds of miles from New York, my friends, everything that's familiar to me."

"But it's close to Allison." Tom put down his towel and grabbed her hand. "Honey, remember, she's the only family you have left."

"I guess it is just the two of us now," she said softly as she stared into the soapy water. She meant it at the hospital when she said she missed Ally. "It's late," Nicole mumbled. "I'm not going to decide much of anything tonight. Let's just finish these and turn in early." They skipped their usual coffee and Bailey's, clicked off the kitchen light, and headed upstairs to the loft.

After a good night's rest, Nicole awoke to the smell of bacon. Tom finished making breakfast while Nicole showered and dressed for the day. After breakfast, she helped with the dishes and packed the groceries while Tom loaded the Tahoe and her Nova. Nicole stuffed her graded exams in her book bag, threw it over her shoulder, and headed out the front door to her car. Tom was just coming back in when they met on the porch.

"I don't have to bend down to kiss you." He stood on the ground while she remained on the steps.

"No. No. You don't." It was easier to kiss him like this.

"You know what else?" he asked with a devilish grin. "In the spring, when the snow thaws, we can make love outside."

"With the deer and the bears? I don't think so." A city girl at heart, the idea of making love outside scared her, especially after learning that bats also lived in the woods.

"Trust me, you'll enjoy it," he said with a smile.

Nicole gently broke away and walked to her car. As she sat down inside her Nova, she felt that there was still so much left unsaid. Tom had helped her deal with her father's death in ways that no one else could have. He really seemed to listen and care, which is exactly what she needed the most. But it was more than that. She had never felt so open with anyone.

Tom was pulling away when Nicole ran toward his Tahoe. He stopped and rolled down the window.

"I forgot to say thank you." She reached through his open window to kiss him one last time.

As if he understood all that was on her mind without her saying it, he brushed her face with his hand and replied, "You're welcome."

Monday morning, Nicole bought an extra large coffee at the Mini-Mart and headed to campus. Over the weekend, the search committee chairman from High Point had called to see if she was any closer to a decision. He again indicated their interest and repeated his job offer. Of course, Dr. Danforth had left another message on her voice mail but she was afraid to return his call. Even though her father just died, Nicole sensed that Dr. Danforth was the type of man who still expected an answer, and she still didn't have one. To him, the question was very black and white—either she wanted to be at Columbia or she didn't.

Nicole managed to get through the day's classes and still hadn't returned Dr. Danforth's call. She decided to wait. Tomorrow would be fine. He'd understand, she told herself, knowing full well that he wouldn't.

She had made plans to see Carol that evening. They hadn't seen each other since the funeral. Carol listened as Nicole rehashed all the reasons to go to Columbia and all the reasons not to go to High Point. By the end of dinner, Nicole was exhausted and no closer to a decision. She headed home early.

Nicole couldn't put off Dr. Danforth forever. Why was she so ambivalent? High Point was never even a serious choice. That night, she smoked nearly an entire pack of cigarettes as Tom's words churned in her mind. With her father's death, Allison really was all the family she had left. Taking the job at High Point would make it possible to visit more often. Greensboro was just a thirty-minute drive away. And she could see her nephews. They were getting older and she hadn't been much of an aunt. She hadn't been much of anything. Over the years, she lived as if she didn't need her sister—like she didn't need anyone. Was she just feeling vulnerable after the funeral or did she really need her family?

She thought about calling Jennifer for advice but she already knew what she had to say on the topic—Columbia was the best choice for her career and she would be back in New York. She thought about calling Allison, but she already knew her answer too—she would want Nicole to go to High Point. She began to cry because the one person she wanted to call was gone.

Tomorrow became today, and Nicole knew she couldn't put off the call any longer. It was three o'clock in the afternoon. Her classes were done for the day and she was alone in her office. Columbia was the best choice. She was just overreacting to Dr. Danforth's attitude toward her. She pictured telling her friends that she was on faculty at Columbia University and being able to write letters on Columbia University stationary. She imagined the smell of chestnuts from New York vendors, the look of Rockefeller Center at Christmas time, and the feel of losing herself once again on the anonymous streets of Manhattan.

Finally, her fingers dialed the phone. "Hello, this is Dr. Nicole Benson for Dr. Danforth."

The instant Nicole heard his voice, she was certain of her decision. There was no hesitation, no ambivalence as she said, "I'm sorry, but I'm calling to inform you that I'm unable to accept your offer." As soon as the words came out of her mouth, a deep sigh of relief flooded from her body. And the next call she made was to High Point College to accept their job offer.

She called Tom immediately. "You'll never believe what I just did," she said. "I accepted the offer at High Point! I can't believe I actually did it."

"I'm so happy for you," he said, almost as if he wasn't surprised.

"I couldn't have made it through any of this without you"

"No, honey, it was all you."

"No, it was you. It's like I woke up from a deep sleep. I was so numb to everything else in my life. Ambition was the only thing that made me feel alive, until you."

"I'm proud of you," he said.

"For once, I'm proud of me too."

They decided to celebrate at the camp that weekend. The next call she made was to Carol, who joked that Nicole was an idiot. Nicole then told Allison, who was thrilled and couldn't wait to tell John and the boys. And then there was the call to Jennifer, the hardest. Jennifer would never understand. Nicole thought of who else in New York city to call, and she suddenly realized that, besides Jennifer, there wasn't anyone. She had lots of acquaintances in New York but Jennifer was her only true friend.

That entire week, Nicole felt a sense of deep relief. She finally knew where she was going. For all that she thought she wanted, she was at peace with her decision to go to High Point, although it seemed on its surface to be the opposite of what she had thought she wanted.

She taught her last class on Friday and packed her clothes for the weekend. She couldn't wait to see Tom again. When Nicole arrived at camp, Tom was on the porch. He came down to help her with her bags. When she unloaded the grocery bags in the kitchen, she noticed his usual Mason jar full of pine sprigs on the table. Tom threw his jacket on a chair and reached over to hug Nicole. His lips still felt so good. His hands still made her tremble as they glided over her body. She unbuttoned his shirt as he tugged off her sweater and tossed it on the floor. She headed toward the loft, but Tom pulled her back and said with a devilish grin, "This is one room we haven't tried."

They made love on the table. The kitchen generally was a room that Nicole had never tried. Afterwards, she headed to the bathroom to freshen up while Tom opened a special bottle of merlot and grilled two large cuts of venison steak for dinner. Nicole sat down at the kitchen table, laughing about how they had just made love on it as she inhaled the aroma of the freshly cooked meat. She had grown to love venison. After dinner, she took a shower before they relaxed in the living room to have their coffees. When she returned, Tom was on the couch reading and had already poured the coffees. Nicole lay next to him on the couch and talked about the hike they had planned for the next day. The weather forecast said it would be sunny.

"It would be a good day to spot deer," Tom said.

"I've got a bunch more papers to grade, so I don't want to be outside too long," she said as she rolled over to pour the Bailey's. The bottle was empty. She got up to grab a new bottle from the kitchen cabinet and spotted a box wrapped in pink paper on the table.

"It was the only paper I could find, leftover from Mildred's party," Tom laughed as he walked into the kitchen behind her.

"What is it? You didn't have to get me anything."

"Well, maybe I wanted to." He smiled. "You gonna open it?"

Nicole started to cry when she pulled out a white hooded sweatshirt with High Point College written in large purple lettering.

"I'm told these are the school colors. I hope it fits."

Nicole trembled as she held the sweatshirt. "How? Where? How did you get this?"

"I called the campus bookstore and had it sent overnight delivery to my office."

"This is so thoughtful." Nicole couldn't stop crying and was shaking as she hugged him tight. It was the nicest gift that anyone had ever given to her. Michael's pearls, sapphire earrings, or the Nikon camera couldn't compare. This came from the heart. "I love it. Thank you so much."

"I figured it'd be good in the evenings when it got cool and maybe you'd think of me when you wore it."

There it was—like a hard slap in the face. Neither had said it until now, that they would be apart. They had talked all the way around the fact, but now, he had said it, and it made her heart ache instantly. Nicole started to sob, this time harder and no longer about the sweatshirt.

"Honey, please don't cry. I love you. Please don't. You know I don't know what to say," Tom pleaded as he reached to kiss her. Nicole pulled away.

"I love you too, and that makes it all that much worse." And then all her pent-up feelings from the past few months just poured out. "I've tried not to say anything. I knew this would be hard, but I didn't plan on it being *this* hard." She paced as she ranted. "I can't deal with it anymore. I wait every day just for your call and it kills me to hang up the phone. I live just to spend time with you, just to talk to you. It's all I want. But I'm supposed to leave this summer. I can't stay here in Bradford. My teaching contract here ends in May. And what does staying mean anyway? I can't live my life at the camp waiting for you on the weekends."

Nicole hated herself the moment it all came out. She had never spoken this way to a man. She had never let a man know that she wanted to see him, that she needed to see him. Still trembling, she sat at the table and covered her face. She wiped her tears with her hand and quietly said, "I just don't know what to do."

Tom finally moved toward her and knelt beside her. "I don't know what to do either," he said. His deep green eyes fixed on her face. "Don't you think this is hard for me too? A day doesn't go by that I don't think of you—a moment doesn't go by that I don't think of you. And don't you think I look forward to hearing the sound of your voice every day?"

Nicole looked into his eyes. If she was only sure of one thing at that moment, she was sure that he loved her.

"I hate myself even more for getting so upset. I'm sorry. I know how you feel," she said as she reached to hug him. But he grabbed her hand, his gaze fixed all the while on her face.

"No. You don't know how I feel," Tom said softly. "You've come into my life and turned it upside down. I was the guy who had it all figured out. I lived each day and accepted my life. I knew Rose and I had drifted apart emotionally, especially after Lisa, but I didn't question it, not like this. I accepted my lot in life, even without Lisa, and my life was good for the most part. I was content, or I thought I was. A few complaints here and there, but nothing earth shattering. Then I met you."

"It's okay. I'm sorry for being so upset. Please. I know how you feel."

"No, I don't think you do. From the moment I saw you, I couldn't take my eyes off you. Your smile still intoxicates me." His eyes were still focused on her face. "Do you know I wanted to call you the day after the dedication ceremony when you gave me your phone number? But the leaves weren't changing for a few more weeks. And do you know that I think of you everywhere I go and I keep hoping I will bump into you. And do you think I ever talk with anyone else the way we talk? About books? Or my father? Or Lisa? Never."

Tears welled up in his eyes. "I've questioned what to do. Every day I question. I have completely reevaluated everything in my life. Please understand. It's been twenty-three years."

Nicole said nothing, but she understood, better than she wanted to. Still, it made her feel better to hear him say the words, to know that he also was confused and conflicted, to know that she wasn't in it alone, and perhaps it was good for Tom to hear that he wasn't in it alone either. In an ironic way, she admired that Tom was so committed and valued that same sense of loyalty from others. Besides, what did she expect him to do—leave his job and family to move down to High Point? Or could she walk away from the job offer to stay with him in Bradford, after all she had been through to get it? And how would they cope with the constant judgment from others, as well as from themselves?

She hugged Tom, who was still on his knees. He kissed her cheek as she wiped a tear rolling down his face.

"Then let's not make it end," Nicole said, kissing him back.

They accepted their situation as best as they could and agreed to make the most out of every free moment that they had together before Nicole had to leave. They held on, not knowing where they were going, but neither could bear to end the relationship any sooner than was necessary.

In the months that followed, the camp became their private retreat. They spent as much time together as circumstances allowed. Tom read while Nicole graded. They hiked and became consummate players of gin rummy, and Tom became the first and only person to read Nicole's poetry. As the thaw of spring came and the Kinzua Valley turned lush green, they sat on the porch with their coffee and Bailey's to watch the sunset over the bridge. And Nicole finally made love in the woods for the first time—and three more times after that.

She was careful to give Carol merely glib answers for her whereabouts and managed to squeeze in another trip to New York over spring break. Jennifer forgave her for turning down Columbia and treated her to a celebration meal at the Gramercy Tavern before the big move.

The end of the semester was fast approaching, almost too fast. It was finals week, and Nicole had one month until her apartment lease was up and she had to leave for High Point. She had already gone down to find a nice two-bedroom in an apartment complex just outside of the campus. Like her place in Bradford, it had a balcony—something she had grown accustomed to having. And it even had a fireplace, not that she needed one very much in North Carolina, but she had also grown accustomed to having one of those. Allison called every week. She promised to show Nicole the best malls and the best places to eat in Greensboro and had already made plans to have her over for dinner to see the boys. As Nicole packed, some days she was excited about her new life and what awaited her at High Point, but other days, the calendar on her desk became an oppressive reminder that the passage of the days meant she was one step closer to never seeing Tom again.

On the last day of classes, her colleagues gave her a small going-away party. The Chair of the department gave her a university mug and Carol gave her a gold bracelet. Nicole even got a dozen boxes of Brown Sugar and Cinnamon Pop Tarts from one of her former students, who frequently noted a half eaten box on the corner of her desk. As she cleaned out her office the following week, she was reminded again of the boxes of paper she had accumulated in her life and how the pile grew with each passing year.

That weekend Nicole met Tom at camp for the last time. As usual, she pulled into the driveway, but tonight her gut ached when she saw Tom waiting for her on the porch. In everything Tom said and did, he always had a way of bringing out her softer side. He touched her someplace deep inside and she was terrified to let go. Worst of all, she didn't know if she could.

She didn't want to ruin their time together by rehashing all the issues. She promised herself to simply enjoy the here-and-now as she ran from the car to hug Tom. His touch, the smell of wood smoke, his shoulders, his eyes, all gave him a power over her that no other lover had—and she knew no other lover ever would. Tom brought in her suitcase while she carried in the groceries. As usual, he had set a Mason jar filled with pine sprigs on the kitchen table, something she now felt comforted by each time she saw it.

They tried to act like it was any other weekend, but there was an unspoken sadness in the air. It was the last night they would eat dinner together, the last night he would wash and she would dry, the last night they'd enjoy their coffee and Bailey's on the front porch while watching the sunset over the Kinzua Bridge.

Like their first night at camp, the moonlight flooded the loft with light as their bodies intertwined and pressed close together. They savored every touch and every caress. They were tender together for hours. As his hands roamed over her body, Tom thought her skin had never felt so good. They drifted in and out of sleep as the night faded and sunlight cascaded into the room. In the early morning, he leaned over to kiss her shoulder.

"You are still the most beautiful thing I've ever seen," he said. "Sometimes I don't understand what you see in me. But I'm glad you do see something. This is the happiest I've ever been."

Nicole turned to him. This didn't have to end. She could visit or he could have business in Greensboro. They could find someplace in the middle to meet, or keep in touch through letters, or even e-mail. Her mind pictured each scenario, but inside she knew, as he did, that continuing to see one another would not work. Not in the long run. The relationship would become something neither of them wanted. This place, this cabin, was something they shared. It was his, of course, but it would not be the same to meet at a motel, which would make what they had seem tawdry somehow. She knew they had to say goodbye. She brushed her hand through his hair. "This is the happiest I've ever been too."

She relaxed back into bed and they held each other as morning turned into afternoon.

The sun radiated over the valley as Tom loaded the suitcases and Nicole packed the last of the groceries. He came back inside to clear out the firewood while she emptied the pantry, took her last two packs of cigarettes from the counter drawer, and grabbed a half full bottle of wine from the cabinet. She would need the rest of the wine later. She lifted the bag and headed toward the porch, but on her way, she broke down crying.

"This is our home. It's hard to say goodbye," she said as she threw the grocery bag on the couch and turned to Tom. She felt the incredible longing as the reality set in that she would never see Tom again after today. What was she doing? Did she have her priorities in order? Could she live a life without him in it? The idea of never seeing Tom again, never speaking to him, never holding him, was too much for her to bear. "I don't want to go," she said with tears in her eyes. You mean everything to me. I can't imagine life without you. I can stay in Bradford and teach part-time, work odd jobs for a while if I need to. We can get a little place for ourselves. I didn't even want to go to High Point. We can make this work if we try."

"You can't give up everything just for me," Tom said. He held her shoulders. "I can picture us together here. I have played that scenario a million times in my head. I want you here with me, but you can't stay, you know that. I long for you to stay. I imagine waking up in your arms every day, to feel the warmth of your body beside me, to grow old together, to have the comfort, tenderness, and intimacy we have shared to never end. I want that more than anything but I can't ask that of you."

"People do it all the time. What makes me so different? I've never felt this way about anyone. I've never felt so complete." Her career had always meant so much to her. Tom Ryan was the first man to make her question her career, her ambition, everything that she thought mattered to her. "Don't you think I've

171

questioned my priorities too? Don't you think I've questioned the decisions I've made? Maybe this is where I'm supposed to be."

With an intense look, his deep green eyes stared into hers as they never had before.

"Honey, don't you see? This isn't just about my responsibilities but about yours, too. Your life is out there. It's not here in Bradford working odd jobs. You've got so much potential. You gave up too much and worked too hard to get where you are headed now to stop. I know you love me, but don't you see, you are destined for greater things."

"Then come with me. We can start fresh. I'm sure there are plenty of jobs at nursing homes in North Carolina. Lots of people retire there, so I imagine there must be dozens of places to apply," Nicole pleaded.

"I've been tempted by that thought a million times. I meant it when I said that this is the happiest I've ever been. I have made choices, things that I can't change even if I wanted to. I love you with every part of my being. You've become a part of me," he said, holding Nicole close. "I know you will never be far from my heart, of that much I am sure. It's not just about Rose, although she's a big part of it. I worry about Robert's respect and that of our families. A job is a job, but it's hard to replace those other things. I can't just walk away. I can't. I can't."

Nicole knew Tom was right. Asking that of him would change him and it would change her and it would change their relationship. There were too many commitments and too many complications involved in both of their lives. "I'll always love you," Nicole said. "Even if we never talked or spoke again, I'll always love you. Do you know that?"

"That goes for me, too," he softly replied. "Do you know that, too?"

They held one another, unable to stop trembling. When they finally broke away, Nicole stuffed the grocery bag in the back of her Nova. Tom locked the front door of the camp behind him, walked her to her car, and kissed her on the lips. Then he turned her around to look over the valley at the Kinzua Bridge in the distance. "I'll always think of you when I see that view."

Nicole looked out over the landscape to absorb every image and slowly turned back to him and said, "I love you, Tom Ryan."

"I love you, Nicole Benson. Always," Tom replied quietly.

She watched him climb into his Tahoe. He waved goodbye, mouthing the words "I love you" before pulling out of the driveway. She sat alone for a moment looking up at the camp that had become her home, and she started to sob as she drove away.

The movers took the last of her boxes from her apartment, and every room but the kitchen had been cleaned. Carol mopped up the kitchen floor while Nicole scrubbed her refrigerator. Even though it had only been a year, she was going to miss Carol. Before she grabbed the last of her cleaning supplies to leave, Nicole hugged Carol goodbye. "Thanks for all your help this year. I couldn't have made it without you. I'm glad you were my mentor."

"Me too." Carol hugged her and promised to visit.

After Carol left, Nicole walked through the empty apartment room by room. Even though she hadn't spent much time there between campus and the camp, she was going to miss that place, too. As she locked the door behind her, she whispered, "Goodbye."

Nicole hoped her old clunker would make the trip to North Carolina. She filled up with gas, bought two packs of Marlboros, and a large coffee. She started to drive farther out of town, but instead of heading south, she headed north toward Tom Ryan. He was waiting in his Tahoe next to the dirt path that led into his special hillside. They didn't have long, just a few minutes before Tom had to get back to the office, but he insisted that he see her once more before she left.

As she drove closer, she was afraid. What if she asked the same questions, made the same pleas? But fear or no fear, she too needed to see him one last time.

It was sunny and warm, much like their first day together at the hillside. But this time, she was appropriately dressed in jeans and sneakers, her new High Point College sweatshirt tied around her waist. Her Nova pulled up behind his Tahoe. As Tom got out to meet her, they were careful not to kiss or hug until they got far enough into the woods. The Kinzua Bridge looked grander than she remembered, the rolling hills were breathtaking as they climbed upon their rock. They quietly held hands until her voice softly broke the silence.

"This is going to be hard. I miss you so much already."

"I started to miss you after our first morning here. And I've missed you every day since," Tom replied as he gently squeezed her hand.

"You know what I wish?" Nicole said quietly. "I wish we had met when we were younger and had our whole lives ahead of us."

"Yes, I think about that too, but we were different people back then. Who knows how meeting then would have been. Besides, when you fall in love at this age, it's that much purer," Tom said, and then he kissed her. As they stared out over the bridge once more, the breeze washed against their faces. They sat there together, becoming more and more aware of the passing time. Tom gently helped her from the rock and they silently made their way back down the path toward the road, holding hands until the last possible minute before they had to let go.

CHAPTER 11

The Right Inspiration

She had been Professor Nicole Benson at High Point College for almost eleven years and had been tenured for five. The High Point faculty had proved to be a friendly assortment of colleagues, and like Bradford, most dressed in the traditional academic garb of the Goodwill clothing rack. But still a New Yorker at heart, Nicole never succumbed to such bold fashion statements. Instead, she finally reached her financial aspirations and now shopped the likes of Neiman Marcus and Saks. The previous year, she even bought her Lexus.

While she toyed with the idea of a new Rolex and looked at several, she settled on a fake Rolex she bought from a street vendor in Manhattan. Somehow she could never justify spending the money on the real thing. Besides, no one ever knew the difference. She had been achieving her goals. She lived in a large three-bedroom townhouse in an affluent neighborhood outside High Point and even owned a timeshare on the Outer Banks of North Carolina.

Over the years, the piles of paper had grown into a neatly organized, though cluttered, mess, her file cabinets overflowing with folders and her bookshelves with books. In the span of her distinguished career, she had received two nominations in the Who's Who of American Teachers, had numerous research citations in prestigious journals, received a substantial grant from the government to study the impact of the media on young voters, and last year, she earned the Heinz Eulau Award for the best article published in the *American Political Science Review*.

As she aged, she had become more self-assured about her accomplishments and finally reached a point that she no longer needed external validation, that is, except for a few material possessions. While she had accumulated things over the years, like her Lexus, she had come to realize that the satisfaction was only fleeting and her true happiness came from being close to her family and from her love of teaching. With a sense of peace, there came a day, years before, when she took down her diplomas, her awards, and her commendation letters and hung artwork in their place. She prominently displayed a beautiful replica of Monet's *Garden at Sainte-Adresse* that she first saw at the Metropolitan Museum of Art after her first year in New York City, a quiet reminder of her old life. Below that was a replica of Monet's *Rouen Cathedral at Full Sunlight* that she saw at the Louvre during her trip to Paris the previous summer, a symbol and rite of her new life.

She had made several friends at High Point, and they often went out for dinner, movies, and happy hours. A little grayer and a little wider, she even joined a gym with a friend to reduce her growing thighs, and she went with a regular group who took in concerts at the Greensboro Coliseum Arena. Once, she even saw Jim Brickman perform again from a front row seat. But of all her new friends, no one ever replaced Jennifer. Jennifer sold her company and freelanced in promotional work. She still lived on the Upper East Side, but she now lived with a retired IBM executive she actually seemed to love. Jennifer made an annual pilgrimage to High Point, usually in March, to enjoy two weeks of North Carolina sunshine and time with Nicole taking in the sights. In return, Nicole made frequent weekend trips to New York to take in a Broadway show, grab a real Manhattan bagel, eat at the Gramercy, and of course to get her brief fix of losing herself amidst the crowds before returning to her rather simple life at High Point.

While Carol e-mailed, she never managed to visit. Over the years, even her e-mails dwindled to just one at Christmas time. The last Nicole had heard of her, Carol had retired and lived somewhere in Naples, Florida with her girlfriend. After all these years, she still wasn't sure what Carol actually meant by "girlfriend".

Nicole still dabbled in photography on and off, but lately, between work and her social calendar, there was little time for picture taking. However, her office was decorated with several of her most prized photos, including one of her and Jennifer with former Mayor Rudolph Giuliani at a political fund-raiser that Jennifer's company promoted. Her favorite picture was of her with her father. He had his arm around her shoulder as they sat together on his new boat that he got a year before he died. There was a picture of her with Allison and Allison's husband in front of Outback Steakhouse to celebrate the opening of his own construction company. There were several pictures with her nephews at their various school events and graduations. But of all her prized photos, none was as treasured—or as sacred—as the one she kept of Tom Ryan.

She framed Tom's photograph the day she got the film developed after Mildred's party. The picture captured his face—his smile and his eyes—perfectly. In Bradford, she had kept the photograph hidden in the top drawer of her desk at work, only taking it out in the evenings after she was sure the other faculty had gone home for the day. Once she moved to High Point, Nicole openly displayed Tom's picture on the corner of her desk. When others asked, she simply said that he was a good friend. Still an intensely private person, no one ever probed further.

The photograph had the power to comfort her, even though she hadn't seen or spoken to Tom since the day she left Bradford. His deep green eyes greeted her at the beginning of each day, and each day she silently whispered, "I love you," at his smile. Tom still touched her heart in a place that no one else ever reached, someplace deep inside that made her forget all her insecurity and all her fear, a place where it was safe to love and to be loved.

She fought the constant temptation to pick up the phone to say hello or to write to let him know that she was thinking about him. She knew these were just excuses and that any contact would be dangerous. She also understood that any contact from Tom would mean that he was free to do so. However, there were those moments when her insecurity got the best of her. She feared that Tom Ryan had simply forgotten about her.

Nicole tried to move on as best as she could, but no one ever replaced Tom. She dated a few times, and then she met a nice biology professor originally from Dallas. He still wore a bolo tie and cowboy hat. He was divorced and his children lived in Texas with their mother. They started dating after serving together on a university committee, shortly after he migrated to High Point College eight years ago. They shared the same interests in museums and art and attended openings at the High Point Theater and Exhibition Center together. They accompanied one another to faculty parties and even took an Art History class together, just for the fun of it. He was a good companion and their relationship was what Nicole termed comfortable.

She visited Allison every week and they talked on the phone almost every day. Allison had become the only other person Nicole ever told about Tom, and despite her fears, her sister never judged and even understood. She took her nephews to watch the Greensboro Generals, the East Coast Hockey League. While the Generals were not a professional team, she simply enjoyed spending time with her nephews before they got too old to be seen with their aunt. Of course, she always spent the holidays with her sister and her family, every holiday that is except for Thanksgiving. Thanksgiving was her day to volunteer at the local homeless shelter to serve turkey dinner to the poor. It had become her annual ritual since moving to High Point, and Nicole even served on the board for the local senior center. Volunteering always made her feel close to Tom.

After her tenure, she quickly rose to the position of Chairperson of the History and Political Science Department and currently served as the President of the Faculty Senate. Still baffled by academic bureaucracy, it seemed strange to her that such highly educated people, smart people, could be so utterly inefficient when doing anything as a group—and inefficient was the nicest word she could think of to describe their dithering. She had just returned to her office from a senate meeting, a political disaster trying to re-negotiate their contracts with the administration. Her office overlooked the campus, and as she often did in the evening, she stood at the window to relax after a particularly grueling meeting. She named the types of trees to herself as the sun's haze fell over the hillside, and while she enjoyed the orange or red color of the Carolina sky, the view lacked the brilliance of the rolling hills of the Kinzua Valley.

While it had already been a long day, she still needed to review the budget for the next fiscal year before tomorrow's departmental meeting. She had just poured herself a fresh cup of coffee from the pot next to her conference table and flipped off her shoes under her desk when a knock came at her door.

Brian Phillips, a former student, popped his head inside her doorway with a cigarette hanging out of his mouth.

"Don't you know those things will kill ya?" Nicole said, now a reformed smoker.

"They haven't killed me yet." Brian laughed. "Sorry to bother you, Professor Benson, but here's a package for you that was too big for the mailroom. It weighs a ton too," he said, lugging a thick cardboard box from UPS that was almost too heavy for him to carry.

"Thanks, Brian. Just put it over there." Nicole pointed to her empty conference table and then slid on her shoes.

"It's too early for Christmas," he said jokingly as he laid the package on the table with the label on the top. When Nicole spotted the postmark, it took only a second to resurrect every emotion she had fought to repress for the past eleven years. *Bradford, Pennsylvania.*

Nicole became dizzy. Only yesterday she had stumbled upon the High Point College sweatshirt that Tom had given to her. It was slightly torn after she snagged it on a nail in her sister's garage, but otherwise, it still was in good shape. She wondered why she suddenly came across it in her closet. Now she knew.

"You okay, Professor Benson?"

"I'm fine. I just need to get something to eat." Nicole tried to collect herself as she thanked Brian for bringing up the package, hurried him out of her office, and closed the door behind him. Feelings flooded her as she tried to imagine what could be that big from Bradford. The label read that it was from a Frederick Garvey, Esquire. She didn't know a Mr. Garvey from Bradford—but she knew the package came from Tom Ryan. Coming from an attorney, she had a sinking feeling that whatever was inside wasn't good news. Tom would have sent it himself if he could.

Nicole hesitated a long time before taking a pair of scissors from her desk. Minutes later, she still couldn't believe her eyes as she reread the letter inside:

> *Dear Dr. Benson,*
>
> *It is with deepest sympathy that I write this letter on behalf of my client, Mr. Thomas J. Ryan. I have been Mr. Ryan's personal*

attorney for the past twenty-five years, and I regret to inform you of his untimely death due to cardiac failure. With his passing, my firm is now handling Mr. Ryan's estate, and in accordance with his last will and his express wishes, I am forwarding the contents of this package to you. Please find enclosed the following items . . .

That was all Nicole could read. Tom Ryan was dead. She was unable to move as she read the words over and over again. Her stomach ached as she carefully examined the contents. As she pictured Tom's face, the memories played in her head. Her first visit to camp, falling asleep in his arms, making love in the woods, waking up to the smell of bacon, taking pictures together, spotting deer, grading papers while he read on the couch, drinking their coffee and Bailey's after dinner. She felt numb at first and then suddenly, burst into tears.

"Why? Why? Why?" Nicole wailed, "Why? Why?" She had always believed that she would see Tom again, somewhere, someplace, somehow. They should have done things differently. They should have made other choices. This wouldn't have happened if she had been with him.

She tugged on the corner of the UPS box and shook loose the framed lithograph of the original drawings for the Kinzua Bridge from 1882 that once hung on the wall of Tom's cabin. Pushing the cardboard box to the floor, she laid the lithograph on her conference table. Perfectly preserved throughout the past years, it was as magnificent and as remarkable as she remembered it.

Taped on the front of the lithograph was a sealed envelope. "*Nicole Benson*" was handwritten on the front in black ink. Although she had never seen his handwriting, she knew it was from the pen of Tom Ryan. Her hands trembled as she reached in the top of her desk to pull out her bifocals and a letter opener. She tore into the corner of the envelope and removed two documents from inside, one a property deed and the other a handwritten letter on plain white paper, unlined, undated, and signed by Tom. A goodbye letter. She mustered the strength to sit down at her desk, the letter in her hand. She leaned back in her leather chair, wiped her tears, and adjusted her glasses as she slowly began to read:

Dear Nicole,

As I write this, I struggle with the same temptation to call that I have felt every day since you left. It was so long ago, but I remember every moment as if it were yesterday. You are never far from me as I walk through our woods and always closest to me as I sit on our porch with my coffee and Bailey's after dinner. I write this letter from our kitchen table on a cool day in autumn, the season of the year that I most associate with you, especially after the leaves have turned and I fondly remember our first trip on the hillside to take photographs.

The camp has your presence all around it and is the one place I feel nearest to you despite our distance. I've given this a great deal of thought, and enclosed with this letter you will find the deed to the camp in your name. My family clearly doesn't want it and would as soon believe that I sold it to a friend. It didn't seem appropriate to will the camp to anyone but you, for the cabin and camp are our home that I have selfishly occupied for these past years and I want you to have it to cherish for us in future years.

At night, I often sit in our living room and stare at my father's lithograph. I have questioned so many things, but never have I questioned the love I feel for you. Nicole, you have changed my life and made me feel whole again, when I didn't think that would be possible, especially after losing Lisa. I have loved you like I have loved no other woman. No woman has looked at me the way you have and no woman has touched my soul the way you have. As I gaze out from our front window at the Kinzua Bridge, I am constantly reminded of how it pales in comparison to your beauty. You have been the sun and the moon of my life, and far more than the bridge, you are my Eighth Wonder in this world.

The lithograph is indeed rare and has always been a constant source of comfort while we've been apart. I especially wanted to send it to you as a piece of our home away from home, and I only hope you find the same comfort in it.

I Love You,

Tom

Nicole read Tom's letter again and again. His words never questioned her love. He never doubted and never stopped believing. He had the faith that sometimes she had lost over the years. She noticed something else in the envelope, and she emptied into her hand a set of keys. Suddenly she felt deeply alone again in the world. Tom Ryan was gone. She missed him more than she ever had before.

She slid the deed, the keys, and Tom's letter back into the envelope and abruptly left her office. Stuffing the envelope and its contents into her briefcase along with Tom's framed picture from her desk; she grabbed her coat and headed for her car. Suddenly, the budget didn't seem important. Tomorrow's departmental meeting didn't seem important. Nothing seemed important. She ran to the store to buy cigarettes, the first carton she had bought in ten years.

By 4 a.m., Nicole had smoked nearly two packs of cigarettes. She considered calling Allison, or maybe Jennifer, but it was very late. Her stomach aching, she took some Pepto-Bismol and ate an entire box of graham crackers that she washed down with a bottle of wine. She didn't even try to sleep. First thing in the morning, she called her secretary to cancel her appointments for the remainder of the week, made up an excuse that she was sick, and proceeded to sit at home alone—smoking and drinking and eating as she reread his letter.

Tom Ryan was dead. Any thought of someday being together that lingered in the back of her mind was now destroyed, but he had not forgotten her, had always loved her as she had him, and there was some comfort in that; but when she thought about the world now without him, she felt an emptiness that she doubted could ever be filled. He was the only man she truly loved unconditionally.

Nicole finally returned to work the following Monday. Being so self-destructive was not what Tom would have wanted from her, not what he would have expected either. If he was watching from Heaven above, he would want to know that he helped her, not ruined her.

Nicole arrived to work early, even before her secretary, and found the lithograph sitting on her conference table exactly where she had left it. She threw her coat over a chair and glanced at the lithograph. Taking a cloth from the cabinet next to her conference table, she cleaned her fingerprints from the glass and dusted the edges. Looking carefully at the walls of her office, she walked behind her desk to remove the Monet paintings and prominently displayed it in their place. She leaned into her leather chair and stared at the blueprints, remembering the first time she saw it at the cabin. The more she stared at it, the more she felt Tom there with her. Now, she felt thankful to Tom for sending her a piece of their home to have with her away from home.

She took out the property deed for the camp and walked over to her filing cabinets. She slid the deed into her folder for legal papers and then walked back to her desk, opened the top drawer, and placed the keys to the camp next to her frequently used yellow highlighter. She put Tom's picture back on the corner of her desk. Now she needed to buy a frame for his letter, which she would keep on the nightstand next to her bed.

The spring semester was nearing its end, only one month left until finals week and graduation. When her secretary came to work, Nicole told her to clear her calendar for the summer. She was taking a trip north to Pennsylvania.

There was a sense of familiarity as she drove through the streets of Bradford. The town had grown substantially since she left—they even had a Wal-Mart now. Her suitcases were loaded in the trunk of her Lexus and her laptop and briefcase were in the backseat as she headed farther out of downtown and deeper into the woods. She pulled into the driveway. She sat in the car for the longest time, afraid to go inside. The cabin looked exactly the same from the outside as when she had seen it last. Then, almost as if Tom's spirit whispered to her, an inner force pulled her from the car.

Turning towards the bridge, she saw its shattered remains that covered the Kinzua Valley. Nicole let out a gasp and covered her mouth. Reading about the collapse of the bridge and seeing it were two different things. The news reported that the tornado hit the bridge on July 21, 2003. The tornado had wind speeds up to 100 mph and was 3 1/2 miles long and a third of a mile wide. It gutted the entire center of the bridge. The tornado hit with such a force that McKean County was named as a disaster area. Nicole saw nothing but toppled trees and debris for miles. The high winds had twisted the train tracks that now dangled down a couple of hundred feet on each side of the valley. The thick rusted steel towers lay flattened at the bottom of the gorge underneath the fallen branches. Nicole felt herself choke up. It was all that remained of the old railroad bridge. Train tracks leading to nowhere. Bits and pieces lay shredded on the ground like the dismembered remains of a dead body. That was all that was left. Nicole wondered what Tom must have thought when he saw it. How he could have survived seeing it torn apart. He loved that bridge. She remembered Tom telling her how much he loved hiking through the woods by the bridge with his father as a boy. How much Lisa loved sitting on the porch watching the sunsets over the bridge. How much she and Tom loved to look at the bridge in the evenings. Now, the bridge, like Tom, was gone.

As Nicole made her way onto the porch, she noticed several planks of the wood floor and awning had been replaced. Tom had taken great care of their home. Her hands shook as she tried to open the front door, and she dropped the keys twice. Finally, she pushed open the door and the sunlight flooded the room. The smell of wood smoke intoxicated her as she stepped inside. The old couch with wooden arms and deer patterns in the cushions was still there, but clearly reupholstered. The large wood stove remained and there was a small pile of firewood next to it. He always removed the wood when he left at the end of the season. Maybe Tom had died before he had a chance to finish his chores around the camp, she thought.

Tom had purchased a new television, this time one with a remote, and a new stereo-system sat on top. He had replaced the end tables, although the old army chest full of extra blankets and pillows was still used as a coffee table in front of the couch. Nicole walked farther inside, again almost pulled by an inner force.

She passed the empty spot on the wall where the lithograph had once hung, and then almost out of habit, she walked to the kitchen. She stood in the doorway to see the same table, the same chairs, and the same white metal cabinets exactly as she remembered. She missed her pine sprigs on the table, but she smiled as she opened the cupboard. There was her ashtray.

Not yet ready to see their loft, she poked her head inside the bathroom and saw Tom's metal razor next to his shaving cream in the medicine cabinet. He would have always taken that with him. Now she knew Tom must have died before he had a chance to clear out his things from camp.

Slowly, she lifted up her foot on the bottom rung of the stairway and made her way upstairs to the loft. Hands trembling, she opened the door and gazed about the room. The sight of the old chest filled with blankets made her smile but also brought tears to her eyes. She imagined opening the chest and smelling Tom's scent on the blankets, but she knew she would have to do that later, when she felt strong enough. She glanced around. He still kept the pewter candlesticks on the nightstands next to the bed and had the same green wool blanket on the bed, slightly faded by the years. She remembered the night he watched her naked silhouette in the front window and recalled their image in the reflection as he held her tight. She felt like she was going to collapse so she sat on the bed. She started to stroke the wool blanket he kept there with her fingertips, and she wanted to cry but somehow the tears wouldn't come. Oh God, she missed him. She longed to be held in his arms and feel the warmth of his chest against her. She wished for so much that wasn't possible. Why did it have to end? Why had she come back? It was all too much to take—she just wanted to die.

Suddenly noticing something stuck to the mirror on his dresser, she walked closer. It was her photograph. Curled from the years and the edges slightly frayed, it was tucked inside the corner of Tom's mirror at his eye level. She pulled the photograph down and tried to remember when it was taken, and then she remembered the pictures he took on the hillside the day he experimented with her camera. She caressed the photograph. It was the most vibrant picture of her that she had ever seen. She imagined Tom dressing in the morning before that picture.

She looked down at the dresser top and saw his hairbrush and a bottle of English Leather. She put down the photograph and opened the cologne. Its familiar odor brought tears to her eyes as she remembered their first time making love. She closed her eyes and imagined his touch on her body. No man had ever made her feel so much like a woman.

As if an inner force guided her hands, she opened the center drawer of his dresser and found the package of photographs from their day at the Kinzua Bridge. She slowly flipped through each picture. The majesty of the bridge, the tapestry of the rolling hillside, the vibrant orange and purple and red and bronze of the leaves was perfectly captured in each photograph. What had Tom told her on that autumn day?

Perhaps you haven't had the right inspiration—referring to her writing. Nicole was on the cusp of her forty-seventh birthday and still hadn't written one creative word.

She looked further inside the drawer and noticed a yellowed piece of paper, folded and torn. She carefully unfolded the paper, held it up to the light, and read in disbelief: *In the depth of winter, I finally learned that within me there lay an invincible summer. Albert Camus.* It was Mildred's quotation that helped Tom heal after Lisa's death, the same quote that helped her heal after her father's death. She almost laughed at the irony of finding it as she tried to confront Tom's death. Could she discover her invincible summer within?

Nicole unloaded the Lexus and unpacked her suitcases. That night, she scrubbed the kitchen sink and shower stall and dusted the furniture. Tom wasn't always the neatest man, and if she was going to be there for a while, she wanted to make sure the place was at least clean. As she cleaned, she considered throwing away his belongings, but there was something comforting about having them around. She put her razor next to his in the medicine cabinet and her perfume next to his English Leather.

In the late evening, Nicole had her coffee and Bailey's on the front porch before retiring upstairs to their loft. She considered changing the bed, but his smell was all over the sheets. In the morning, she made a large pot of coffee and drank two cups at the kitchen table before she showered. Dressed in Tom's High Point College sweatshirt and a pair of jeans to start the day, she took an inventory of the furniture. She carried an old wood desk from the spare bedroom to the living room, pushed it all the way across the room, past the television and wood stove, and placed it directly in the front window. It was the best view. She grabbed one of the chairs from the kitchen and placed it next to the desk, then set up her laptop on the table.

Nicole poured a fresh cup of coffee, walked back toward the front window, and looked over her office for the summer. As she sat down, she stared at the view of the valley and the torn remains of the Kinzua Bridge in the distance and remembered a thousand little things that made Tom Ryan special. She knew from the beginning that there was a great risk in loving him, but in that moment, she finally understood that Tom Ryan was the inner force that had guided her all these years, and that he had always been with her and always would be.

She sighed and took a sip of coffee as she opened up her laptop and began to type:

> *The Kinzua Bridge had changed everything in her life. As the familiar smell of wood smoke filled the cabin, Nicole Benson gazed out the window at the rusted steel girders of the fallen bridge in the distance, the bridge that was called the Eighth Wonder of the World but that had much more meaning for her than a mere wonder. The large potbelly stove smoldered as she glanced at the empty wall where his lithograph once hung and sensed the quiet, much as she did on that summer day when she first came to Bradford.*

The Eighth Wonder—Book Club
Discussion Questions

1. New York City plays a small role in the novel overall but plays a significant role in Nicole's life. She has lived there for 17 years, going to college, working on Wall Street, and then going to graduate school at NYU. What elements of New York City play a role in Nicole's life? What emotional needs does living in New York City fulfill for Nicole and why does that make it so difficult for her to move to a rural town like Bradford, Pa.?

2. Tom appears stable and content in the choices he has made in his life. Married twenty-three years and having a family is what he wanted. After going to college in Pittsburgh, moving to Bradford for Tom was returning to home. He loved living in a small town and the simplicity that came with it. Yet, Tom appears to be longing for something more. What is Tom longing for and how does he find that through his relationship with Nicole?

3. Nicole is clearly a hard-working, independent, and ambitious woman. Despite having a Ph.D. in political science from NYU, Nicole still views her career as unsuccessful. How does Nicole measure career success at the beginning of the novel and how does that view change at the end?

4. How does Nicole's childhood and relationship with her mother influence her decisions about having children and raising a family of her own?

5. After Lisa died, Tom had a difficult time dealing with her death. He withdrew from Rose, and Rose withdrew from him, he drank more, he was unhappy, and he withdrew from his patients at the nursing home. His life was spiraling downward until Mildred's note shook him back to reality. How does Mildred's

note impact Tom's view of life and community? How does Mildred's note go on to impact Nicole's view of her father's death and ultimately, how does Mildred's note help Nicole heal at the end of the novel?

6. What keeps Tom and Nicole from making love to each other when they go to the camp for the first time together?

7. Michael was the cliché. Rich, good-looking, and single, something that every Manhattan woman would have wanted to marry. Do you think Nicole was ever really in love with Michael? Did Nicole trust Michael? How would Nicole's life have been different had she married Michael?

8. Tom is placed in an emotional dilemma the closer he becomes to Nicole. Ironically, as the story progresses his relationship with Nicole changes his relationship with Rose for the better. How does Nicole influence Tom's relationship with Rose? What is the pivotal moment in their marriage? How would the story have been different if Rose had discovered Tom's relationship with Nicole?

9. At thirty-five, Nicole felt by that age that she should have accomplished more with her life. Any kind of accomplishment would do. She thought if she was already ahead in her career instead of just starting it, if she was financially secure, or if she was married with children that she would have felt more like a success, even though that is not what she really wanted. How does Nicole's perspective on her life change after her relationship with Tom? How does Nicole's views on family over career change after her relationship with Tom?

10. Do you think that Tom made the right decisions in the end? Do you think Nicole made the right decisions in the end?

11. After reading the book how do you feel? Are there any immediate thoughts that come to mind or scenes you keep replaying to yourself? What do you think about the ending? Would you change it, why or why not?

Acknowledgements

I want to thank so many people that I have loved and who have loved me, and in their own special way, have been part of this book. There are too many to name them all but with special consideration, I do wish to acknowledge a few extra special folks:

To Gayle Bauer—my dear friend and the first person I asked to read my manuscript. Thank you for being tougher than any editor could have been and for your constant encouragement throughout the writing process.

To Anita Dolan, Kim Durrance, John Egbert, Brigid Flanigan, Connie Horan, Rich Johnson, Kathy Jones, Ann Lehman, Chris Merry, Dr. Todd Palmer, Dan Parker, Fred and Betty Pysher, Kevin Quirk, Sandy Rhodes, Joneen Schuster, and The Sturm family—for taking time to read early versions of my manuscript and for your encouraging words and helpful insights.

To Michael McIrvin—the best editor I have come across.

To Bev Verbeke and Ed Bernick—you were great to work with.

To Dr. Amy Justice—my friend and colleague—for giving me hope that someday I would see again after my retina surgery and for being the only person to know exactly what I was going through.

To John Peverley—my dear friend and eternal pal—thank you for being my tour guide of Manhattan over the years and for introducing me to the Gramercy and the Gotham.

To Dr. Mary Lou Zanich—my dissertation advisor and mentor—for letting me become your protégé and helping me to learn in the words of Albert Camus that 'In the depth of winter, there lay an invincible summer within me'.

To Jennifer Buchanan—my best friend and personal diary—thank you for always being there for me and letting me obsess. You have helped me in so many ways that you will never know. Now, let's see about our prophecies and how the next ten years will turn out.

To Michael and Diane Mitchell—my guardian angels—thank you for having the uncanny ability to show up in my life when I need you the most.

To Susan Evans—for giving me the final push I needed to get my novel published—your words made me believe in my writing again.

To Suzie Maras—for always watching over me as my big sister and for giving me the family I never had.

Most of all, to Jim O'Mara—my true inspiration—thank you for being the wind beneath my wings.

About the Author

Kimberly S. Young is a licensed psychologist and a professor at St. Bonaventure University. She has received several honors and awards for her research on Internet addiction and has authored numerous articles and several books on the topic including *Caught in the Net*, *Tangled in the Web*, and *Internet Addiction: A Handbook and Guide for Evaluation and Treatment*. She lives in Bradford, Pa. *The Eighth Wonder* is her first novel.

Made in the USA
Lexington, KY
15 August 2013